DRAGON SECRETS

Also by Thomas E. Sniegoski
and Christopher Golden

Magic Zero

Coming soon

Ghostfire

MAGIC ZERO
BOOK TWO

DRAGON SECRETS

Thomas E. Sniegoski

and

Christopher Golden

Aladdin

New York   London   Toronto   Sydney   New Delhi

ALADDIN

An imprint of Simon & Schuster Children's Publishing Division

1230 Avenue of the Americas, New York, NY 10020

First Aladdin hardcover edition April 2013

Copyright © 2004 by Christopher Golden and Thomas E. Sniegoski

Originally published as the series title Outcast.

All rights reserved, including the right of reproduction in whole or in part in any form.

ALADDIN is a trademark of Simon & Schuster, Inc., and related logo
is a registered trademark of Simon & Schuster, Inc.

Also available in an Aladdin paperback edition.

For information about special discounts for bulk purchases, please contact Simon & Schuster Special Sales at 1-866-506-1949 or business@simonandschuster.com.

The Simon & Schuster Speakers Bureau can bring authors to your live event. For more information or to book an event contact the Simon & Schuster Speakers Bureau at 1-866-248-3049 or visit our website at www.simonspeakers.com.

Designed by Tom Daly

The text of this book was set in Bembo Std.

Manufactured in the United States of America 0213 FFG

2 4 6 8 10 9 7 5 3 1

Library of Congress Control Number 2003116535

ISBN 978-1-4424-7310-2 (hc)

ISBN 978-1-4424-7309-6 (pbk)

ISBN 978-1-4391-1354-7 (eBook)

For Jake Golden
—C. G.

For Emily and Julia Stanley
—T. S.

Thanks and love to Connie and our brood, Nicholas, Daniel, and Lily. Thanks to Tom, as ever, and to the ever-patient Samantha Schutz, for all her hard work. Thanks are also due to my whole clan, with love, as well as to: Jose Nieto, Rick Hautala, Amber Benson, Bob Tomko, Pete Donaldson, Lisa Clancy, Allie Costa, and Ashleigh Bergh.

—C. G.

Special thanks to LeeAnne for putting up with my nonsense and to Mulder for being . . . Mulder. Thanks to Mom and Dad Sniegoski, Dave Kraus, David Carroll, Kenneth Curtis, John and Janna, Harry and Hugo, Lisa Clancy, Bob and Pat, Jon and Flo and the cast of crazies down at Cole's Comics in Lynn, Lynn the city of sin.

—T. S.

PROLOGUE

P erched on the edge of one of many turrets adorning
the floating fortress of SkyHaven, Verlis unfurled his
leathery wings and basked in the rays of the early
morning sun. The warm sunshine was pleasant, but it caused
the dragonlike creature a pang of guilt. He had no right to
feel even the slightest joy until he had accomplished the task
that had brought him to this world in the first place. There
was a civil war going on among the Wurm in their world of
Draconae, and his kin were losing badly. He could not rest
until his tribe was safe from harm.

Verlis sighed and smoke vented from the nostrils on either
side of his blunted snout. A roiling flame burned within every
member of his race, a species descended from the great
Dragons of Old, and there was nearly always smoke or fire
rising from their snouts.

Verlis had come to Terra, a world forbidden to his kind, to

seek out the help of a mage known not only for his vast, magical power, but also for his great wisdom and kindness. He needed the help of Argus Cade. Yet almost immediately upon passing through the dimensional barrier separating his world from Terra, he had known that something was wrong. He had used magic taught to him by Argus himself to slip through the barrier, appearing inside the old mage's home, but there had been something in the air. *No,* he corrected himself. *There was a* lack *of something.*

His taloned feet gripped the edge of the stone tower, and he tilted his horned head to look down at the vast ocean surrounding this great fortress suspended above the emerald waters by powerful spells.

How peaceful it seems here, Verlis mused. But no one knew better than he that looks could be deceiving.

He had come to this world of mages only to find that his friend and confidant, his last hope, had died. But now it seemed that Argus might not have been his last hope after all. Verlis had learned of the mage's passing from Argus's own son. The boy looked like the child of any mage, and yet he was as much an outcast in this magical world as Verlis was. Timothy Cade had been born with a most unusual malady. Terra was a world of magic; the entire planet hummed with interconnected lines of magic, a kind of power matrix. Everything had been built by magic. And every person in that world had magic inside them, the same way the Wurm had fire.

But Timothy Cade was without any magic at all. He had been born empty of it. He was an un-magician—the only one that Terra had ever seen. Timothy could not perform even the simplest spell. Worse, magic broke down at his touch. He was like a blank spot, a hole ripped into the magical matrix of the world. Timothy was a most unusual creature indeed, and Verlis had learned that the mages feared the boy nearly as much as they feared the Wurm. Perhaps more. For Timothy was something they could not understand, a boy fast becoming a young man to whom none of their rules or expectations applied.

A gentle breeze blew in from across the ocean, caressing the hard, scaled body of the winged creature, and again Verlis felt that brief respite of pleasure, but promptly dismissed it. His clan, his family, was in danger.

Timothy had promised to help his clan just as Argus would have, but first he had had to resolve a crisis on Terra, in the city of Arcanum. Nicodemus, the Grandmaster of the Order of Alhazred, had murdered others of Verlis's kind and used his position for foul purposes. When Timothy and his loyal companions had attacked SkyHaven, Nicodemus's home, Verlis had flown into battle alongside them.

Now Nicodemus was no more, and they were preparing to slip through the dimensional barrier again. Timothy was going to return to Draconae with Verlis and do whatever he could to help. The Wurm did not know how much help the boy would be, but he had faith in Timothy, and he was pleased to be going home.

Verlis turned to face the rising sun. It was truly glorious, and he struggled to recall the last time he had experienced a joy so simple. Images of his own world filled his mind—the sky so often darkened with clouds of thick, volcanic ash and the dreaded ice barrens that bordered his home city on Draconae. The harshness of that environment, however, was nothing compared to the situation his clan was in now, hunted by their own kind, in the midst of a terrible civil war. Time was of the essence, and Verlis prayed to his ancient dragon gods that he would not be too late.

Spreading his wings to their full span, Verlis prepared to take flight. It was nearly time for them to depart. He would need to find Timothy and review their plans once more. There was far too much at stake to leave anything to chance. His powerful wings beat the air, and as he rose up from his perch, he noticed out of the corner of his eye something was moving. He turned his great horned head, but it was not Timothy, nor any of his loyal friends, who moved quickly toward him.

Six mages approached, four males and two females, dressed in vestments of solid black, the morning sunlight glinting off diagonal rows of golden buttons that adorned their chests. The Wurm was about to address them when the first one lashed out.

A bolt of pure, crackling magic erupted from one of the men's hands, striking the dragon's left wing. Verlis cried out in surprise and fell to the rooftop, his wing immediately numbed.

"What treachery is this?" he roared.

But the six mages remained eerily silent, their eyes devoid of all emotion.

"I am a guest of Timothy Cade and Grandmaster Leander Maddox," he explained, certain that there must be some kind of mistake.

Still the humans said nothing, their hands glowing and sizzling with magical energy.

The Wurm surged to his feet as his attackers encircled him. "If it is a fight you seek," he snarled, his voice like the rumble of an approaching storm, "then I am more than happy to oblige."

A female was next to attack, her voice high and shrill as she uttered a spell that created spheres of solid magic in the air. Verlis spoke a spell of his own, erecting a shield of pulsing blue force only a heartbeat before those spheres streaked toward him. They would have battered him, and even with his tough Wurm hide, they might have shattered his bones. Another mage shot a hand forward and sent a blast of blistering crimson magic searing through the air at him. Verlis turned his reptilian body to counter the assault. The attack sparked and flashed as it smashed into his shield, and the Wurm stumbled backward with the intensity of the blow.

He was hit from behind by three enchanted strikes and spun around with a ferocious roar. Verlis tried to deflect the magic, but his attackers' spells were relentless, pummeling him with their combined strength and driving him to his knees. The Wurm's magical shield shattered with a sound like breaking glass and the aggressors closed in, their spells raining mercilessly down upon his weakening form.

Liquid fire, the most destructive of weapons in the

Wurm's arsenal, churned in his chest. Verlis raised his horned head and gazed at his assailants through angry eyes. He inhaled, opening his mouth of razor-sharp teeth, flames roiling at the back of his throat, and let loose a stream of fire from his gaping maw.

"How careless," he heard an authoritative voice say from somewhere up on the tower. But he was more concerned with the enemies before him. First things first.

The flames blossomed outward, hungrily reaching for the first of the attackers. The men and women recoiled as his burning breath drew near, but it did not touch them. Something had stopped the fire, freezing the tongues of flame in midair. The Wurm took a deep breath and expelled another incendiary blast, and again the flames hung petrified in the air like strangely beautiful sculptures of angry orange and red.

A tall, older mage in a long gray cloak appeared before the stunned Verlis, eyeing him with a curious tilt of his head. "How careless indeed," he repeated, a long-fingered hand reaching up to smooth the ends of his long mustache. His hair was black and his eyes a gray that matched his cloak.

Verlis snarled.

"My, you are a fearsome devil, aren't you?" the cloaked stranger observed.

Then, as quick as a thought, the stranger extended his hand and a powerful bolt of magic exploded from his fingertips, striking Verlis in the center of his broad, barrel chest. The Wurm was thrown violently backward, the world spinning crazily as he struggled to remain conscious.

"Rule number one," the man announced to the others, holding up a single finger for all to see. "Know your enemy as well as you know yourselves."

Through bleary eyes Verlis watched the newcomer pace before his attackers, who now stood stiffly at attention, hands clasped behind their backs. He brushed his cloak back with a flourish.

"Know his every action, even before he decides to take it," he continued, looking sternly into each of their faces. "That is how you will survive in a world fraught with danger."

"Yes, Constable Grimshaw," the six mages responded in unison, eyes straight ahead.

Mustering his strength, Verlis climbed unsteadily to his feet, standing to his full height, still refusing to succumb. "I have done nothing, yet you attack me." His legs trembled beneath him. "I want to know why."

The constable's back was to him, and the man slowly turned, a cruel smile on his face. "I would think that rather obvious, monster," he answered. "Your kind does not belong in this world."

The constable walked toward him. "Wurms, savages, freakish little boys who cannot wield magic, but can make men from metal. None of you belongs, and that is why I have been called."

Verlis was stunned. The constable was speaking not only of him, but also of Timothy Cade and his companions.

Grimshaw raised his hand again and allowed the magic to flow. This spell was even more brutal than the first, and Verlis cried out in agony. Drained of the strength to fight, Verlis slumped to the rooftop as the constable's assault pounded him into unconsciousness.

"I am here to restore order from chaos," Verlis heard the Constable say as he slid into the embrace of dark, cold oblivion.

Order from chaos.

CHAPTER ONE

Timothy Cade stood on the ocean floor, rocked by the rhythm of the water, and he gazed around at the wondrous undersea landscape. It was so peaceful beneath the waves. He had always found a cool serenity there, as though it were a dream. Reeds flapped like banners, pushed and pulled by the deep tide. Dozens of breeds of fish swam in these waters, a kaleidoscope of colors in motion. Burrow crabs skittered from beneath clumps of prickly plants into the warrens of coral that jutted from the ocean bottom, pale castles that looked as though they had been carved of bone.

He wore a tunic into which he had sewn pockets that were filled with enough sand to weigh him down. In his hands, Timothy carried a speargun, a device that had been simple for him to construct. All he needed to do was pump the barrel several times to increase pressure inside the chamber and then pull the trigger, and the short spear would fire, its flint-rock tip slicing the water. In his first excursions below the waves, he had quickly learned that though some fish were good to eat and some served other purposes, none of them was easy to catch. And some of them were truly dangerous.

Timothy breathed slowly, hearing his inhalations inside his head, and he was careful not to disrupt the air tube that trailed behind him, leading up to the surface and then to the shore. At his end the tube had a mouthpiece he fastened to his face with Yaquis tree sap and straps that tied behind his head. On the other end, back on the shore, was the air pump, a device that used the crash of the waves, the pull of the tide, to drive the bellows that sent air down the tube. As a young boy, Timothy had been single-minded when an idea for a new invention struck him. At the age of eight he had discovered that a hollowed-out length of Lemboo plant was pliant, durable, and waterproof. Weeks later, he had laid enough of it end to end—connections wrapped in an elastic sheath of boar skin—that he could walk a full minute straight out from the shore into the water and still have air.

The combination of his speargun and the air tube made it simple to catch fish or to scavenge other things off the ocean floor. Yet it was not fishing that had drawn him beneath the waves to begin with. He still preferred the calming, almost meditative experience of fishing off the jetty to submerging himself in search of dinner. No, what he loved best about the underwater world was the sense of discovery.

Until recently, Timothy had spent his entire youth on the tiny Island of Patience, which sat in the vast ocean of an unknown world. There might have been other islands, entire continents, species of intelligent creatures, on that world, but Timothy had never encountered them. The island had been his only home, and it was small enough that he could have walked all the way around it in a day and a night. It was so small, in fact, that when he had realized he could venture into the ocean, it was one of the happiest days of his young life.

Timothy had found a mystery to explore.

In time, of course, he came to know the ocean floor all around Patience as well as he knew the island itself. But with the surge of the tides and the migrations of the ocean life, the sea changed far more than the land. And so he returned from time to time to explore the waters, examine a plant he had not studied before, or capture a fish whose flavor he had not enjoyed when cooked over a fire, wondering if his tastes had changed with age. More Lemboo tubes were added, to give him greater range in his marine exploration, but he knew that his crude breathing apparatus would never let him explore as deeply as he wished.

The ocean remained a mystery that he had only begun to investigate.

Now, as he walked along the spongy bottom, speargun in hand, eyes long since grown immune to the sting of salt water, he recalled the lingering sadness of curiosity. He had been curious about what lay beyond the island, above and below the water. But he had been far more curious about the world of his birth and about the city of Arcanum where his father was still living—his father, the great mage Argus Cade.

A whiskerfish darted past Timothy, only inches from his face. He smiled, catching himself before the smile grew too wide. If he stretched his face too much, it could unseal the sap he had used to glue the mouthpiece to his skin.

Troublemaker, he thought, glaring at the whiskerfish, which paused and then came back toward him, dancing in the water, wanting to play. Several others came out from the cover of the reeds and soon they were flitting about, chasing one another.

Then all of them froze, sensing the arrival of something else, something they feared.

The small school of whiskerfish scattered, hiding, and a moment later a muck eel sliced through the water, shimmying to the ocean floor and snaking along the bottom in search of prey. It ignored Timothy completely. He was so alien to this place that most of the predatory marine life did not seem to take an interest in him. Most. Poison sponges and bladefins could be very dangerous, but they rarely came into shallower waters when the sun shone brightly above.

Most of the marine life Timothy had been forced to name himself. Some of them were similar to creatures from the world of his birth, and those he had named based upon the pictures he had seen in books his father had brought.

Father. Once more his mind turned to Argus Cade.

All through Timothy's youth, his father had visited him

regularly. A magical doorway would appear above the red sands of the island's shore, and his father would arrive to bring him supplies—food and fabric and books—and sit with him and talk of love and magic and of his mother, who had died giving birth to Timothy. His father had taught him to read and to write and the basics of numbers and science. But by the age of four, the boy had already learned much of what could be taught from those books, and he had yearned for more, longed to explore with his mind just as much as with his body.

That was his own type of magic. For though his body was confined to the island, his mind could wander as far as his imagination and his intellect could take him. So he had built his workshop, and he had begun to invent the things that made his life on the Island of Patience more comfortable and more interesting.

Patience. Timothy had given the island that name himself. It was his life, really. Everything he had. He had to have patience between his father's visits, and patience each time he asked the old mage if he would ever be able to return to the world of his birth.

"Some day, I hope," his father would say.

But Timothy could hear another answer in his voice. The world of mages, the realm from which he came, was ruled entirely by magic. It was in the air, in the ground, in every structure, and in every man, woman, and child.

All except for Timothy Cade.

He was a freak, a monster, an abomination, who never

should have been born. Or, at least, those were the slurs Argus Cade feared would be hurled upon his son. He had been certain that Timothy would be in danger, that there would be those who would want to destroy him, as if this infant un-magician could infect the world with a contagion of un-magic.

So Argus had used his great power to hide his son away, to open a door to another dimension and keep Timothy safe.

Though the boy had been lonely, he had been safe, and he was not without friends. There was Ivar, the last survivor of the Asura tribe, whom Timothy's father had placed upon the island to save the warrior from those who wished him harm, years before Timothy himself had arrived. And the boy had also constructed a friend. He had built a steam-driven, mechanical man whom he called Sheridan. The warrior and the metal man had taken a very long time to adjust to each other, but they had been courteous because both of them were fond of Timothy. Over the years they had developed a grudging respect for each other. So though the boy was lonely, he was not entirely alone.

Yet he had always longed for more, to explore not only this world, but that of his birth, and any others that might exist. But he had been safe, and that was as his father wanted.

Now Argus Cade was dead.

His father would never visit the shores of Patience again, would never smile and clap him on the shoulder, would never bring him another book, never wrap him in a tender embrace and say those words he had always said upon his departure.

You will see me soon.

But Timothy would not see him soon. Not ever again, except perhaps after his own spirit moved on. His own soul. If he even had a soul. The Order of Alhazred—to which his father had belonged—believed that a person's magical essence was their soul. This was the part of them that lingered after death, that lived again in a realm of spirits. Many of the other guilds that belonged to the Parliament of Mages believed the same.

If they were correct, then what did that mean for Timothy, who had no magic?

Now, striding across the ocean bottom, he tried to stop the thoughts from coming, stop the questions that came into his mind. Shafts of sunlight knifed down through the warm water and sparkled like a rainfall of gems in the currents. He narrowed his eyes and searched for any sign of a Bathelusk, the fish he had come searching for today. A large, dark shadow moved beyond the columns of sunlight, and he moved toward it.

But ugly thoughts snuck back into his mind. Memories both thrilling and unsettling. Things to celebrate, and others to grieve.

One morning the door had opened on the sand and it had not been his father come to visit, but Argus Cade's favorite student, a burly, red-bearded mage named Leander Maddox. He not only brought the terrible news that

Timothy's father was dead, but he also brought freedom. Despite Argus's cautions, Leander had not believed that Timothy would be reviled, that he would be a freak, an outcast in the world. He had convinced the young man to return with him, to enter his father's house for the first time since birth.

Timothy and his friends had taken up residence in his ancestral home, and Leander had introduced him to Nicodemus, the Grandmaster of the Order of Alhazred. The boy had allowed himself to hope, to become excited over the prospect of investigating the world of his birth, this realm of magic and mages.

The tragedy was that Argus Cade had been correct.

For it was not long after Timothy had left the Island of Patience that the first attempt upon his life had come. Assassins had infiltrated his father's house and tried to kill him. For his protection, Nicodemus and Leander had suggested he move into SkyHaven, the Grandmaster's fortress, which floated in the air above the ocean, just offshore from the city of Arcanum.

Yet even there he was not safe. Other assassins came. Nicodemus explained to him that some of the magical guilds wanted him dead because they felt he was an abomination, a blemish on the face of the world. But others wanted to kill him because they feared what he was capable of. Without magic, the Grandmaster had explained, he could be the perfect spy. The spells they used to defend their homes, to sense intruders, would neither notice Timothy, nor keep him out. And the many guilds in the Parliament of Mages were always suspicious of one another, so the idea that such a person existed did not sit well with them.

Afraid for his life, frustrated and angry at having become their target, Timothy decided to become what they feared— a spy for the Order of Alhazred. But in so doing he discovered a terrible truth. Nicodemus had the darkest heart imaginable. He was a killer, and worse. The Parliament of Mages had assigned Leander as a special investigator to look into the mysterious disappearances of a number of mages. Nicodemus had killed them all and trapped their spirits as wraiths, as his ghostly slaves.

As the truth began to reveal itself, Leander had confronted Nicodemus and been captured. Timothy and his friends had attacked SkyHaven to rescue Leander. During their invasion the boy had come face to face with the Grandmaster—who had been leeching the magical life force from his victims to extend his own life—and destroyed him.

Now the Parliament of Mages was attempting to make sense of it all, and Timothy had retreated to the Island of Patience so that he could center himself, although briefly, before he fulfilled his promise to Verlis.

And every time he allowed his memory to go back to that fateful day, when they had flown across the ocean and stormed SkyHaven's battlements, one single image lingered: a girl in a long, gauzy green dress with ghostly pale skin and flowing, bright red hair. She had stood atop one of the towers amid that fortress and gestured to him, as if guiding him toward the most strategic, the most vulnerable, place to infiltrate SkyHaven.

Then she had disappeared.

Even after Nicodemus was destroyed and the battle was over, even after the Parliament had taken over SkyHaven and begun to discover its secrets, there had been no sign of this mysterious, beautiful girl. Leander had even suggested that Timothy might have imagined her.

But Timothy knew she was no product of his imagination. He had seen her, and the images of her red hair blowing in the wind, of her graceful form atop that tower, lingered in his mind.

Even here beneath the waves he could not escape her.

He sucked air through the mouthpiece of the tube, and with thoughts of the mystery girl in green flitting across his mind, he smiled.

The sap he had used to glue the mouthpiece in place cracked, and water began to seep in. Timothy's eyes went wide in alarm and he nearly dropped his speargun. His pulse sped up and he clapped his free hand over the mouthpiece, pressing it into place and pausing to steady his breathing. Time to get back to shore. In his mind he cursed himself for being so foolish. Now he would return to the surface without a single Bathelusk, the fish he had come down here to catch in the first place.

Frustrated, Timothy turned back toward shore and began trudging along the ocean bottom. He had been careful to avoid touching it before because he did not want his vision obscured, but now his feet kicked up clouds of dirt and sand.

Then he froze.

In the brown cloud amid the green water was a pair of fat, yellow fish as big as his head, each of them covered with cruel-looking spikes that would prick anyone foolish enough to try to grab hold.

Bathelusk.

Timothy raised his speargun.

But he did not smile. He prided himself on not making the same mistake twice.

Timothy was in his workshop, surveying the various tables and shelves for anything that might be useful for his trip to Wurm World, as he had come to think of it. Verlis had found a way to slip between dimensions in search of Argus Cade, to plead for the mage's help in saving his family from the terrible civil war among the Wurm. Timothy's father was dead, of course, but the young man had promised to do whatever he could to help Verlis. In return, Verlis had offered to help him defeat Nicodemus.

Now that Grandmaster of the Order of Alhazred was no more, Verlis had done his part, and it was time for Timothy to do his.

He scratched his head and looked at a wooden crate he had begun to pack. The speargun was in there, along with a weapon he had built for hunting birds, a crossbow. A smaller box containing two fresh and several dried Bathelusk went in as well. There was a slingshot. Now he stared at his forge and wondered if he would have time to hammer some of the metal in his workshop into armor for his torso, or even a helmet.

It wouldn't be a terrible idea.

More importantly, though, he wanted to make sure that the saltweed cloak he was making would be ready. The garment would be ugly, but it would also be fireproof.

"Time, time, time," Timothy whispered to himself, rubbing his mouth where the tree sap was still sticky. "Once all I had was time, and now there isn't enough of it."

On another table was a rack of various herbs and potions in Lemboo tubes he wanted to bring with him. There were healing remedies there, as well as other things, tinctures to darken the skin, mixtures that would start a small fire when exposed to air, and—

His thoughts were interrupted by a loud clatter at the reed door of the workshop. It swung open and Sheridan— the mechanical man Timothy had built—clanked in, moving backward. Steam whistled from the pressure valve on the side of his head. Together, he and Ivar were carrying a large barrel into the workshop. The Asura warrior frowned as Sheridan bumped the open door.

Timothy flinched.

"No, no . . . please, you two, be careful!"

He rushed across the workshop. Ivar's face was stoic as always, the tribal markings on his flesh shifting fluidly, beautifully. The Asura's skin was covered in pigment that could be changed simply by willing it, so that he could blend into his surroundings and effectively become invisible. Timothy had often been mesmerized by the movements of those marks. Now, though, he was only panicked.

Ivar raised a fleshy brow.

Sheridan's head turned around halfway, but his body remained forward, holding up his end of the barrel.

"What's wrong, Timothy?" the mechanical man asked. "We've upset you."

"No, it's . . . Look, you should've taken that around the front," the young man said. Then he shook his head. "Go through the shop and out the front door. But whatever you do, don't drop it. It might be completely safe . . . but it might not be."

"Not safe?" the Asura warrior asked, one corner of his mouth lifting in amusement. "What will it do? You expect a barrel to attack us?"

Timothy smiled, but his heart was still pounding. "No. But since the barrel is filled with Hakka powder and coal, I can't promise you it won't explode."

Sheridan's eyes lit up, blindingly bright in the gray light of the workshop, and steam hissed from the side of his head. He swiveled around to stare at Ivar. "Be careful."

"Oh, yes," Ivar replied.

He was kind enough not to mention that it had not been him bumping into doors with a barrel of explosive powder.

Timothy turned to make sure their path was clear. Even as he did, a black shape flashed through the open front door with a flutter of dark wings and an excited cry. It was Edgar, the rook that had been the familiar of Timothy's father, and now of the boy himself.

"Caw, caw!" the bird called. "On the beach! The door. The door has returned!"

Timothy smiled and would have gone straight out the door, but in that moment Sheridan bumped a workbench and nearly dropped his end of the barrel. Ivar muttered an Asura curse that Timothy had heard him use hundreds of times, but that the warrior had never been willing to translate. With a sigh, the boy waited to make sure his friends managed to get the barrel outside without blowing up the workshop, or themselves.

Then he took off, sprinting toward the beach.

He had spent his lifetime with only Sheridan and Ivar for company. Much as he loved them both, in his brief time in the world of his birth he had come to appreciate the companionship of others. Timothy Cade was deeply grateful for the friendship of Leander Maddox, and hoped he would build other friendships as well. Lacking even a single blood relative, he was gathering around himself a different kind of family. One of his own choosing. And in that strange family, Leander Maddox would certainly be counted as his favorite uncle.

Red sand flew up from beneath his feet as he ran toward the shoreline. The surf rolled up the beach, dampening the sand only inches from an ornate door frame that stood impossibly alone. The door hung open, and in front of it was a massive figure in flowing robes of green and gold, a hood shading his face from the suns. Upon his chest, and upon the crest of his hood, was the insignia of the Order of Alhazred, the sleeping dragon.

"Leander!" Timothy shouted.

The man reached up with both hands and slid back his hood so that it cowled about his neck. His shaggy mane of red hair and full bushy beard shone in the sunlight. But that gleam did not reach his expression. His eyes were dark.

Timothy slowed nearly to a stop, as though the breath had been stolen from his chest. He could not keep himself from remembering, all too clearly, the first time Leander had come through that door with an expression much like this one. On that day, the mage had come to tell him his father was dead.

"What?" he asked as Leander strode up the beach to meet him. Timothy shuddered and his shoulders slumped. "What is it?"

Anger passed across the mage's features like the surf upon the shore, and then receded. Leander collected himself and gazed steadily at Timothy.

"I have not wanted to burden you with bad tidings," the mage said. "Not here. Not until you returned to the world, to your father's . . . or rather, to *your* home. But circumstances force my hand."

Timothy saw that he was deeply troubled and reached up to lay a small hand upon the thick arm of the burly mage. "What's happened?"

"Since the truth about Nicodemus was discovered—and

I was made acting Grandmaster of the Order—relations amongst the guilds have only worsened. With their greatest enemy gone, you would think otherwise. Unfortunately, the Parliament of Mages has only grown less trusting of one another, fragmenting further. Suspicion is rampant. Accusations of espionage and treason to the Parliament fly daily. A constable has been appointed."

Timothy frowned. "What is a constable?"

"A peacekeeper. A single mage given far more power than any one person should have and assigned the task of setting things right. A constable is the law."

"But that sounds as though it should be a good thing."

"It ought to be," Leander agreed. "But the man they have appointed, Constable Grimshaw, is cruel and arrogant. He has waited for power most of his life, and now he that he has it, he means to use it. When your father feared that there would be those who considered you a monster, a freak, because you have no magic, Grimshaw was precisely the sort of mage he was worried about."

Timothy shook his head. "You think he means me harm?"

"Not directly, no. But he will watch you very closely because he sees you and any being who is not a mage—not a member of one of the guilds—as somehow less than other beings. And also, as a threat."

Leander hung his head a moment and took a long breath. His thick hair cast his face in shadow and curtained his features from the sunlight.

"Wurms, for instance, would be considered quite a threat.

Constable Grimshaw has ordered his men to capture Verlis. They have imprisoned him."

A dark anger passed through Timothy. His eyes narrowed and his nostrils flared. Sadness pierced his heart, but he did not try to fight it, for it only made him angrier.

"Take me to him."

CHAPTER TWO

The elegant sky carriage that bore the family crest of Leander Maddox hovered in the air, beginning its descent from the heights of August Hill, a wealthy neighborhood on the outskirts of the city of Arcanum. August Hill was the highest peak in the area, and many of the homes built near its apex hung suspended in the air by the power of magic, anchored to the hill itself only by a single corner. Among these was the Cade estate.

Once again Timothy had to leave his father's house behind. Caiaphas, Leander's navigation mage, sat up on the high seat on top of the carriage in his night-blue robes and veiled hood, blue magic crackling from his fingers. Timothy sat safely within the craft, arms folded angrily across his chest, as far away from Leander as possible.

"Timothy, please understand," Leander pleaded. "There was nothing I could do."

The boy refused to make eye contact with the burly mage, choosing instead to gaze out the craft's window as it soared above the greatest city in the nation of Sunderland, although not even the splendor of Arcanum could raise his spirits this day.

Upon hearing the news of Verlis's imprisonment, Timothy had demanded that they depart from Patience at once, leaving Edgar, Sheridan, and Ivar the task of packing up his workshop. He hated the way they had looked at him as he left without explanation, but he didn't have the heart to tell them what had happened. He was too ashamed.

"I understand that you're angry with me, but you need to realize that—"

"I'm more than just angry, Leander," the boy interrupted, his voice trembling with emotion. "I'm hurt and disappointed. How could you? How could the Grandmaster of the Order of Alhazred allow this to happen?" he demanded. "Verlis is our friend, never mind the fact that he's done nothing wrong."

The great mage sighed, sliding closer to Timothy. "I did all I could to sway the Parliament, but they're still reeling from the realization of the heinous things Nicodemus was doing right beneath their noses. The Parliament is in chaos, and all too susceptible to the recommendations of Constable Grimshaw."

"But you're a grandmaster," Timothy complained. "It has to mean something."

Leander nodded. "Yes, that's true. But I am grandmaster of an order whose former leader was responsible for foul deeds.

The most treacherous mage in modern history. Needless to say, my words don't carry much weight these days."

Timothy turned to face his friend, pulling his leg up beneath him on the padded bench. "Verlis hasn't done anything wrong. He came to us—to my father—for help. I don't care how paranoid they are. What justification do they have for locking him away?"

Leander closed his eyes, squeezing the bridge of his nose between his thumb and forefinger. "I'm afraid my answer to that question will be just as unsatisfactory, my boy," the Grandmaster said. "The constable's reaction is a carryover of mistrust and hate from another age. It is not that Verlis is accused of a crime. Constable Grimshaw has arrested him solely because he is a Wurm, and his species is considered a danger."

Timothy knew he ought to have been shocked. The idea that Verlis would be imprisoned just for who and what he was certainly struck him as horrible. But the words were disturbingly familiar. Ivar had spoken of the Parliament's intolerance for different races. The warrior's own tribe, the Asura, had become extinct thanks to the suspicion and hatred of the world's most powerful mages. And Timothy had experienced these attitudes firsthand from those who feared or hated him because he was an un-magician.

It was even worse for the Wurm. Verlis explained that once the Wurm had lived in the wild places of Terra, in jungle caves and the mountain caves of the hottest parts of the world. Their only natural predators were their enemies, the Asura tribe. Wurm and Asura continued to struggle over territory for centuries as both breeds expanded. They evolved together, locked in a mutual hatred upon which both seemed to thrive. The average lifespan of a Wurm was more than two hundred and fifty years, an Asura more than three hundred, so new generations learned old hatred fresh from those who had kindled it for centuries, and the animosity between the two never had a chance to die out.

The mages changed all of that. Verlis had been a child when it had begun, but he remembered still. When the Parliament of Mages was still brand-new, the many guilds were beginning to come together, to make peace, and to look at the world as *theirs*. Offshoots of Wurm and Asura tribes were springing up far beyond their usual homelands, with their own types of magic and with powerful warriors as well. Yet with no loyalty to any guild. The Parliament would not have welcomed them, of course. They were different, monstrous, to the eyes of a mage. But the mages might have been content if the monsters had been willing to bow to the Parliament's authority. Neither Wurm nor Asura would ever have bowed to anyone. So they were seen as a threat.

It had begun quickly after that. In the areas where the Wurm and Asura existed, locked in their eternal struggle, the mages began to oppress them. Alhazred, who had only recently founded his own guild, the Order of Alhazred, drove the Parliament into a panic over the danger of these so-called savage races. He pushed Parliament to create laws in an attempt to control them. Or better yet, enslave them.

Both Asura and Wurm were driven out of their homes, but the mages were not content with that. Alhazred whipped the Parliament into a frenzy of hatred against both tribes, but the mages hated the Wurm even more. The Asura, after all, were humanoid. They were different—their skin, their eyes—but at least they were shaped like mages.

The oppression had become so bad that the Wurm and the Asura began to cast aside centuries of feuding and work together in some areas to fight against the mages.

The Parliament would have none of that.

Timothy had heard the entire, ugly truth from Verlis, and the boy's own research and conversations with Leander confirmed it. One hundred and seven years ago, the Asura were wiped out. Thirteen months later, the Parliament of Mages set out to do the same to the Wurm. Timothy's own father, Argus Cade, had saved Ivar—the last of the Asura—by secretly moving him to the Island of Patience, which existed in a parallel dimension. This had inspired Argus to do the same for the Wurm, but on a grander scale. Though he was a member of Alhazred's guild, he spoke against his own grandmaster in opposition to the slaughter of the Wurm. He offered a gentler solution.

Banishment.

Now, though, Alhazred was dead. Argus Cade was dead. And there was a Wurm on Terra, in the city of Arcanum, for the first time in over a century. But Alhazred had been wrong. All of the Parliament had been wrong, then, to oppress the Wurm. They weren't savage as a race. They were no different from mages. Perhaps some were cruel and vicious, but some were kind and gentle.

Verlis was more civilized than most of the mages Timothy had met.

"He's not dangerous!" the boy insisted, shooting a hard look at Leander. "I know the history. All his kind ever wanted was to be left alone. Now there's a civil war in his dimension, in Draconae, and his clan are being killed. All he wants is help! He risked everything to get here. I promised to help him, Leander."

Leander glanced out his window, avoiding Timothy's gaze. "They understand completely, but it has done nothing to sway their judgment." The Grandmaster smoothed his thick tangle of red beard with one hand, then glanced at the boy again. "They have retracted your offer of aid to the Wurm."

Timothy felt as though he'd just been slapped. "Retracted my offer? How can they? It's my offer, not theirs. It isn't as though I promised Verlis that Parliament would help. I told him I would go to Draconae with him, and that's exactly what I plan to do."

The Grandmaster gazed at him solemnly. "They have forbidden it," he said softly, his face drawn, eyes filled with woe.

To Timothy, the man looked to have aged at least ten years in as many days, but that did little to restrain his anger. "I promised."

"And they have negated that promise," Leander stated. "I'm sorry, Timothy, but no one is going to Draconae. You have no choice but to abide by the Parliament's decision, especially during this time of upheaval."

The sky carriage slowed, and from his high seat, the navigation mage called down to his passengers. "We have arrived, Master Maddox."

"Very good, Caiaphas," Leander called. "Bring us down. I'm ready." He began rolling up sleeves as though preparing to cast a spell.

Timothy watched out the window as the carriage glided over an abundant expanse of forest, and then the ocean came in sight. He frowned. "I thought you were taking me to see Verlis."

"I am," the mage replied, flexing his fingers as he began to utter a strange droning incantation.

"I don't understand. I see nothing out there except ocean. Where have they taken him, Leander? Is it hidden by magic?" Timothy pressed his face to the window and the spell-glass dissipated at the touch of his forehead. Air blasted into the carriage, buffeting him, but as he withdrew, the glass restored itself.

"Timothy," Leander said, his tone grave.

The boy turned to find the mage staring at him with brow furrowed as though in anger. "Do not do that again," he said sternly.

Then Leander extended his arms. Bolts of pure magical force arced from his fingertips through the walls of the craft and coalesced to form a transparent bubble of emerald energy around the hovering carriage and its navigation mage. The magic hummed, tinting everything outside the windows green.

"The Wurm has been brought to Arcanum's most notori-ous prison," Leander explained as the sky craft began its descent toward the churning ocean. "The prison is called Abaddon, and its ugliness, and what it represents, is hidden from sensitive eyes by neither spell nor glamour."

Within the translucent sphere of magic, the sky carriage bobbed as it touched down on the waves. Timothy gasped when the craft began to sink, plunging the cab into darkness as water rose above the windows.

They seemed to descend forever, and Timothy only real-ized he'd been holding his breath when his lungs began to burn for air.

"No need for concern," Leander said. He conjured a float-ing bubble of silently spinning energy to cast light within the darkness of the carriage, yet still there remained a kind of eerie gloom. "We're quite safe."

The protective bubble glowed, and Timothy received his first view of the strange world beneath the ocean. The water seemed gray, as if the color had somehow been drained away. Even the sea life darting behind rocks or plants was devoid of any color.

"What a sad, cold place," Timothy said, pulling his atten-tion from the drab world outside the carriage to look across the seat at his friend.

Leander nodded in agreement. "Yet appropriate."

The sky craft stopped short of touching the muddy bot-tom and glided forward through the murky waters as if moving through a stormy night sky, propelled by the expert skills of the navigation mage. Leander dipped his head to look out Timothy's window. Slowly he raised a hand, pointing out into the ocean depths.

"There," he said. "Just ahead."

Timothy squinted, looking in the direction that the mage was pointing. At first he saw nothing, and then it was there, massive and foreboding, on the ocean floor.

"Abaddon," Leander said in a whisper, as if to say the name too loud might be a crime all its own.

The enormous structure appeared to be made from slabs of gray stone, its surface shiny and slick, most likely from an accumulation of algae, Timothy guessed. Circular windows like multiple eyes shone in the darkness, and Timothy could not help but be reminded of some fearsome sea beast, lying in wait for prey to swim by.

"What a terrible-looking place," Timothy said as they drifted closer, his concern for Verlis already on the rise.

"Constructed to house Sunderland's most dangerous criminals," Leander said. "It is as if the face of Abaddon reflects the evil that dwells within its walls."

Timothy fixed Leander in a fierce stare. "Verlis isn't evil," he said emphatically. "He doesn't belong in a place like this."

The Grandmaster lowered his gaze, sighing with obvious regret. "You must believe me, if there was anything I could have done—"

A strange humming sound filled the carriage, startling its occupants.

"Attention, unauthorized craft," said a cold voice of

authority. "You have entered the perimeter of the Abaddon Penal Institution. State your business at once, or suffer the consequences of your trespass."

Timothy looked out the window at the prison and could see movement up on the structure's flat roof as multiple weapons of some kind were trained on their approaching carriage.

"Abaddon Control, this is Leander Maddox, interim Grandmaster of the Order of Alhazred," the mage said with equal authority. "I believe we are expected."

The voice was silent as it verified the Grandmaster's claim.

"Visitation authorized, Grandmaster Maddox. Please have your craft piloted to the designated airlock."

A light came on, illuminating a circular entrance in the front of the prison, and Caiaphas guided the sky carriage toward it. A pulsing barrier of mystical energy that seemed to act as a gate faded briefly away, allowing them to pass into the facility before it sparked to life again behind them.

Once inside the submerged chamber, the craft began to rise through a circular shaft to Abaddon's docking bay. Timothy's ears popped uncomfortably as they rose. The carriage broke the surface and Caiaphas guided it gently to the floor of the docking area. Leander muttered another spell and the bubble of magic surrounding them dissipated in a silent flash.

Timothy pushed open the door, cautiously stepping out onto the stone floor. The air was stale, and he found breathing it unpleasant. He moved away from the carriage and surveyed his surroundings; the inside of the prison facility was just as oppressive as the outside. Strange crafts bobbed on the water in other nearby bays. He briefly studied them, his inventive mind already figuring ways to improve upon their basic design.

"Timothy," Leander called, pulling the boy from his reverie. "Stay with me." His stare was fixed on the doorway at the far end of the room, and as Timothy moved to join him, he heard the sounds of multiple sets of footsteps drawing closer.

Six guards entered the room, dressed in high-collared uniforms a rich shade of red, a startling introduction of color to the cold, drab surroundings of the prison. Each of the stoic men and women clutched a long cylindrical object made of polished metal that tapered to a point. Even though he was unable to wield the power of magic, Timothy had made certain to learn as much about the practice as he could, and he knew that those objects were called focus rods. He also knew that the rods enabled magic users to wield powerful forces that would normally be harmful to them by allowing them to focus vast amounts of destructive energy through the special metal.

The guards aimed their gazes at Timothy and Leander and the boy gasped, startled by the show of aggression. Leander placed a calming hand upon his shoulder, clearing his throat before addressing them in his most official voice.

"I am Leander Maddox, Grandmaster of the Order of Alhazred. Who is in charge here?"

A tall woman with sharp features strode into the bay, the shoulders of her uniform decorated with golden stripes. "I am Captain Simons, Grandmaster Maddox," she said, casually adjusting the sleeves of her blouse. "Please excuse our cautionary measures, but this is a maximum security facility. We can't be too careful, now can we?"

Captain Simons smiled a smile absent of all warmth and humor, and Timothy felt a cold chill cascade the length of his spine. At the same time, he found it odd that there were so few guards, and that there had been no one in the chamber when they had first arrived. It might have been a maximum security facility, but he had the idea that they had a minimal staff, relying mostly on magical defenses. After all, their prisoners were incarcerated, and the enchanted weapons on the exterior would sense any uninvited guests.

The woman gestured with a black-gloved hand and the guards snapped to attention, lowering their focus rods.

"I believe you've come to see our latest resident," Captain Simons noted. "If you follow me, I will take you to the monster's containment cell."

"He's not a monster," Timothy said sharply. "He is a Wurm, and he has a name. Verlis."

The woman fixed him in an unwavering gaze, the corner of her mouth gradually rising in a sneer. "Of course," she said. "Calling a fire-breathing eater of children a monster, how thoughtless of me." The captain abruptly turned on her heel and started for the door. "This way, gentlemen."

Timothy opened his mouth to argue. *Eater of children!*

Verlis would never have done such a thing. It was just the sort of thing Verlis had told Timothy the Parliament would say about his kind to stir up fear of them among all the world's mages. But the captain was already walking away before Timothy could come up with the words to defend his friend. Leander laid a gentle hand on his shoulder and ushered him along, and so the boy could only grumble angrily and follow, walking quickly to keep up with the woman's brisk stride.

The facility was like a maze, filled with winding hallways and doors locked to anyone unable to produce the correct spell-key. The guards followed close behind them, as if expecting some kind of trouble. Timothy gazed back at them nervously, meeting their emotionless stares. There were at least a million other places he would rather have been at that moment, but he had no choice. He had to see Verlis—he had to be sure that his friend was all right.

At the end of yet another winding hallway, Captain Simons uttered a short, guttural incantation and waved her hand in front of a glass orb that resembled a gigantic insect eye set into the door frame. The heavy door rose up into the ceiling with a snakelike hiss, and they stepped onto a catwalk that spanned an enormous room. They were in a vast chamber, hundreds of feet wide and just as deep. Everywhere Timothy looked he saw prison cells of solidified magic, floating weightless within the open space. He could feel the prisoners, peering out from their cages with hungry eyes, desperate to be noticed. Timothy wasn't sure he had ever seen anything quite so disturbing. He flinched when he felt Leander's powerful arm wrap around his shoulders.

"Come along, Timothy," the mage said. "You shouldn't see any more of this than you have to."

They made their way across the chamber, Captain Simons leading the way. She had obviously noticed how much her prisoners had disturbed Timothy. Standing before the door at the far end of the catwalk, she gestured toward them.

"Better they be in here than out there. Trust me, the world is a much safer place," the captain said.

Another magical lock was undone, and the door rose to allow them access to another room. It was much smaller than the one they had just left. A single cage rested on a platform, and within the cage stood Timothy's friend.

"Took no chances with this one," Captain Simons said, her eyes upon the cell. "We thought it wise to keep it separated from the general population."

Timothy barely noticed the captain's words, and the way she called Verlis *it*. The boy called out his friend's name and ran toward the cage.

"Come back here!" Captain Simons barked. "Utmost caution must be used around the prisoner at all times!"

The guards standing in the doorway immediately snapped to attention, raising their focus rods.

"Wait, please. You need not worry," Leander said, appealing to the guards. "They are friends. The boy and the Wurm. Verlis would never hurt him."

Timothy slowed as he reached the perimeter of the cage.

Verlis's cell was constructed not from magic as the other cages were, but out of thick black metal.

"Verlis," he whispered, peering through the bars. "Are . . . are you all right?"

The Wurm did not respond, standing motionless in the cell's center. As Timothy moved closer, he saw the reason for his friend's silence. Verlis's mouth was covered in a kind of muzzle—a precaution against breathing fire, Tim supposed. The Wurm was chained and his talons covered with gauntlets, most likely to hinder any magics that could be conjured by gesture. Even his friend's mighty wings had been bound closed, strapped against his back with a band of metal that appeared to be made from the same material as the prison cell.

Timothy's heart ached. "I'm so sorry," he told the dragon, gripping the cold bars tightly. "Don't worry," he assured his friend. "Leander and I are going to do everything in our power to get you out of here."

He reached into the cage to lay a hand on the cold metal restraints that had been placed over the Wurm's hands. Verlis pulled away, his dark eyes raging with anger and hurt.

"Verlis, please . . . ," Timothy pleaded, but the Wurm turned his back. The boy stepped away from the cage, smarting from the rejection. "I know you probably hate me now—probably hate all of us—and I can understand why."

The Wurm did not turn around.

"But I want you to know, I will get you out of here. I promise."

"Is that so?" boomed a voice Timothy did not recognize.

He spun around in time to see a figure clad in a starched uniform of solid black enter the chamber, a long cloak swaying behind him. Captain Simons stood at attention and Leander did his best to hide a scowl. The man was tall and powerfully built, with hard eyes and a black mustache that slashed across his chiseled features.

"You must be Timothy Cade," said the stranger, his hand reaching up to smooth the ends of his mustache. "Allow me to introduce myself," he said, striding further into the room.

"I am Constable Grimshaw."

"You're the one who put Verlis here," Timothy said, glaring at the constable and gesturing to the cell behind him.

Grimshaw's eyes gleamed with pride and he smiled politely. "Correct," he said, moving toward Timothy and the cage. "The Wurm posed a serious threat to the security of our world, and to all of the guilds in the Parliament of Mages. We can't have vicious beasts wielding that kind of power and running free. It would be chaos. That is why the Wurm were banished from Terra in the first place."

"That's not the way I heard it," Timothy muttered.

The constable raised an eyebrow and shot a suspicious glance at Leander. "Really. I would be quite interested in how *you* heard it. And from whom."

Leander only stared back at Grimshaw defiantly.

Verlis had turned to eye the approaching constable. A rumbling growl from somewhere deep within his broad chest filled the chamber, and Timothy could see that his friend was fighting uselessly against his bonds.

"He's done no one any harm," the boy said.

"Yet," Grimshaw stressed, holding up a long index finger to make his point. "He's done no one any harm *yet*." The constable clasped his hands behind his back and began to pace in front of the boy.

"You see, Tim—I can call you Tim, can't I?" Constable Grimshaw asked, stopping in midpace to glance at the boy.

"No," Timothy snapped.

Grimshaw chuckled as he began pacing again. "You see— young Master Cade—you look at this caged beast and see a noble creature, a friend even, but I see something far more dangerous. I look at the Wurm and I see our great cities in flames, our citizens destitute, injured, or worse, eaten. I see the seeds of a threat that must be stopped before it is given the opportunity to take root."

The constable stopped pacing and glared at Timothy with cold, calculating eyes. "Do you wonder what I see when I look at you, boy?"

The chamber was eerily silent, their eyes locked upon one another.

"Constable," Leander called from across the room, and Timothy could hear the warning in his friend's voice.

"It's okay, Leander," the boy spoke up. He knew that the man was dangerous, but could not bring himself to back down. He was reminded of one of Ivar's many lessons about the art of combat: Never show your adversary that you are afraid. Timothy was doing everything he could at that moment to follow that lesson.

"What do you see, Constable Grimshaw?" he asked. "I'm curious."

Again Grimshaw raised a hand to his mustache and smoothed one of the ends. "You're a smart boy," the constable said. "But you're not a mage. In your way, you're no different from the Wurm, except perhaps for the fact that you are not in a cage."

Timothy gritted his teeth to stop the shudder that went through him, for he could almost hear the unspoken word that would have finished that sentence, the same way Grimshaw had finished his sentence before. *Yet.* The constable saw him the same way that many members of the Parliament of Mages had seen him when he was first introduced to them. They saw a threat—something to fear.

He looked away from Grimshaw and studied the metal bars of the cage that held his friend. It all made sense to him now, and like a spark of hungry fire setting Hakka powder ablaze, he felt his anger flare.

"It's because of my . . . affliction that you've used no magic to keep him prisoner."

Verlis growled again, straining against his restraints, his dark, terrible eyes boring into the constable. Grimshaw smiled coldly, turning to admire the cell. The constable gripped one of the unyielding metal bars in his hands and tugged on it.

"Precautions were taken to assure that the prisoner would remain with us." Grimshaw looked back to the boy. "Every possible contingency was considered. Even little boys with the ability to disrupt magic."

Timothy sneered, glaring at him, and again studied the cage, committing to memory the angles of its construction, the points where the metal was joined together. He could build a cage like this if he was so inclined, or perhaps even take this one apart.

"How long, Constable Grimshaw?" he asked in all seriousness. "How long before you try to put me in one of these cages?"

The constable placed a hand to the front of his black, gold-buttoned waistcoat and gasped theatrically. "Young Master Cade, you wound me. One would have to be a great threat against the nation of Sunderland to be imprisoned here. Are you suggesting that you pose such a threat?"

Timothy seethed, unable to remember a time when he'd ever felt as angry—or as helpless. He had to leave this place before he said anything that could get him or his friends into trouble.

He reached through the bars into the cage.

"Be careful, boy," Grimshaw warned.

Timothy paid him no mind, laying a tender hand on the metal sheath that encased Verlis's hands. This time, the Wurm did not pull away.

"I have to go now," he said softly. "But I'll come back to see you again very soon." Timothy looked into his eyes, hoping to reinforce the message that he would do everything in his power to set his friend free.

With a final nod, the boy turned away from the cage and went to where Leander waited, surrounded by guards. "I'd like to go now," he told the Grandmaster, and the mage obliged, placing a comforting arm about the boy's shoulder and escorting him through the doorway and out of the room.

"It was a pleasure making your acquaintance," he heard the constable say from the chamber behind him. "I hope we have another opportunity to chat again soon."

Timothy turned to stare back at him, even as the door swung closed.

"You can count on it."

CHAPTER THREE

Timothy had spent almost his entire life on the Island of Patience, where he only had to answer to himself. The idea that the Parliament could imprison Verlis, that they could effectively erase the promise Timothy had made to him, was deeply horrifying. Never had he felt such frustration, such utter and complete helplessness. When he had an enemy, like Nicodemus or the Nimib assassins who had once tried to kill him, it was easy to know how to fight back.

But how could he fight Parliament?

The underwater prison of Abaddon was a marvel, and Timothy's analytical mind had wished to linger, to examine it and figure out how it had been constructed. He had been so furious and so sad for his friend that he had not been able to focus on such things. Even so, there were things he had noticed about the place and logged away in the back of his mind.

One way or another, he was going to get Verlis out of there. The Parliament was simply wrong. The Wurm's imprisonment was unjust. And since nobody wanted to treat Timothy like a citizen of the nation of Sunderland, he didn't consider himself bound by its laws or by the rulings of the Parliament of Mages.

On the other hand, he was no fool. He knew that if he crossed the Parliament, there would be nowhere in this world that would be safe for him, and he might end up down in Abaddon himself.

Once they emerged from the ocean, Caiaphas guided the carriage south, along the air currents that would lead them to SkyHaven. When they came in sight of it, that magnificent fortress floating above the ocean, Timothy shivered. His memories of the things that he had experienced there still made his skin crawl. The wraiths, the bloodshed, the deception of Nicodemus—he doubted there would ever come a day when those things did not echo in the halls of SkyHaven.

Now, though, the place was in Leander's hands. As Grandmaster of the Order of Alhazred, he had inherited a job he had never really wanted. Leander wanted to go back to the University of Saint Germain, to return to his students. Despite the work he had undertaken in secret, as an investigator answering only to the Parliament, in his heart, Timothy knew the mage would always think of himself as Professor Maddox, and never Grandmaster.

But Grandmaster he was. And commanding the order was a job Timothy did not envy.

Atop his high seat, Caiaphas guided the sky carriage over the floating fortress. Banners flew above SkyHaven, and Timothy could see mages practicing their spellcraft on the grounds inside the walls. The ocean was a deep blue-green far below . . . and then he could see it no longer, for Caiaphas had flown them in among the towers of the fortress.

The veiled navigation mage guided the craft to a gentle landing in front of the main entrance of SkyHaven. Even as it set down, Timothy glanced out the window and saw a thin man running toward them, his face pinched with a strange combination of urgency and superiority, as though he hated having to run out to the carriage like some servant. Which was, of course, precisely what he was.

"Him?" Timothy asked, unable to contain himself. "You kept *him* here?"

The door swung open for Leander, and he had begun to step out when he paused and glanced back in at the boy. "Carlyle is my chief aide. He knows more about the inner workings of the order than anyone. He's been invaluable."

"But . . ." Timothy scowled and shook his head.

Leander smiled. "That does not mean I like him."

The massive mage got out of the sky carriage, the wind immediately whipping at his hair and beard. Timothy hesitated a moment before following.

"Good day, Grandmaster. Welcome home," Carlyle said. He bowed his head as he spoke, a gesture of respect that seemed empty to Timothy.

Carlyle wore a green robe, cinched tightly at his waist, the fabric of it hanging as neatly as if it had been painted into place. Everything about him was precise. But when he glanced past Leander and spotted Timothy, his nostrils flared and one eyebrow twitched in disapproval.

The feeling's mutual, Timothy thought, but he did not speak the words. Right now, Constable Grimshaw worried him a lot more than the annoying, arrogant Carlyle.

"What is it?" Leander asked.

Carlyle nodded. "You have received a message from the Parliament. You're ordered to appear before them immediately, Grandmaster. There was no mention of the purpose of this audience."

Leander thoughtfully stroked his beard. Timothy noticed that there was more than a little satisfaction in Carlyle's tone, as if he thought his new master might be in trouble, and the idea pleased him. Leander seemed not to notice, or not to care.

"All right. Has Master Fraxis arrived?"

Carlyle frowned. "He has. But the message—"

"Can wait for a few moments of common courtesy. We'll go inside and explain why our meeting must be delayed, and then you will offer him every comfort until I return."

The aide seemed about to argue, but then he relented. "Of course."

Leander turned to Timothy. Carlyle glared at the boy, but Timothy ignored him.

"I wish I could let you feel what I feel," Leander told him, his eyes sad. "There is a spell for that very thing, but of course it will not work on you. I'll be inside for a few moments, and then I must go."

"Because Parliament commands you," Timothy said, unable to hide the bitterness in his words.

Leander nodded gravely. "Yes. Yes, they do. This is the way of the world, Timothy. Along with my teaching, the order and the Parliament are the things I've built my life around. I wish you could understand that. I am very sorry for what has happened to Verlis. I was not yet born when the Wurm were banished, but you can be sure I would have stood against their treatment, just as your father did. I do not always agree with parliamentary decisions, but I must abide by them."

Timothy only shook his head. Leander hesitated a moment, then turned and strode quickly toward the entrance to SkyHaven. Carlyle sniffed and then followed his master inside.

"You're being quite hard on him, young one."

Frowning, Timothy glanced up at Caiaphas. The navigation mage sat on his high seat, draped in the blue robes of his station, sparks of magic still dancing around his fingers. In moments, Leander would return and they would be off again. It occurred to Timothy for the first time that though he had focused his magic upon a particular skill, Caiaphas must be very strong to be able to propel a sky carriage all day.

"He deserves it," Timothy replied, watching the eyes that showed through the mage's hood. "He could have fought harder for Verlis."

Caiaphas sighed wearily. Only his eyes could be seen above the veil that covered his face, but those eyes were expressive enough. "He is doing his best, Timothy. Professor Maddox always does his best. At present, he is torn in many different directions. It is more of a burden than you imagine, becoming Grandmaster. Every mage in the order has been made to appear at SkyHaven in recent days, and to submit to questioning. Even those as respected as Master Fraxis. Most of them have turned out to be more loyal to the order than to Nicodemus. But I have heard the professor—pardon me, the Grandmaster—speak of others whose eyes are dark with malice. Others who cannot be trusted.

"That is a precious commodity of late. Trust. Grandmaster Maddox is attempting to serve the Parliament, and the best interests of the order, as well as his own heart when it comes to the university and to his feelings for you. But you and I both know that it is impossible to please everyone. Yet he tries, Timothy. Trust in that much, at least. He will do anything in his power to protect you, even if it means his own life. If nothing else, at least give him your trust."

Timothy gazed at the sparkling blue eyes of the navigation mage and felt ashamed of himself. Guilt welled up within him. Caiaphas was right. Leander was doing his best, of course. But the situation was far more complicated than Timothy was willing to admit.

"I will," he whispered to Caiaphas. "I do."

The navigation mage nodded, but then his gaze shifted, and Timothy turned to see that Leander was returning.

"Thank you. I needed to hear that," Timothy said.

Caiaphas said nothing.

The young man hurried toward SkyHaven. He did not want to discuss Verlis's situation any further at the moment, and Leander surely had other things on his mind, but Timothy stopped him and gave him a quick hug before continuing on to the entrance. Ivar, Edgar, and Sheridan would be waiting for him.

At the door he paused to see Leander watching him, surprised by the embrace he had received. Timothy smiled and waved to him.

Leander waved back, a curious expression on his face, but he had pressing business and so he hurried to the sky carriage. A moment later blue magic spilled from Caiaphas's fingers, and the craft lifted up off the ground and whisked away across the sky.

What now?

This question echoed through Leander's mind over and over as Caiaphas guided the sky carriage high above the city of Arcanum. Normally he was soothed by such a journey. The elegant spires of the city's towers were breathtaking, their pale reds and gleaming turquoises creating a sort of elemental color scheme, earth and fire and ocean. But there had been so much political strife in the aftermath of the revelation of Nicodemus's crimes that he never seemed able to relax anymore.

It wasn't only the politics and this new summons from the Parliament that worried him. Timothy was on his mind as well. The young man meant well—he always did—but he had to learn how to fight injustice from within the system. No one boy, no matter how special he might be, could take on the entire Parliament of Mages. Even Argus Cade, who had earned the respect of all mages, had not been able to sway the Parliament's hatred of the Wurm, only to convince them that banishment was a more civil punishment, and that continued, unnecessary warfare was just as barbaric as the sort of acts they so often accused the Wurm of. Leander was only seventy-six, barely middle-aged for a mage, but he wished he had been alive to see Argus Cade in his prime, arguing before Parliament. Argus had mastered the art of working within the system to improve it. His son, however, knew no such nuances in the world, only right and wrong.

Leander sighed. He and Timothy were going to have to have a long talk when he returned from this meeting. There was more than one way to fight.

The sky carriage banked to the left, and through the window Leander could see the Parliament complex ahead, a sprawl of buildings at the very heart of the city. There were stone structures, traditional Arcanum spires, and vast, cavernous halls. At the center of it all was the Xerxis, the oldest surviving structure in all of Sunderland. Once it had been the palace of Xerxes, one of the greatest of the legendary Wizards of Old. Now it housed the grand meeting chamber of the Parliament of Mages. Yet the Xerxis was only the core of the complex, which had been built up around it over the ages and now spanned three entire blocks, filled with libraries, residences, offices, and restaurants. Its greatness was appropriate, for it was the center of guild relations, commerce, and politics for the entire world.

Long ago the world had been composed of countries whose fierce national pride put them at war with one another. But over time the guilds had grown more and more powerful, each with members scattered around the world. Mages were no longer divided by nationality, but by guild membership. Now national boundaries had all but disappeared. Arcanum might be the capital city of the nation of Sunderland, but such geographical definitions meant little these days.

The Parliament ruled the guilds, and the headquarters of Parliament was in Arcanum. In a very real sense, that made Arcanum the capital city of the world.

Arcanum was a large, busy city—the lights and spires of its towers stretched as far as the eye could see from Leander's current position. Sky carriages filled the air, but the air traffic was much worse around the Parliament complex. It took Caiaphas several minutes of avoiding collisions with reckless navigation mages before he was finally able to guide them toward the entrance to the Xerxis.

Leander stepped out of the carriage and glanced up at the Xerxis. The four corners of the tower were formed by stone beams that began to curve halfway up, twisting in upon themselves so that the tower grew narrower and narrower, ending in a solid, rounded stone cap far, far above the ground. It always gave him perspective, staring up at that structure. The Xerxis had been there thousands of years before he was born, and it would likely remain thousands of years after, and it represented to him the very best that magic could accomplish, the best that could be found in the hearts of mages. For the legends of the wisdom and leadership of Xerxes were an example to them all.

It was an honor for him every time he set foot inside. Even today, with all the stress weighing upon him, he took a moment to acknowledge that honor. He paused, then turned to look to Caiaphas, up on the high seat of the carriage.

"I've no idea how long this will be. Be at ease. Find refreshment. I will summon you when I am ready to depart," Leander said.

"Certainly, Master Maddox," the navigation mage replied.

Then the sky carriage was sliding away into the air.

The tall doors of the Xerxis opened for Leander as he approached. Sentries eyed him warily, in case any of the defensive wards and spells that protected the Xerxis should identify him as an intruder or an impostor. At the interior doors he identified himself to the final sentry, though the woman knew him on sight. She touched two fingers to her forehead, then to her chest, and executed a courteous half bow.

"Grandmaster Maddox. Kind thoughts on this day," the sentry said.

Leander smiled and repeated the woman's gesture. This was a traditional greeting dating back, or so it was said, to the days of Xerxes himself.

"On this and all days," he said, it being the traditional reply.

She stood aside and let him pass, and Leander hurried

down a long corridor. He passed several aides as he rushed toward the massive parliamentary chamber, and noticed two men whisper to each other when they saw him. A frown creased his forehead. Gossip did not bode well, and now his curiosity about the nature of this urgent summons took on an ominous bent.

There were four sentries at the ornate double doors of the chamber, two on either side. They opened the door as he approached, and the corridor was suddenly flooded with the noise of dozens of voices speaking at once—the buzz of conversation on the chamber floor.

"Professor Maddox," one of the sentries said in greeting as he passed.

Leander was already inside the chamber when it struck him. *Professor.* The sentry had called him Professor, rather than Grandmaster.

The circular chamber was vast, with twenty rows of seats ringed about a bare floor where anyone wishing to speak would stand to address the Parliament. The room was the heart of the Xerxis, and its walls went all the way up to the apex of the tower itself. There were no openings on the lower walls, no windows save for one, at the very tip of the tower, where a single broad pane of spell-glass allowed a view of the sky. Unless it was midday, however, daylight did not reach down onto the floor of the parliamentary chamber, and so ghostfire lanterns flickered from wall sconces and from posts at the end of each aisle.

At the moment the only mage on the speaker's floor was

Alethea Borgia, a silver-haired woman of advanced age who was both Grandmaster of the Order of Tantrus and the Voice of Parliament. As the Voice, it was her place to conduct all of the parliamentary meetings, to make certain procedures were followed, and to oversee the various committees established. She was, for all intents and purposes, the most powerful mage on Terra.

When Leander entered the chamber, all conversation instantly ceased. All eyes were upon him.

Alethea had been a friend to Argus Cade. There had been some who had suggested that the two—who had known each other before many members of Parliament had been born—were more than friends. But Alethea's first loyalty would always be to Parliament.

"Grandmaster Maddox," the Voice said. "Thank you for coming so quickly. There is an urgent matter that must be . . ."

She continued speaking, but though he held her in very high regard, Leander was no longer listening to her. His eyes had gone, only naturally, to his own seat in Parliament, the first row on the second aisle to the left of the entrance. As he was standing, his seat ought to have been empty.

It was not.

In the place that had for over a century belonged to each successive grandmaster of the Order of Alhazred, there was a beautiful girl, only a few years older than Timothy. Her long hair was a rich red and it gleamed in the ghostfire light, giving her an almost ethereal aspect. She wore robes of gold.

Stitched in emerald green on the front of her robe was the sleeping dragon, the symbol of the Order of Alhazred.

Alethea Borgia had at last noticed that he was not paying any attention to her. She cleared her throat. "Grandmaster Maddox."

The red-haired girl crossed her arms and shot a withering glance at the Voice. "I do wish you wouldn't call him that."

"You will be silent for the moment," Alethea instructed her. "I have the floor."

Leander stared at the girl, then at the Voice. "What is the meaning of this, Alethea?" he asked, breaking protocol by using the familiarity of her first name.

The girl leaned forward, studying them both, and her fiery hair spilled across her features, hiding her eyes from him.

"Professor Maddox," Alethea replied. "Your appointment as Grandmaster of the Order of Alhazred has been challenged by the granddaughter of the previous Grandmaster, who claims the right of ascendancy."

"Granddaughter?" Leander repeated, mystified. He stared at the girl, even as the Voice continued.

"Yes. His granddaughter indeed. Leander Maddox, may I introduce you to Cassandra Nicodemus."

Timothy had a workshop in the lower levels of SkyHaven. There, just offshore from Arcanum, it was far easier for him to get materials for his inventions than it was on the Island of Patience. Yet in the time he had spent back on the island, he had realized he still preferred that isolated workshop to this one. Leander might be able to remove all of the bad elements from the Order of Alhazred, but Timothy would never be able to eliminate the bad memories from his time as a guest here, when Nicodemus was still in charge.

He hoped there would come a time when things quieted down enough so that he could move back into his father's house—into his house. But for now he knew he and his friends were safer at SkyHaven. Or, at least, most of them were. It seemed Verlis wasn't safe anywhere in the world of mages.

"I should be doing something!" he snapped as he paced through the workshop. Ivar, Sheridan, and Edgar were there, and he was glad to have his friends about. Leander had arranged for Caiaphas to go to Timothy's father's house and use the door to Patience, to retrieve them and bring them here. If the boy wasn't going back to the island anytime soon, he wanted his friends with him.

"Caw! What can you do?" Edgar asked. The rook perched on one of Timothy's worktables, head tilted to one side, regarding him with black eyes. "Parliament has made its ruling. Your father used to say Parliament was created so that there would be one place in the world where mages fought with words, not magic. It's civilized."

Timothy spun and glared at him. "Civilized? They've locked Verlis in a prison underwater, just because he's different from them! Is that civilized?"

The bird ruffled his feathers, but said nothing.

A hiss of steam came from the valve on Sheridan's head, and the mechanical man took several steps forward. He had been working on a new gadget for the arsenal that was stored inside his metal torso, an extendable arm that, when deployed, would give off a friction shock. Now his eyes glowed a pale red as he gazed at Timothy.

"No. It is not civilized. But it is not entirely unexpected. Your father used to bring books to Patience. There were history books among them. We both read them, Timothy. Mages have always defined living creatures by their differences, and conflict has often resulted."

Timothy sighed. "I know. But that doesn't make it right." He strode across the room to the large window and stood looking down at the churning ocean beneath. The sun shone brightly upon the waves. It was a beautiful day, but the plight of his friend left him unable to enjoy it.

He heard the ruffle of feathers and then the flap of wings, and Edgar settled down on the windowsill beside him. "Not right. Of course it's not right. But until the Parliament understands that . . ."

The rook did not finish his thought.

Timothy shook his head.

"And what if they never understand?"

The boy glanced up. He had just thought this very thing, but the words had not come from him. In a shadowed corner of the workshop, Ivar sat in a crouch, whittling a piece of wood into a startlingly realistic image of Verlis, wings and all. Timothy had nearly forgotten that the warrior was there, for Ivar had used his ability to alter the hue of his skin to blend into the shadows.

The warrior's face was grim. "Verlis is a prisoner because of what he is. Sheridan is correct about history. Mages have no love for the Asura. They exterminated my tribe before they attempted to do the same with the Wurm. If they do this to Verlis, can the day be far away when they will come for me, as well?"

Timothy stared at him. His heart ached with the sadness in Ivar's voice, and his face burned with anger at the injustice of it all.

"That's it!" he snapped. "That is it! I'm going to tell Leander to ask the Parliament if—no. No, no. I'm going to tell him that—as a friend of Verlis—that I demand the right to defend him, that I demand an audience. My father did it, and I'll do the same. One way or another, they're going to let him go, and let me get him back to his own world."

CHAPTER FOUR

Timothy stood before the mirror in his bedroom gazing at his reflection. He tugged on the bottom of the fancy dinner jacket and stepped back to scrutinize his attire. The high-collared shirt was tight against his neck, and he pushed a finger between the starched material and his throat, trying to loosen it. He briefly regretted his decision to dress formally for dinner with Leander, but tonight he wanted to express how serious he was about taking Verlis's plight to Parliament, and Timothy felt that these uncomfortable clothes would lend credence to his views.

He had never bothered to wear any of the myriad outfits Nicodemus had provided him upon his arrival at SkyHaven, choosing instead to wear the more practical and more comfortable clothes he had brought from Patience. Tonight was a different story, however. Timothy had to prove to Leander Maddox how important this was to him.

A knock on the door interrupted the boy's thoughts. "Come in," he called out, tugging on the sleeves of his rich brown jacket, catching the reflections of his friends as they entered through the door behind him.

"Caw! Caw! Look at you," Edgar said from his perch atop Sheridan's head.

"What do you think?" Timothy asked nervously, looking down at the heavy black trousers and ankle-high boots. "Do you think Leander will take me seriously?"

A short burst of steam hissed from the valve on the side of Sheridan's head. "I think you look very serious," the mechanical man said politely. "As a matter of fact, I'm not certain I have ever seen anybody look *more* serious. What do you think, Edgar?"

The rook ruffled his feathers, looking the boy over once again. "If Leander can't see how serious you are, he isn't really looking."

Timothy caught movement out of the corner of his eye, a distortion in the air, moving across the room. "Hey, Ivar," he called. "What do you think?"

The warrior appeared as if by magic, his skin turning its natural pale coloring as he leaned against the windowsill. "I think you are wearing too much," he said with a scowl. He circled around Timothy, reaching out to feel the fabric of the clothing. "How is it even possible to breathe—never mind do battle?"

"But this is the way people dress here—when they want to impress someone—and I don't think I'll be fighting with anybody tonight. At least, I hope not."

Ivar shook his head sadly. "I mean no disrespect, Timothy Cade, but I am not impressed."

Timothy chuckled, checking his image one more time in the mirror before making his way toward the door. "And no disrespect to you, either, but the only person I have to impress tonight is Leander. Wish me luck," he said to them as he went out the door with a wave.

The Grandmaster's dining room was in the west wing of the floating citadel. Timothy made his way through the winding corridors of SkyHaven and only took the wrong turn twice before he managed to reach the room. He took a deep breath, letting it out slowly to calm himself. The doors had been left open, and he strolled in, hoping he exuded an air of maturity, of seriousness. Leander was seated at his usual place at the head of the table, his back to the door, but there were other people around the table as well. When he saw the red-haired girl at the table, he froze and his eyes went wide.

She was the same mysterious girl who had aided him on the day he and his friends had attacked SkyHaven to stop Nicodemus. She had pointed out an entrance that had led him swiftly to the evil Grandmaster. And then she had, seemingly, disappeared. Yet here she was, sitting down for dinner.

"It's you!" he said, far louder than he had intended.

"Ah, Timothy," Leander said, rising from his chair and turning to face him. He looked the boy up and down and smiled, obviously taking note of his attire, then placed a friendly arm around his shoulder. "As you can see, we have some special guests tonight, and I'm pleased that you dressed appropriately."

"Leander, it's her," Timothy said in a shocked whisper, looking from his friend to the mysterious girl sitting across the table. "She's the one I was telling you about. She wasn't a figment of my imagination at all."

The mage arched an eyebrow. "No, she is very real indeed. Allow me to introduce to you Cassandra Nicodemus and her aides, Nadda and Cybil," he said as he extended his arm toward the young woman and the others at the table.

The aides bowed their heads politely, but the girl did not. Cassandra Nicodemus stared at him, her emerald eyes holding Timothy's, as if daring him to look away first.

"Cassandra," he found himself repeating as he swam in the intensity of her stare. "Nicodemus?" He broke the gaze and looked up at his mentor.

Leander nodded his large, shaggy head. "She is the grand-daughter of the former master of our guild."

"And you must be the renowned Timothy Cade," Cassandra said. "The un-magician, as they call you."

Timothy looked back at the girl, suddenly self-conscious, her scrutiny making him feel as though he'd been placed beneath a magnifying lens. The uncomfortable clothing made his skin begin to prickle and itch.

"I—I never knew—Nicodemus—," Timothy stammered, suddenly finding it difficult to stand still.

"That the former Grandmaster had a family?" Cassandra interrupted. "I arrived at SkyHaven two weeks before you.

My parents were killed in an accident with their sky carriage, and my grandfather thought it best for me to be brought here to recover."

Though her words were plain enough, Timothy sensed pain beneath them, a kind of hurt immediately recognizable to one who shared a similar loss. "I'm sorry," he said, attempting to let her know that he understood, that she was not alone in her sadness.

For a moment he sensed a connection between them, a mutual understanding, but then it was gone, and she recoiled from his words as if slapped.

"And what on Terra could you be sorry for?" she asked, a frown marring her pretty features.

"I—I recently lost my father," he began, feeling even more foolish. "It's just that I know how it feels to lose somebody close."

"My grief is very personal, Timothy Cade," Cassandra stated coldly, precisely adjusting the place setting before her. "I do not wish to discuss it with strangers."

The tension in the room was almost palpable, and Cassandra's two female aides looked supremely uncomfortable.

Timothy frowned. "I didn't mean to—"

Always the diplomat, Leander stepped in. "Of course you didn't." He directed the boy to a chair on the opposite end of the table and gestured for him to sit. "I am certain that our guest took no offense. But perhaps we ought to turn the conversation to less intimate matters."

Timothy sat as Leander returned to his own seat.

"Now that the introductions are out of the way, we shall enjoy a nice dinner, hmm?" Leander asked, a warm smile on his face. The mage raised his hand, tracing a symbol of magic in the air, and the gentle peal of a tiny bell was heard. Within moments, the room was filled with waiters bringing their meals.

For a while they ate in silence. Timothy was anxious to discuss Verlis's predicament, but he knew this was not the time. Instead he focused on the magnificent food on his plate. The razorboar meat was delicious, and he wasn't sure he'd ever had vegetables prepared quite as tastily as these. *The chefs of SkyHaven have outdone themselves tonight,* he thought, cutting another slice of the tender meat and popping it into his mouth.

"How does it feel?" someone suddenly asked, and Timothy looked up from his plate to see Cassandra staring at him.

"Excuse me?" he asked, dabbing at his mouth with a cloth napkin, swallowing the last of his bite.

The girl studied him closely. Her aides seemed uncomfortable again. "How does it feel to be not connected to the magic around you?"

Timothy thought for a moment. "It really doesn't feel like anything to me," he said with a shrug.

Cassandra picked up her crystal water goblet and sipped daintily. Her eyes were wide and curious and a little sad. "It must be very lonely, to be the only one like you."

There was pity in the girl's voice, and Timothy smarted

from it. But she had known magic as part of her life since birth, and he had known no such thing. It was like feeling sorry for the mudtoad because it was unable to fly above the clouds.

"I'm not lonely at all, really," he told her. "When I was on Patience, I had my friends Ivar and Sheridan to keep me company, and now that I'm here"—Timothy looked to Leander and smiled—"and now that I'm here, I have even more."

The mage returned Timothy's smile affectionately, and suddenly the boy felt that this was the opportunity he had been waiting for.

"But one of my friends has been taken from me," he said, watching the expression on Leander's face turn to one of disapproval.

"Timothy, please," he said, not without a little exasperation. "I've told you, I have done all I can."

"Then it's true?" Cassandra asked, eyes wide and excited. "You actually befriended a Wurm?"

"Yes," Timothy answered. "Verlis is my friend, and they've put him in prison without any reason. He's done nothing. It's unfair. Unjust."

Cassandra's aides gasped, gazing at each other nervously.

"Wurm are the enemy of all humankind," Cassandra stated. "Everyone knows that. It was only a matter of time before your supposed friend betrayed you. They're like that, you know."

Timothy's anger flared. "What do you know about my friend?" he demanded. Cassandra brought a delicate hand to her chest in shock. "Have you ever even met a Wurm, let alone talked to one?"

Cassandra looked away indignantly. "Wurm are nothing more than monsters. My grandfather taught me that—"

"Your grandfather was more of a monster than Verlis could ever hope to be."

"Timothy!" Leander snapped, rising to his full height at the head of the table. "I will not allow you to be rude to our guest. Apologize at once!"

The boy rose as well, throwing his napkin down onto the tabletop. "I don't think so. The world knows what Nicodemus did. It's no secret. I meant no disrespect, but I can't stand the way the people of this world talk about Verlis and his clan. He is no more a monster than I am—and yes, I am aware that some see me like that."

Save for Leander, no one would meet his gaze.

"I want to speak to them, Leander," Timothy continued. "I think I can convince Parliament to set Verlis free."

"*You* want to speak to Parliament?" Cassandra asked, aghast. "If I were Grandmaster I would allow no such thing."

"*If* you were Grandmaster, but you're not," Timothy snarled.

"Not yet," she retorted, placing her hands atop the table on either side of her plate. "But that's only a matter of time."

Leander sighed and slowly nodded.

"What is she talking about?" Tim asked in confusion. "*You're* the Grandmaster. How could she—"

"Cassandra is the heir of the former Grandmaster," the

mage explained. "By right of ascendancy, she has the authority to remove me and assume the title of Grandmaster of the Order of Alhazred."

Cassandra shook her head. "I'm not yet ready for such a daunting position, but possibly, in the near future."

Timothy was growing frustrated. "Well, she's not Grandmaster yet, Leander. Please, let me talk to Parliament. I'm sure that if I could get them to listen . . ."

Leander sighed heavily, shaking his head from side to side. "I don't think that would be wise right now."

"Whatever you asked of them, they would deny you," Cassandra added curtly.

"She's right. Now is not the time for you to be talking to Parliament."

"I understand your doubts, and why you hesitate," Timothy said slowly, quietly, attempting to remain calm. "But I can't let that get in the way of what I know is right." He had made up his mind, and nothing was going to change it. "My father was Argus Cade. In his name, I demand an audience. Out of respect for him, if nothing else, I know they'll comply. I've done my research. I know the customs. Please inform Parliament that I am coming to speak with them tomorrow," he said with finality.

Leander was speechless as Cassandra lowered her eyes to her plate.

"Now if you'll excuse me, I'm not feeling very well and would like to go to bed." With those words Timothy took his leave of them, their disapproving stares boring into his back as he walked from the room.

Sheridan's visual sensors activated with a faint click, and the mechanical man looked about the darkened bedroom.

He wasn't sure what it was that prompted him to awaken before his designated time, but he knew it had something to do with his friend and creator, Timothy Cade. Sheridan's head slowly swiveled, taking in every detail of the room. The large bed, where he had last seen the boy sleeping, was empty, and Timothy was nowhere to be found.

The boy had returned from his dinner with Grandmaster Maddox quite furious. When pressed by Edgar, Timothy had begun to rant about Leander Maddox and the mystery girl with the red hair, who, it seemed, was actually the granddaughter of Nicodemus.

He had gone to his bedroom, frustrated, and removed his fancy clothes, tossing them into a rumpled heap in the corner. Sheridan had followed, hoping the boy would confide in him once they were alone, but instead he had crawled into the bed and buried himself deep beneath the covers. The mechanical man had decided to remain functioning in case Timothy decided to talk, but as the evening wore on, and the boy didn't move, Sheridan had shut himself down. He hoped that a good night's sleep would give his young friend a fresh perspective, and that he would be able to share his feelings in the morning.

Sheridan moved away from his position against the wall, heavy metal feet clomping across the hardwood floor as he made his way to the bedroom door. Carefully he opened it and peeked into the living room.

"Timothy?" he whispered. "Are you here?" There was no answer, but Sheridan thought he knew where the boy might be.

He left the suite, striding down the nighttime corridors as quietly as he could. Sheridan reached the workshop in the lower level of the floating estate and saw that the heavy wooden door was ajar. His suspicions confirmed, he pushed open the door.

"Timothy?" he called quietly.

"Over here."

Sheridan followed the sound to a corner of the cramped room, where the boy sat at the desk he had recently constructed, illuminated by a lantern that contained a single bright flame of hungry fire.

The boy placed a finger to his lips, cautioning him to be quiet. Sheridan rotated his head completely around to see a sleeping Edgar perched atop the autogyro flying machine, and Ivar curled up on a blanket beneath the large, shuttered windows.

"I reactivated early and found that you were not in your bed," the mechanical man whispered. A short burst of steam hissed from the valve on the side of his head. "I was concerned. Are you well?"

"I'm fine," Timothy replied, setting his pencil down atop the many pages of notes and drawings he had done since leaving his bed. "Thanks for your concern—especially after I behaved so badly tonight."

"That's quite all right," Sheridan said, dismissing the boy's behavior as irrelevant. "I've got quite the thick skin, you know." He thumped on his rounded chest with a metal fist for effect.

Timothy smiled, and it made the mechanical man feel good to see that his creator had at least partially escaped the dour mood that had weighed upon him earlier.

"I woke up and couldn't go back to sleep, my thoughts were racing so fast," Timothy explained, picking up his pencil again. "I figured this was the best place to go."

"It is quite inspiring, isn't it," the mechanical man said, placing his hands on his rounded hips and looking around at the fully functioning workshop. It had only been a few months ago that this had been an empty storage room, but now it was a place where Timothy Cade's creative skills could run wild.

"I decided I should have a backup plan, just in case Parliament doesn't listen to me."

"I don't like the sound of that," Sheridan said cautiously. "Please tell me that you won't do anything that will get you into too much trouble."

Timothy chuckled, starting a new drawing on a fresh sheet of paper. "Don't worry about me, Sheridan. I'm always careful."

Something tickled the cogs and springs of Sheridan's mechanized brain, telling him otherwise, and he immediately began to worry about the safety of his best friend.

"Will you be returning to bed soon?" he asked, watching as the boy continued to draw, fabulous ideas spilling from his brain to the paper.

"I want to finish this design first," Timothy said, not looking up. "Why don't you go back to the room and wait for me there. I should be along shortly."

"Very well," the mechanical man said, leaving the boy to his designs, knowing that it would be quite some time before his young master again sought the comfort of sleep.

Timothy sat nervously in a tiny room in the Xerxis, awaiting his summons from the Parliament of Mages.

The morning had come, seemingly with the snap of a finger. The sun had barely risen when he was awakened, still seated at the desk in his workshop, startled to discover that he had never found his way back to his bedroom.

"Parliament will hear you this morning at the ninth hour," Leander had said firmly, barely making eye contact. "I suggest you put on some clothes and fortify yourself with a hearty breakfast." And with those words, he had turned and left the workshop.

Timothy had been stunned by the coldness of his friend, but understood that Leander was still upset with his defiance. His chair creaked loudly under him, disturbing the fragile silence of the waiting room as he crossed his legs, musing upon his morning.

He had done as the mage suggested, and as he had dressed he considered another fancy outfit from his crowded closet, but decided against it. He wanted there to be nothing artificial about his appearance, eager for the various guild masters who composed the Parliament of Mages to see him for what he actually was, not for what they believed him to be.

After hurrying through his breakfast, he had found Caiaphas and Leander waiting for him at the main entrance to SkyHaven, and they were off. The ride to his appointment had been spent in an uncomfortable silence, and he had briefly considered apologizing to his friend, but his father had taught him to stand firm in his beliefs, and he believed that what he was doing was right. Someone had to speak up for Verlis, despite what the majority believed, and it had to be him. There was no one else.

From the air the Parliament complex was even more incredible than in the pictographs he had seen in his books, and Timothy had found himself nearly breathless as the sky carriage descended through the early morning traffic toward the sprawl of buildings at the center of Arcanum.

He had stood staring in awe at the grandeur that was the Xerxis until Leander hurried him along, desperate to be on time. They entered the building through tall doors held open by two armored sentries.

Since the building's defensive wards and spells would not work on him, Leander was required to vouch for the boy's identity. Once that was done, he was ushered into the tiny room with the single chair where he now impatiently awaited Parliament's summons.

Timothy wasn't sure how long he had been kept waiting— it felt like days. He stood and began to pace around the tiny room, trying to imagine what his audience with the ruling body of mages would be like, and how he would handle them.

His thoughts drifted toward the plans he had devised the previous night in case Parliament denied Verlis his freedom, but he pushed them quickly away. They were imaginings for another, more desperate time.

A door opposite the entrance to the tiny room opened silently, and a sentry dressed even more elaborately than those guarding the Xerxis filled the doorway.

"Parliament summons you," he said in a booming voice, and stepped back to allow the boy to pass.

Hesitantly Timothy walked through the doorway into the meeting chamber of the Parliament of Mages. *This is it,* he thought, each step feeling heavier than the last. The sentry directed the boy to a circular dais in the center of the high-ceilinged room, where he stood, turning his attention to those gathered around him. Twenty rows encircled him, each of the one hundred and sixty-nine seats occupied. His father had taught him that in the days of old, only thirteen guilds had made up the Parliament. But as the years passed, other guilds had formed, and now there were thirteen times that original number. Today the Grandmaster of every guild was present, and Tim could feel their scrutinizing eyes upon him.

It was eerily quiet within the chamber, the silence almost deafening, but an anticipatory buzz suddenly arose, spreading through the vast chamber as another door opened and a tall, older woman with silver hair, dressed in robes the color of dawn, walked toward him. She moved as though she was gliding across the floor, holding a staff that appeared to be carved from a gigantic piece of bone. In his nervousness, Tim tried to think of the animal from which a bone so large could have come.

The silver-haired woman stopped before him and struck the base of her bone staff three times on the floor—a signal, Tim guessed, that his audience was about to commence.

"I am the Voice of the Parliament of Mages," she said, her words echoing throughout the auditorium. "Who is it that has requested we gather this morn?"

Timothy hesitated, not sure of the protocol, not knowing if he should answer the question.

"I have called for this gathering," said a voice that he recognized, and he turned to see Leander Maddox striding toward him, dressed in his emerald finery. "I, Leander Maddox, interim Grandmaster of the Order of Alhazred, have asked you here this glorious morning."

The Voice again stamped her staff upon the floor. "The Parliament recognizes Leander Maddox," she cried out, looking about the room. "Tell us why you have asked us here, Grandmaster."

Timothy scanned the crowd before him, his eyes finding familiar faces, representatives of some of the more powerful guilds. He saw the rat-faced Lord Foxheart, Grandmaster of the Malleus Guild, and the enchanting Mistress Belladonna of the Order of Strychnos. Timothy shuddered in fear as his gaze fell upon the fearsome, armored visage of Lord Romulus of the Legion Nocturne, his eyes seemingly burning red from within the confines of his horned helmet.

"The son of the late Argus Cade has requested the

opportunity to address this assembly," Leander boomed, looking about the chamber.

"And do you vouch for this stranger to our gathering place?"

Leander bowed deeply toward the woman who was the Voice. "I do," he proclaimed as he straightened. "And I shall be his advocate, if it is so allowed."

Timothy glanced at Leander, a smile of thanks gracing his tense features. Maybe the burly mage wasn't as mad as he thought, or maybe he was and it just didn't matter. Leander caught his eye, dragging a hand down over his shaggy beard, and then the mage quickly looked away as the Voice again began to speak.

"The Parliament recognizes your role as advocate, Grandmaster Maddox. Now it is time for this convocation to begin." The woman lifted her staff and turned slowly in a circle, showing all present the symbol of her authority. "What is the name of the one who wishes this audience?"

Timothy was about to speak when his advocate did it for him.

"His name is Timothy Cade," Leander proclaimed. "And I beg of you, brothers and sisters, keep an open mind as you listen to his plea."

A flash of something scarlet and gold caught Timothy's eye, and he noticed the stiff and proper form of Cassandra Nicodemus seated in the gallery, her red hair in a large knot atop her delicate head, adorned with golden ornamentation. He wasn't quite sure how to feel about the girl. On one hand, he found her superior attitude extremely obnoxious, but at the same time, he suspected that her behavior might be hiding something far more vulnerable.

But those were musings for another time, he knew, as the Voice pointed her ivory staff at him and directed his attention to those seated around him.

"Timothy Cade," she pronounced. "I give to you the ears of this Parliament of Mages."

Timothy froze. The gazes of all those gathered pummeled him like a rain of hail, but then he remembered why he had come, and for whose freedom he was about to petition.

Verlis.

"Grandmasters," he began, his voice trembling softly. "Kind thoughts to you on this morning." Looking out over the crowd, he touched two fingers to his forehead, his chest, and then he bowed, the traditional greeting of mages.

"On this and all mornings," the gathered guilds responded as one powerful voice.

He felt his courage bolstered by the courteous greeting and continued with his address. "Thank you for granting me this audience." He felt his voice growing stronger, more powerful. "I have come to you with an important request, one that I hope you will give your complete consideration after hearing my plea."

"What do you ask of the Parliament?" asked the Voice.

"I ask that you release the Wurm, Verlis, and grant me permission to travel with him through the dimensional barrier back to his home world."

The Voice's eyes grew wide as she turned her attention to the mages seated around them. "I will allow response to this boy's request."

"The child is mad," said an elderly figure from the top row. He was clad in a hooded robe that twinkled like the stars in the night sky. "I have been Grandmaster of the Order of the Winter Star for one hundred and twenty-three years. Though only a handful of you were also members of Parliament then, there are others among us who were alive in those dark days when the threat of the Wurm was real, when villages burned from their fire and children were stolen by night. When Alhazred's voice thundered in this very chamber, exhorting us to defend ourselves, I was the first to second his motion.

"I say this so that those of you who do not remember will know that these are not myths, but memories. You see a young boy before you, son of the wise but soft-hearted Argus Cade, and despite what he is, this abominable nonmagical thing, you might be tempted to look kindly upon him. He is his father's son, after all. But push aside all such thoughts. The world was rid of the monsters for a reason. To allow a doorway to be opened from this world to theirs would certainly invite disaster upon us."

Timothy looked to the Voice, eager to respond, but not sure if he needed permission. "May I answer?" he asked politely.

The Voice nodded. "Proceed."

"I have lived only thirteen years and most of that time in another place, not even of this world. But I have learned the history. If the Wurm were a threat in those times, might it not have been because they felt threatened, because they were in danger?"

An angry muttering came from several spots around the room, but Timothy went on. "Never mind that. You can't blame an entire race for the crimes of a few. Verlis came to our world not to menace us, but to seek the aid of my father, who, unbeknownst to him, had passed on." Timothy felt a painful lump of emotion form in his throat. "I did what I felt my father would have done, and I agreed to help the Wurm and his people."

A figure seated not far from Cassandra jumped up from her seat. "You're lucky to be alive, son of Argus Cade!" she shrieked. "The Wurm would just as soon burn you to ash as look at you! They are monsters of the worst kind. Retract your request and leave the abomination to rot at the bottom of the sea."

This time he didn't ask for permission to rebuke the hurtful words. "Verlis is not a monster! He is a thinking, feeling creature from a race of thinking, feeling creatures. Are there bad among them? Wurm who could wish to do us harm? I'm sure there are. But remember there is evil among us, as well, or have you forgotten Grandmaster Nicodemus."

A collective gasp escaped the gathering at the mention of that name, and Timothy could not help but look in Cassandra's direction. The girl hung her head in shame. He didn't mean to hurt her, but he had to make his point.

"Verlis and his clan are not evil," Timothy continued. "A

civil war has broken out in Draconae. They are being oppressed by their own kind and are in danger, and they have asked for our help—my help. I beg you to allow me to do this."

"I say we let him go," said a booming voice like the rumble of thunder, and Timothy saw the foreboding shape of Lord Romulus rise to his feet, causing those seated around him to cringe in fear. "I say we let the boy go and close the doorway permanently behind him!"

A scattering of cheers and claps erupted from around the chamber, and Timothy felt his heart sink. They weren't listening to him, their fear and ignorance not allowing them to think beyond their petty prejudices. He hung his head, as the weight of his sorrow sat heavy upon his shoulders.

"Please, show some respect," said a powerful voice, and Timothy realized that Leander now stood beside him. "You may not agree with his request, but at least show him the same courtesy that he is showing you."

Mistress Belladonna was the next to rise, seeming to grow up from her seat like one of the beautiful and unique flowering plants that the Order of Strychnos was known for. "As his advocate, how do you feel about the boy's appeal, Grandmaster Maddox? Do you think that we should allow the Wurm to go free, and a doorway between our two worlds to be opened?" she asked. "I'm sure I could tell you how the former Grandmaster of the Order of Alhazred would have answered."

Leander sighed, clasping his large hands behind his back as he studied the hem of his robe. "My opinion would have very much mirrored the responses I have heard this morning." He gazed up at his peers. "If I had not the pleasure of meeting the Wurm, Verlis. Yes, he is monstrous in appearance, but within him, there beats a heart very much like our own. Verlis is a father and a husband and a son, and he fears for his family."

The Grandmaster paused, looking about the room. "And if you are still wondering how I would respond to young Master Cade's request, the answer is, I would grant it to him."

A murmur went through the crowd. The fact that a respected member of Parliament like Leander Maddox had taken Timothy's side had certainly thrown the proceedings into turmoil, and the boy dared to wonder if his request might actually be granted.

"But of course you were the one to bring the boy over from where he had been hidden away for years, isn't that true, Professor Maddox?"

Another player had suddenly come onto the scene. Timothy felt his heart skip a beat, and he flushed with anger as he watched Constable Grimshaw saunter arrogantly into the chamber.

"I would imagine that you've grown fond of the afflicted youth," the constable added, his hand reaching up to smooth the end of his thin, black mustache.

"Yes, I have grown quite close to the boy, but that fondness has very little to do with what I see as the merits in his request."

The constable sneered, turning his attention to the Voice of Parliament. "My deepest apologies," the man said with a bow. "The tribulations of my position as constable kept me from arriving in a more timely fashion. I'm afraid another mage has disappeared from the streets of Sunderland, and I was called to the scene to investigate."

The crowd murmured at this revelation, and Timothy was perplexed. He had thought the mystery of the vanishing mages solved with the death of Grandmaster Nicodemus. He was disturbed to discover that this was not the case. For if Nicodemus was gone, then who was responsible for the recent disappearances?

"Your apology is accepted," the Voice replied. "Do you have anything to contribute to our gathering this morning, Constable? Something that might help our representatives to make their decision?"

"And what, exactly, has the boy asked of Parliament?" The constable glanced at Timothy with a hint of a smile.

Leander began to answer, but Grimshaw quickly raised a hand, silencing him. "Let the boy respond," he purred.

Timothy met the constable's gaze without wavering. "I want them to free Verlis from Abaddon and let me go with him to Draconae to help his clan."

Grimshaw's eye grew wide as he turned toward the assemblage. "Surely he jests," the constable said, his astonishment obviously a pretense. "Free a creature from captivity whose sole desire is to see our kind wiped from existence, and then open a doorway that could allow more of its fearsome kind access to our world?"

The constable narrowed his gaze and glared at Timothy as

though he himself were the worst kind of criminal. "If you are indeed serious, Master Cade, I would have to say that it is my belief that you have lost touch with your sanity."

The crowd growled, emotions stirred by the constable's forceful words.

"Why should the esteemed members of Parliament even consider a request from one such as you?" he asked. "With all that has happened since your arrival—the turmoil and the discord amongst the guilds—why would they even entertain the idea?"

"See here, Grimshaw," Leander said. "To blame Timothy for the mistrust within the guilds is outrageous and—"

"He's right!" yelled a mage from the gathering. "Things were fine until the boy showed up! He's unnatural!"

The guild members began to speak at once, each of them stirred to opinion by the constable's insinuations.

"The son of Argus Cade is to blame!" shrieked Lord Foxheart. "His presence in this world must be responsible for all the disharmony. How else can one explain it? An abomination, that's what he is! I've said it before, and it's time you all listened."

Timothy was shocked and disappointed. He had always known that they were afraid of him—afraid of his difference— but never could have imagined how much. Leander moved swiftly toward him, as if to put himself between the boy and the angry Parliament members.

"You have to do something!" a mage dressed in robes of scarlet screamed.

"You're the constable, it's your job to restore order!" bellowed another.

The Voice strode to the center of the circular room, her staff of bone held aloft. "Silence!" she demanded, but her cries fell on deaf ears.

"Do you hear them, Cade?" the constable asked. "They demand that I do something about you." He smiled predatorily. "And I believe I know just the thing."

CHAPTER FIVE

Tiny beads of sweat rolled down Timothy's forehead. He was bent over a table in his workshop, the flicker from a hungry fire lantern casting eerie shadows on the wall. His chest rose and fell, the furnace of his heart stoked with anger, and he narrowed his gaze as he studied his handiwork. *Not long now,* he thought. *Not long at all.*

With a grave sigh he snatched up a rag from the table and mopped his brow. Then he set to work once more.

Something disrupted the shadows dancing in the lantern light, flickering at the edge of Timothy's vision. He glanced up and realized it was Ivar, moving closer to see what he was working on. The Asura's skin matched the color of the wall, the lantern light playing the same whispers of shadow and light on him. If Timothy had not been familiar with the color-shifting of the Asura, he would never have noticed Ivar's approach.

"What do you have in mind, Timothy?"

The young man frowned and stared at his friend. "I don't think anyone's seeing all of this clearly. I need to talk to someone who has better perspective."

Ivar crossed his arms, brow furrowing with contemplation.

From behind him there came the fluttering of wings. Timothy turned to see Edgar perched on the windowsill. The rook cocked his head slightly to one side to regard the boy.

"Caw! You're being awfully cryptic. Not to mention that I'm tempted to take it as an insult. We're your friends. I think we see the situation pretty clearly."

In the far corner Sheridan stood quietly, as though he had been shut down. But the mechanical man's eyes glowed, and so Timothy knew he was not resting. He was merely observing. As if to confirm this, a hiss of steam escaped from Sheridan's valve.

"Indeed," he said.

"You know that isn't what I meant," Timothy replied, exasperated. His friends were all watching him expectantly. He threw his arms up and gestured to the workshop around him. "You're just as much prisoners here as I am. So I don't think you qualify as having much better perspective, do you?"

His face felt warm, flushed with his frustration. Constable Grimshaw had confiscated his gyrocraft and confined him to SkyHaven under guard. And not only him, but Ivar and Sheridan as well. He could move about the floating fortress, mostly from his quarters to his workshop to the dining room, and sometimes out on the grounds. But for the past day and a half, he had been escorted everywhere by guards. It was not quite the same as being held captive in Abaddon, but it was not very different, either.

Sheridan's eyes brightened. "Please, Timothy, do not do anything rash."

Ivar only studied him quietly.

Timothy smiled grimly. "I don't think the constable left me with many options. Anything I do now is likely to be rash by his standards."

A heavy knock came on the door. Timothy started, glanced around anxiously, then snatched up the rag he had used to wipe his brow and spread it out to cover up his current project.

"Come in," he called.

The door swung open. A pale, wispy-haired guard with dangerous eyes stepped inside, glanced around as though searching for some hidden threat, then moved out of the way to allow Leander into the room. The Grandmaster—he *was* the Grandmaster to Timothy, no matter what the debate— nodded to the guard, who removed himself from the room and closed the door once more.

Leander glanced around the room, taking in each one of them in turn. He frowned, as though he had a sense that something out of the ordinary was going on here but could not quite figure out what. At last his gaze stopped on Timothy.

"I am so very sorry," Leander said, and his words nearly collapsed under the weight of the genuine sadness and guilt in his voice. "I knew that they would not be pleased to hear from you, but I never imagined it would come to this."

Timothy crossed his arms and leaned against the worktable.

"It probably wouldn't have, if not for Grimshaw," he responded. "But they all seem pretty bad. One worse than the next. They hate anything different, and they treat the Wurm like vermin. But it's as if all they needed to take their suspicion and hate one step further was permission from the constable. And he gave it to them, all right."

The burly mage shook his head, his shaggy mane falling across his face. He crossed the room and put both strong hands on Timothy's shoulders, gazing into the boy's eyes.

"Don't you understand? Before this, the guilds were split over how to deal with you. Some wanted you dead, though they would not speak the suggestion aloud. Others wanted to exile you. You know they fear you. Magic cannot harm you. Your touch can nullify any spell. They cannot really keep track of your comings and goings . . . without guards like this." He gestured toward the door.

"But there were others who wanted to believe the best of you because you are Argus Cade's son, or because they were sympathetic to the hardships you have faced. There were those who were grateful to you for your participation in exposing the evils of Nicodemus. And there were others who simply believed that you should not be discriminated against because you were born without magic."

Timothy stared at him. He glanced at Ivar, who looked on without expression. A soft whisper of steam escaped the side of Sheridan's head. Edgar's wings ruffled.

The young man shook his head sadly. "There *were*. But now that I've come to Verlis's defense, now that I've publicly said I want to help the Wurm, to go to Wurm World, they *all* hate me, right?"

"'Hate' is too strong a word," Leander told him. "Let us simply say that those who might have supported you do not dare to speak in your favor now. And you are right about one thing. Constable Grimshaw has only made it worse."

"Why?" Timothy shouted, throwing up his hands. "Some of the Wurm are vicious. I know that! But not all. Verlis's clan are being slaughtered. They're living, breathing, thinking, and feeling creatures. How can the Parliament simply turn their backs?"

With a loud click, the door to the workshop swung open. The pale guard stepped into the room again.

"Professor Maddox," he said. "Your time is up."

Professor, Timothy noticed. *Not Grandmaster. Professor.* He had to wonder what his address to Parliament had cost Leander. Apparently it had tipped the balance in Cassandra's favor. No matter what the girl had said about not being ready to be Grandmaster herself, it seemed the choice might be made for her.

The fire of Timothy's anger burned even higher.

Leander gazed at him, face heavy with regret. "You're fighting more than a century's worth of perception that the Wurm are monsters, Timothy. Savages, incapable of kindness or reason or morality. Most of Parliament is too young to remember a time before such attitudes were prevalent. And those old enough to recall those days will be loathe to even entertain the idea that they might have been wrong."

"But why?" the boy pleaded.

"If they were wrong about the Wurm," Leander said, "that would make *us* the savages."

Hours after Leander's visit Timothy was still in his workshop, but he was no longer working. The project he had been finishing was now completed. He stood by the broad window and glanced nervously at the workshop door. The guards had only interrupted to let Leander in. There was no reason to think they would try to enter. But still, he could not help being nervous.

"What do you wait for?" Ivar whispered from the shadows by the door. The Asura would be there waiting if anyone tried to enter.

Timothy smiled gratefully and shook his head. "Nothing. I'm going."

"I am not at all sure I like this idea," Sheridan said, his whisper almost indistinguishable from a slow hiss of steam. The mechanical man was prepared to make noise from time to time in the workshop, so the guards would think Timothy was still at work. But Sheridan was clearly worried.

Edgar cawed and beat his wings, gliding across the room to land at Timothy's feet. "Well, I'm sure I don't like it," the rook said. "Not at all. But since none of us has come up with any better ideas as to what we should do next, I vote for Timothy's plan."

The boy gazed at the bird. "It isn't up to a vote. It's up to me."

The rook's feathers ruffled, and he preened a moment. "So it is. Which brings us back to Ivar's question. What are you waiting for?"

Timothy glanced around the workshop, his gaze stopping again on the door. His heart pounded in his chest. He felt as though he could almost see the sentries through the walls, but that was only his imagination working. Ivar shifted in the dark, drawing his attention. The Asura nodded.

The boy nodded back.

His gaze went to the windowsill, where he had set down the items he had made. They were gloves, in a way, but not like any gloves any mage had ever seen. They were made from the dried, yet supple skin of the Bathelusk fish, complete with dozens of its deadly sharp, unbreakable quills, attached to the palms and fingertips. The Bathelusk quills were tipped with an acidic enzyme that continued to be produced long after the fish's death. The acid helped the quills penetrate almost any surface.

On the Island of Patience Timothy had made Bathelusk gloves once or twice a year as the enzymes dried. He had used them to climb various trees to retrieve fruits or fronds or other items of interest. But he had never used them for anything like this before.

His mouth felt dry, his lips rough, and he moistened them with his tongue as he carefully picked up the first glove. Great caution was required with this invention. A single quill could put a hole right through his hand if he did not take care. Slowly, he slipped his right hand into a Bathelusk glove, then cinched it tight with the straps at the back of the hand. He was forced to wiggle his left hand into the other glove. Timothy was prepared to ask Ivar for help, but he managed all right, though he had to use his teeth to cinch the straps on that second glove.

"Okay. Here goes," he said softly.

His friends were silent, watching as he turned to the window and reached out a hand. It was not real glass that kept the wind and the elements out, but spell-glass. Pure magic. Timothy pressed the back of his hand against it, and even through the fabric of the glove, his proximity to the spell disrupted the magic, and the barrier disappeared. The wind rushed in, rustling his hair.

At first Timothy had thought that he had to touch a magical object to disrupt its inherent sorcery. But it was in his nature to experiment and he had been doing a great deal of experimenting recently. Though he had said nothing yet to Leander, he had discovered that if he focused his mind enough, the nullification effect he had on magic could be extended beyond him. He wondered if there was some enzyme he exuded, like the Bathelusk, that was the cause. Whatever the explanation, though, he had learned that if he could concentrate enough, his touch was not necessary. At present he needed to be within inches of the spell. But he was still experimenting.

Timothy took a deep breath and leaned out the window. Outside there was a sheer drop to the ocean far below, and in the darkness he could see the tips of the waves gleaming by the light of several moons.

He heard Edgar's wings flutter again, but he ignored the sound. The boy turned and sat on the windowsill, his entire upper body outside of the fortress now. With his right hand he reached up and pressed his palm against the outer wall. The Bathelusk quills slid into the stone as easily as if it were loose sand. A smile spread across Timothy's face. He glanced back in through the window and saw the glow of Sheridan's eyes looking at him from the darkened room.

"Just like home. There's nothing to it," he said.

And, imagining the Yaquis trees back on the Island of Patience, he began to climb.

The moment Timothy was out the window, Edgar hopped up onto the windowsill to watch him go. And to report to the others. Timothy tried not to look down. Instead he watched the straps that bound the gloves below his wrists. They were impossibly tight, but he had never done a climb so flat and vertical before, and he feared that the strain would tear them, sending him plunging into the ocean below.

It was something he tried not to think about.

The wind tugged at him, whistling past his ears. It was chillier than he had expected, and he shivered. His muscles burned with the exertion, and he was grateful he was skilled at climbing with the gloves, and that he and Ivar had kept up their sparring regimen. If he had not had enough upper-body strength, he would have ended up stuck there on the wall, like a skuib trapped in the web of a Sundin spider.

By the time he had dragged himself hand over hand and passed the window just above his workshop, he was already gritting his teeth. At the next level of the fortress there was a small balcony, and he considered pausing there to rest. His muscles felt as though they were on fire. But he did not dare stop there, for fear he might be seen.

Once he had passed the balcony, he paused for a rest. With one hand above him, and one below, he hung there, catching his breath. His cheek was pressed against the cold stone, and he debated the wisdom of looking up to see how much farther he had to travel. He decided against it. At this point, becoming discouraged could spell his end.

After several more minutes of climbing, Timothy did look up. Off to the right, along the curve of the fortress wall, he saw the window he was searching for. As he was moving his right hand to start in that direction, the wind gusted, pushing him away from the wall.

He swayed, his whole body twisting in the wind, hanging only by the grip of the Bathelusk quills on his left hand. Timothy held his breath. An image of his father, smiling at him as they sat together on the sands of Patience, swam up into his mind. But Timothy was not ready to join Argus Cade in the spirit realm. Not yet.

Pain lanced through his shoulder. Something popped. The muscles felt as though they were tearing. With supreme effort, Timothy twisted himself back toward the wall, fighting the wind, and slapped his right hand against the stone. The Bathelusk quills sank in deeply, and anchored him there.

For a long moment he felt paralyzed. Moisture welled in his eyes, but he gnawed at his lip and refused to let the tears come. Then the wind tugged at him again, and a grim determination seized him. He tilted his head back to check his position, then continued on toward his destination.

Moments later he reached the window that had beckoned him from below.

And then he paused.

The truth was that he was not entirely certain this was the right window. He had gauged its location from the internal layout of SkyHaven, for he had never, of course, scaled its walls before. But Timothy had not come all this way to hesitate. And he could not climb back down without giving his muscles a real chance to rest.

Tentatively he reached up toward the spell-glass of that window, and it disappeared. Bathelusk quills sank into the window frame as he climbed into the room, as quietly as he could manage.

"Thank the spirits," he whispered, and a triumphant smile came to his face. He uttered a soft laugh and shook his head in amazement. Only then did he allow his gaze to survey this extraordinary room his courage had brought him to.

The Repository, it was called. Leander had shown it to Timothy after the defeat of Nicodemus. On that day it had seemed fascinating, but somehow not as wonderful as he had imagined. Now, though, with only the light of the moons streaming through the window, it was eerie and imposing. Fantastically so. The vast chamber was filled with artifacts and relics, ancient scrolls and magical charms that the Order of Alhazred had collected over the course of centuries.

Somewhere in this room were the Rings of Alhazred himself, along with the Eye of Phaestus, and other items that had been salvaged from the wars that had ended the days of the Wizards of Old.

Moonlight gleamed off strange, ornate boxes, medallions, engraved swords, and a myriad of other objects. Timothy hoped that one day he would be able to explore the Repository to his heart's content. But this night it was not to be. Tonight he had come here seeking only one object—an object that wasn't really an object at all.

"Hello?" he called into the gloom of that chamber, his voice barely above a whisper. "Are you here? It's me. Timothy Cade."

For a long moment he waited, his hopes sparking, and then beginning to fade. "Hello?" he asked again, a bit louder.

His heart sank.

And then the reply came.

"Timothy?"

He narrowed his gaze, tracking the voice, and then he saw what he had come for. On a shelf beside a strangely distorted skull and a hand that looked as if it had been carved from beeswax, there sat a beautifully carved box: the Box of Vijaya.

Now that he had found it, a tiny alarm went off in Timothy's mind. He remembered Ivar guarding the door of the workshop below and tried to calculate how long he had been gone. There was no way to know if the guards would wonder how late he was going to be in the shop, or if they would inquire, but he thought he must hurry, just the same.

Swiftly he navigated through the Repository, trying not to let his attention waver, though several items he saw tempted him sorely. Now was not the time, however.

He reached the box and opened it, pushing back the lid, and then stepping away so his presence would not affect the contents.

The contents. That isn't very polite, he told himself. *Not a nice way at all to refer to someone who has helped you before.*

The Oracle of Vijaya was just a withered head in a box. Yet more importantly it—he—was also a true seer of the future. The oracle knew things that no one could possibly know. This had been his magic in life, and now, hundreds or even thousands of years after his death, that magic still survived.

"It is nice to see you, Timothy," the oracle said, gazing at him with dark eyes that gleamed with pinpoints of moonlight.

"You too," the boy replied. And though it was strange conversing with such a creature, he found that he meant it. The oracle had been fair and kind to him before. He hoped the same would be true now.

"Your friend, the Wurm, is in trouble," the oracle said.

Timothy's eyes widened. The oracle knew! But of course he did. Knowing was what he did. It was everything he was.

"Yes." He nodded. "I can't just leave him there, in prison. It isn't right. I wonder what he must be thinking. Does he think I've betrayed him? I know he must be worried about his family, his clan. I promised to help him, and I will. But I don't know what to do. The Parliament—"

"Hush," the oracle said, so sternly that Timothy blinked in surprise.

"But—"

"Hush," the oracle repeated, dark eyes squinting, withered flesh crackling. "You have only moments before you must leave."

Timothy wanted to ask why, to ask what was coming, but he thought better of it. If the oracle said he had to hurry, then that was good enough for him.

"Go on."

"A moment of great change is upon you, Timothy," the oracle said. "The future is in turmoil, and difficult for me to see. It seems that where you are concerned, this is often the case. I find it . . . disturbing. Still, there are several things I can tell you.

"There are forces at work upon this world that will expose the secrets of the past. These revelations will ignite a fire that will smolder for some time before at last blazing brightly, wreaking havoc, throwing the Parliament into chaos. These things have been set in motion and are immutable. Mages will die. Others will be cast down in shame."

The words chilled Timothy, but he could only shake his head in confusion. "I don't understand. What does all this have to do with me? What should I do? About Verlis, I mean."

The edges of the oracle's mouth creased, as though in a smile. The effect was unsettling. If the boy had gotten used to speaking with a disembodied head, it would still take him a very long time to become accustomed to the oracle's whims and moods.

"I cannot tell you what to do. All I can tell you is what I see."

"And what do you see?" Timothy asked.

"You," the oracle replied, its voice a dry rasp. "You, in the Wurm world, Timothy. In Draconae. Whatever else you do, whatever else happens, you will go to Draconae. You must."

Timothy's mind was filled with questions, but the oracle blinked several times, eyes wandering.

"Now," the oracle said. "You must go *now*. Hurry!"

The descent always went far more quickly than the ascent. But the problem with the swiftness of climbing down, with his weight pulling at him, was that he was always tempted to move too quickly. With the ocean below, he dared not. Hand under hand, he moved down the wall, now bracing himself with his feet and elbows, legs splayed against the stone.

He had been gone from the Repository only briefly when he realized that the Oracle of Vijaya's insistence that he rush had made him forget the strain in his muscles. He ought to have rested longer. Timothy winced now each time he lowered his right hand, for doing so meant putting all of his weight on his left arm . . . and on the shoulder he had torn.

Timothy hissed air in through his teeth, jaws grinding with the pain. He slid the quills on his right glove into the stone and paused a moment. Still, the urgent voice of the oracle was in the back of his mind, prodding him to hasten his pace. He had no idea why the seer had rushed him, but the boy had visions of guards coming into the workshop, of his friends thrown in Abaddon with Verlis for their complicity in his traitorous deeds.

Ivar would die in a place like Abaddon. Somehow he knew it. The Asura could endure almost anything, but imprisonment in some cold cell, so far from nature and the open air . . . Ivar would not survive.

With this haunting thought, he began to move again. Hand under hand. Down and to the left. Moving toward the balcony that had tempted him before. Out of the corner of his eye he could see it, and its lure was even greater this time. Two stories farther below was his workshop. He would get there. He was certain of it, but at the moment it seemed so very far away.

When next he stretched out his left arm, he reached too far. As he pressed the Bathelusk quills into the stone and released his right hand, his body slid along the wall, the momentum putting even more strain on his shoulder.

Timothy groaned aloud, barely aware he had made any noise at all.

"That looks difficult."

He had his eyes tightly closed, wincing with the pain. Now they flew open and he twisted his head around to look up.

Cassandra Nicodemus stood on the balcony, her red hair blowing behind her and her pale skin gleaming under the caress of three moons, as though their light were hers and hers alone. One eyebrow was arched, and she gazed at him with a certain amusement that held none of the cold distance he had seen in her before. Instead a sweet benevolence danced in her eyes.

"Perhaps you'd better rest here for a few moments," she suggested.

Timothy stared at her, speechless.

He was caught! Her words made no sense to him at all. She had found him out. No matter how beautiful she was, she was still Nicodemus's granddaughter. She wanted to be Grandmaster of the Order of Alhazred. This girl was not a friend to him, nor to Leander. She was . . . the enemy?

"Or," she ventured, "you could just hang there until your arms tear out of their sockets and the rest of you plummets into the ocean. You'd have a difficult time swimming for shore without arms, I imagine."

This time, there was no mistaking it. Cassandra was smiling.

Timothy could barely breathe. He had no idea what to make of her words, or that smile.

"You've been to see the oracle, I take it?"

At last he summoned words. "How—how d-did you know?" he stammered.

Cassandra tucked a strand of red hair behind one ear and shrugged. "It's what I would have done, if I were in your situation. Though I suspect I'd have found a way to get there from *inside* SkyHaven."

For another long moment she watched him, obviously waiting for him to speak. Timothy's shoulder was throbbing with pain, but he could only stare at her.

"Ah, well. Do as you wish. If you decide to rest here, take as long as you like. But you'd be well advised to be back in your workshop before sunrise. The guards are unlikely to bother you tonight, but they will come to escort you to breakfast."

Once again she arched an eyebrow. "Good night, Timothy. And good luck. I do hope you survive the night. This world is far more intriguing with you in it."

With that, she slipped through the open balcony door, then closed it firmly behind her, disappearing into the darkness of her room. Timothy waited several moments longer, but the strain was too great. If he did not get to the balcony, he *would* fall.

He pulled himself, grunting softly in pain, onto the balcony. Whatever the reason for the oracle's urgency, there was nothing he could do now. He had to rest his arms.

For perhaps half an hour he sat on the balcony, forcing himself not to try to peer through the spell-glass set into the door. He wanted to see Cassandra, but he did not dare look for her. His mind was awhirl with confusion. Was she his enemy, or might she be a friend?

It was only when he began at last to descend once more, with great care and great pain, that another thought occurred to him.

What if the oracle had known Cassandra would see him, there on the balcony? What if that was why the seer had hurried him along?

By the time he climbed back in through the window of his workshop, every muscle on fire with the strain, he was more confused than ever.

CHAPTER SIX

Αnd do not forget your noon appointment with Professor Phineas about his assuming your ancient Arcanum classes at the institute this coming semester," Carlyle said, reading from a scroll of items that Leander would need to address this day.

Leander nodded, but he was not listening; his thoughts were elsewhere this early morning. He couldn't stop thinking about Timothy Cade, and for the first time in his long career, Leander Maddox felt ashamed to be associated with Parliament.

What would Argus think? he wondered as he sat at the table in the dining room, awaiting the boy's arrival. In his mind he pictured Argus Cade as he had been just before falling ill. Leander could imagine the great mage sitting across the table, slowly shaking his head in disapproval.

"Excuse me, sir?" Carlyle asked, startling the Grandmaster from his reverie.

"Yes, Carlyle?" Leander asked, trying to refocus his attentions.

"You said it was out of your hands. What is, sir? What's out of your hands?"

The Grandmaster ran a hand through his thick red beard, his thoughts in turmoil. "Nothing, Carlyle," he said, realizing he must have spoken his concerns aloud. "That will be all for now."

"But we must still discuss the menu for next week's celebration of the Feast of—"

"I said that will be all," Leander repeated with a growl of finality, pounding his fist on the tabletop and making the place settings jump. There were times when he was all too aware that his aide had previously been employed by the last Grandmaster of the Order of Alhazred. Leander had grown to rely upon Carlyle, but he would not have called the man his friend.

Carlyle bowed graciously and quickly departed, leaving the Grandmaster alone with his troubled musings.

Leander still imagined Argus sitting across from him, a look of disappointment on his face, and felt ashamed. Argus had been the spitfire, the one who often challenged the judgments of Parliament, and had developed quite a reputation before his death. Leander had always wanted to be more like his mentor, but it was often so much easier not to question. Still, he *had* questioned. He had protested their treatment of Timothy, but

Parliament had insisted that it agreed with Constable Grimshaw's judgment, and Leander had acquiesced. There seemed little room for further struggle. Parliament had spoken.

"You would have fought them tooth and nail, wouldn't you, Argus?" he said to the memory of his friend, knowing full well how the mage would have answered.

And with that thought, there came a knock, and the doors opened to admit Timothy flanked by two of Constable Grimshaw's men.

"Timothy Cade for breakfast, Grandmaster," said one of the guards.

"We'll be waiting outside to escort him back to his quarters as soon as he's finished," said the other.

And the two left the boy in the dining room to assume their posts outside the door.

"Good morning, Timothy," the Grandmaster said in his cheeriest voice. "I hope you're hungry." He picked up his plate and headed to the buffet at the side of the room.

Timothy followed silently, taking his own plate from the table. Once again, the cooks had outdone themselves. Leander helped himself to some diced fruit, numerous strips of smoked meat, and some freshly baked bread.

"How are you faring?" he asked, watching as the boy spooned a heaping portion of eggs onto his own plate.

"Well enough, I guess," Timothy replied with a shrug, eyeing the items on the elaborate breakfast table.

Leander almost apologized again, but decided against it. The damage had been done; now was the time to move beyond it. And if he was correct in his assumptions about the boy's rebellious personality, Timothy was doing just that. He was planning something, the mage was certain, locked away in his workshop from early morning to late evening. But the mage would expect nothing less from the son of Argus Cade.

Leander filled a delicate-looking cup, emblazoned with the crest of the Order of Alhazred, with steaming hot brew from a silver decanter. "I just want you to know that I'm willing to help, if I can."

"Help?" Timothy asked, using tongs to place a spiny jagger fruit on his crowded plate. The boy studiously avoided looking at him. "Help with what, exactly?"

Leander dipped a spoonful of honey into his drink and stirred. "Don't play the fool, boy. Others might be deceived by it, but I believe I know you well enough by now. I have no doubt that you've already concocted some way to escape the watchful eyes of Constable Grimshaw's guards and free Verlis from Abaddon, though for the life of me, I can't imagine how you could do it."

Taking his plate and drink, Leander returned to the table. Timothy paused by the buffet, his back still turned toward the Grandmaster, as though he were biding his time, trying to determine how best to respond. It pained Leander to think that the boy might no longer trust him, but he knew he had not given Timothy much reason to have faith in him of late. At last Timothy joined him at the table.

"If I told you that you weren't wrong, would you be mad at me?" Timothy asked.

The mage chewed on a slice of smoked meat, wiping his greasy fingers on the cloth napkin in his lap. He studied the boy a moment and then swallowed, hesitating only a moment before speaking his mind. The words about to issue from his mouth were treason, and as such, the hardest words he would ever speak. Leander reached out and placed a comforting hand over Timothy's on the table. The gesture made the boy meet his gaze, all pretense falling away. Leander saw all the pain and doubt his young friend was feeling, but also saw his determination. How could he be any less determined in the face of injustice than this remarkable boy?

"What they have done to you and Verlis is wrong, Timothy," Leander said grimly. "For your sake, as well as for the memory of your father, and not least, to save my own honor, I offer whatever help I can to rectify the situation. And no, I most certainly would not be mad at you."

The boy smiled, the first real smile Leander had seen grace the lad's face in what seemed like months. It was as warming as a late summer sun, and he realized again that there was something incredibly special about this youth, something that went far beyond his inability to do magic.

"I know you think I'm brash, that I rush into things without thinking them through," Timothy began, a bit sheepishly. "But I was not unrealistic in going to see Parliament. I knew there was every chance that they would deny my request. So I began to work on an alternate plan."

Timothy grinned excitedly and shoveled a forkful of orange egg yolk into his mouth, barely stopping to chew. "I would never have expected to be held captive in SkyHaven, but it's given me time to—"

"Tim," Leander said, his mug of brew pausing halfway to his mouth. "Please, you're not a captive. Parliament is being cautious. Observing you."

The boy's smile dissipated. "If you want to help, the first thing you can do is to stop making excuses for them!" Timothy snapped. He looked away, obviously embarrassed by this show of emotion. When he raised his eyes once more, there was an apology in them. "I'm sorry. I know you're stuck in the middle of all this. But, Leander, did you see the two guys that are waiting for me outside this room? They're outside my door when I wake up, and when I go to bed. They aren't observers. They're guards. I'm a prisoner, no matter how you word it."

The Grandmaster set his cup down with a heavy sigh. The boy was right. If he really was going to help Timothy, he was going to have to confront his own reservations about Parliament. Certainly he felt that it was possible, and preferable, to change mage society from within . . . but that could take time. Years. Generations. And Verlis's clan back on Draconae did not have years. Even if they had, Leander did not know how many nights he could sleep comfortably in SkyHaven knowing that Timothy—a boy he had vowed to care for—was a prisoner under his own roof.

"You're right, of course" he said, carefully wiping his mouth with the napkin. "Now, tell me as much as you feel you can about what you have planned, and how I can help set these plans in motion."

The boy had placed his jagger fruit in the center of his plate with a fork and was using a knife to slice it open, revealing its bright green core. "I have to get out of SkyHaven undetected and reach my father's estate." He spooned a mouthful of the sweet fruit into his mouth. "Are you willing to help me do that?"

Leander thought of what was being asked of him, and of the danger that he and Timothy could be facing in going against Parliament, but saw no alternative. Mages were being murdered, creating an undercurrent of fear and paranoia within Parliament. The appearance of the un-magician and an Asura warrior, and now the arrival of a Wurm on Terra, were only making things worse. The Parliament of Mages was in chaos, ancient fears, suspicions, and prejudices governing their every move. There would be no change unless it was forced.

The Grandmaster picked up the last piece of smoked meat from his plate and bit it in two. "How shall we proceed?"

Timothy's radiant smile returned, but almost as quickly, it was dashed. With no knock to signal his arrival, Constable Grimshaw swung the door open and strode into the room.

"Ah, just in time for breakfast," the constable said, hands clasped behind his back as he eyed them both suspiciously. "May I join you?"

Leander caught Timothy's gaze and saw that it was filled with alarm.

"Why, good morning, Constable Grimshaw," he said, politely rising from his seat, as if genuinely pleased to see the man. "Please, do join us. Timothy and I were just discussing matters of the day."

Leander winked pleasantly at the boy, letting him know that it was not a time for panic.

It was a time for courage, and for subterfuge.

"Caw! Caw! So what, exactly, are we waiting for?" Edgar asked as he alighted upon Sheridan's head, talons scratching against the metal.

"I'm not sure," Timothy said, dropping an armload of blankets and pillows from his room onto the floor of the workshop. "But Leander promised he would help me get out of here."

Sheridan released some steam and rubbed a segmented hand across his metal chin. "But won't the guards be coming shortly to escort you to your room for the night?"

Timothy smiled slyly, stepping over the pile of bedclothes to get to his small desk in the corner. "I told them I was really close to finishing a project, and that I wanted to stay in the workshop. They'll be out there, but I doubt they'll bother us again tonight." He began to read over his notes, discarding some, and placing others inside a leather satchel that he wore slung over his shoulder.

A familiar scraping sound filled the workshop, and Timothy saw that Ivar had stealthily joined them and was in the process of sharpening the knife that Timothy had made for him back home on Patience. The Asura had been meditating earlier, reconnecting with himself, as he liked to describe it.

"This place is like a large beast with many eyes," Ivar said, never allowing his concentration to waver from his blade, the strange black patterns writhing over his pale flesh. "How will you leave SkyHaven without being seen?"

It was a question that Timothy had been asking himself repeatedly since leaving breakfast that morning. He and Leander had been unable to finish their discussion after Grimshaw's untimely interruption, and the boy was left to wonder exactly how his friend intended to help him escape the scrutiny of the constable's watchdogs. He had to admit he was a bit worried, but held on to his faith in the Grandmaster.

"I have no idea," he answered in all earnestness as he continued to peruse his notes and drawings. "But I'm sure it will happen."

The room was silent, except for the sound of Ivar's metal blade sliding over the rough surface of the sharpening stone. The boy gathered that his friends did not share his confidence, and was spurred to rally them.

"That's why I need you all to be ready with the next phase of the plan when the time does come," he said, focusing his attention on Sheridan and Edgar. "Are we clear on what you're to do?" He closed the flap on his satchel and approached them.

Something whirred and clicked inside Sheridan's head before he answered, and Timothy knew that the mechanical man was having some trouble with what was being asked of him. But there was no other way.

"I am not especially skilled at lying, Timothy, but I'll do my best."

"Thank you, Sheridan."

"Caw! Don't worry about me, kid," said the rook. "Working with your father for so many years, and dealing with the likes of Parliament, I'm an old hand at creative fabrication. Not that I have hands, but you get the picture. The steampipe over here may not be able to lie very well," Edgar added, nodding his black-feathered head toward Sheridan, "but I'll make sure he doesn't get too close to the truth."

"Excellent." Timothy turned to the Asura. "Ready, Ivar?"

The warrior scrutinized his knife, then picked up a stray piece of parchment from the floor. He tossed the paper up into the air and let it drift down upon the waiting blade, slicing the parchment in two with the mere flick of his wrist. Both halves fluttered to the floor.

"Ready," he confirmed, carefully sliding the knife into a leather sheath at his hip.

Then they were all silent, waiting. At first the apprehension in the air was suffocatingly heavy, but as the hours passed and there was no sign of Leander, the intensity began to rise. Timothy didn't know what to think, and the first seeds of doubt began to blossom. As the night wore on, they grew. His gaze was drawn again and again to the timepiece he had built. It hung on the wall, its pendulum slowly swinging with the incremental passage of time.

Timothy drifted off briefly, and when he woke, found that it was only a few hours before dawn. He began to wonder if Constable Grimshaw had somehow found out about Leander's plan to help him escape SkyHaven, and put a stop to it. Or, even worse, that Leander had abandoned him. Timothy hated even to think such a thing, but he knew how torn Leander was about acting against Parliament.

Edgar dozed, still perched atop Sheridan's head. The mechanical man had long ago shut down his primary functions to review the workshop's inventory of supplies and building materials stored in his automated brain. Only the smallest light glowed in Sheridan's eyes.

Exhausted, his own eyes burning, and his head muddled from the little sleep he'd had, Timothy sighed and looked into the shadowy corner. He could barely make out Ivar there, blending into his surroundings. Even then, he could only see the Asura because he knew what he was looking for, and how to focus his eyes to perceive the shape of the warrior against the identically shaded background.

"We might as well get some sleep," Timothy said glumly. He sat down on his blankets, put the pillow behind his head, and leaned back against the wall. "I don't think we're going anywhere tonight."

The Asura warrior did not stir, and Timothy wondered if his friend was even awake.

"Did you not say that you were sure it would happen?" Ivar asked, breaking the silence and startling the boy.

Timothy shrugged. "Well, yeah, but now I don't know."

"Is your faith such a fragile thing that it can be so easily shattered?" Ivar asked, his flesh returning to its natural tone, his dark eyes slowly opening.

"But look at the time," Timothy said, pointing to the timepiece. "We've been waiting all night."

"It has not happened because it is not yet the proper time," the warrior said. "Remember the name of the place where we once dwelled," he said. "The island that is more your home than this world will ever be. Its meaning will serve you well in times such as this."

Patience, Timothy thought, understanding fully what his warrior friend was trying to teach him. They had lived for years on the island, their days the very definition of simplicity. Rise with the sun. Build and learn. Eat and think. Then sleep when the sun hides behind the horizon and the night comes on.

I have to have patience.

As difficult as it was, he forced himself to do just that. He was so tired now that it would not serve him well when the time finally came to escape. A lack of sleep over the past few days was finally beginning to take its toll on him, and he found himself gradually drifting down into a deep, dream-filled slumber.

In his dream he had escaped the confines of SkyHaven and freed his Wurm friend from prison with ease. Now all that remained was to travel to Draconae and help Verlis's tribe. As he stood with his monstrous friend, the Wurm seemed to grow before his eyes, standing as high as one of Arcanum's tallest towers, like one of the Dragons of Old.

We have to take you home, he yelled up to the enormous Wurm, and Verlis slowly nodded his great head, reaching down to snatch the boy up by the shirt, bringing his tiny form close to his gaping, smoking jaws.

Timothy was speechless, staring wide-eyed as the Wurm

opened its cavernous maw to reveal the roaring fires that seethed at the back of its throat.

You wish to go to Draconae? asked a voice that he did not recognize. Timothy began to struggle as he was dangled closer to the fires that bubbled and churned inside the mouth of the dragon. *Then go!* screamed the voice that was not his friend's, and he felt himself dropped into the liquid flame, his body consumed by the ravenous blaze.

At that moment he knew the identity of the one responsible for his horrible fate.

Grimshaw.

Timothy came awake with a start, his body prickling with a cold sweat. Ivar had shaken him and was pointing to the large window of the workshop.

"Look," the Asura whispered.

The boy did as he was instructed, banishing the horrible dream from his mind. He blinked, as if to accuse his eyes of lying to him. But his dream had not lingered. This was real. A sky carriage hovered outside the workshop window.

"Caiaphas," Timothy whispered, crawling out from beneath his blanket to quickly cross the room. He reached a hand out to the spell-glass in the window's frame, which dissipated at his touch. The chill night air breezed into the room.

"It is time," the navigation mage whispered from his perch atop the vehicle, which hovered outside of SkyHaven, far above the churning ocean below, with only a low crackle of magic to give away its presence.

Timothy turned to his friends to see that they all had

gathered around him. "Are we ready?" he asked in a near breathless whisper, and from the looks in their eyes, he could see that they were.

The time, at last, had come.

It was one of Timothy's favorite fantasies, to have the Cade estate as his own. Not just in name, but truly belonging to him. He wanted to live there all the time, exploring the corridors of the big, old house anytime of the day or night. But the way things were going, he doubted his fantasy would ever become a reality. Could he ever live a normal life in this world and not be looked upon as a freak or something to be feared? He really didn't know, and at the moment, he didn't have time to indulge in fantasies.

Caiaphas had taken Timothy and Ivar from SkyHaven, expertly piloting the carriage away from the floating citadel with no one the wiser. The navigation mage had explained that he was there at the behest of his master, and that he was to offer them aid in any way he could. Timothy had thanked the coachman for his assistance, directing him to take them to his father's home, where all that he needed to set his scheme in motion would be found.

He instructed Caiaphas to moor the carriage to an entrance at the rear of the estate, away from curious eyes, and they had all gone into the grand house beneath the cover of what little remained of the night.

Entering the home of Argus Cade was like wrapping oneself in a down-filled quilt on a cold winter's night. Though large and somewhat foreboding in its design, there was something welcoming about the old mansion, almost as if the kindly attributes of the man who had lived there for so many years had somehow permeated the structure. There would have been nothing Timothy would have enjoyed more at that very moment than to curl up in one of the large, overstuffed chairs in his father's study and just soak up the atmosphere of the place. It would have been almost like having his father back again.

Almost.

But there were other, more important things that required his attention, and hopefully there would be time for comfort later.

Timothy went toward the door that led to Patience to inspect the supplies that Ivar and Sheridan had brought from the island for Timothy's trip to Draconae.

"Is this all of it?" Timothy asked Ivar, examining the baskets, barrels, and crates as he reviewed a mental checklist.

"Yes," the Asura answered, "as well as some items that you did not ask for, but Sheridan suggested might be useful."

"Excellent," the boy said, removing the lid from one of the crates to verify its contents. He grinned. "That Sheridan, always thinking."

"It is like a wholly new kind of magic," Caiaphas observed, his voice a whisper as he studied the inventions, tools, and building materials brought from Patience.

The navigation mage had been both startled and amazed by the few renovations Timothy had made to the mansion in the short amount of time he had lived there. He marveled at the oil lamps that illuminated the household with the light of what mages called hungry fire, and the system of metal piping that allowed non-magical access to the flow of water.

"Wondrous," Caiaphas had muttered over and over again, eyes wide above the blue veil.

"Not really," Timothy said in all modesty. "It's just what I do to get by—what I *need* to do if I'm going to survive in a world of magic. I look at all the magical things that everybody else can do, and try to imagine how the same thing could be done without it, and then, most of the time, I make it happen."

Caiaphas had been gazing into one of the crates. Now he lifted his eyes to gaze at the boy. "They wrongly call you the un-magician. There is more true magic found here than in half the hands of Parliament."

"And it's going to be this kind magic—my own special magic—that's going to allow us to free Verlis," Timothy said, opening the leather satchel that he still wore at his side and removing the folded notes and pages of drawings that made up his plans for the Wurm's rescue. He spread them out atop one of larger crates, using it as a workstation, then gestured for Caiaphas and Ivar to come closer.

"Forgive me, Master Cade," the navigation mage said in earnestness. He shook his veiled head as he looked over the boy's pages of scribbles and strange drawings. "But I cannot imagine how this will be possible. You have been to Abaddon. I took you there myself. It is far beneath the ocean's surface, unreachable without the aid of magics that are not among my skills. I have neither the power nor the social station to possess such spells."

Timothy shuffled through his stacks of drawings, searching for one in particular.

"Trust me," he said, locating the design he was looking for and holding the intricate drawing out so that his companions could see. "We're going to build this," he told them. The excitement he always experienced when inventing was building inside him.

Caiaphas took the drawing from Timothy's hand and studied it.

"Hmmm," Ivar said, scrutinizing the drawing as well, standing alongside the navigation mage.

"Wondrous," Caiaphas said yet again. "Absolutely wondrous."

CHAPTER SEVEN

Heavy fists pounded on the workshop door.

Edgar ruffled his feathers, tilted his head, and glanced at Sheridan. He was perched on a pile of blankets laid out on the floor, and the mechanical man stood by the door, on guard. As the rook was Timothy's familiar, he should have been with his master at all times. But the boy had been away from him far too often of late, and Edgar did not like it at all. He would do whatever was necessary to see that Timothy came back to him safely, and he knew Sheridan felt the same.

"Looks like this it," the rook muttered, crawling beneath the rumpled covers. "Give me a minute to make sure I'm hidden before you open the door."

Again the fists banged on the thick wooden door. "Timothy Cade, it is time for us to escort you to breakfast," called one of the sentries from the corridor outside the room.

"Are you ready?" Sheridan whispered, modulating the volume of his voice as he tentatively reached for the door latch.

"When you are," Edgar replied, his voice muffled under the bedclothes.

Sheridan's jointed metal hand closed on the door latch, his mechanical brain revisiting his master's instructions. He didn't want anything to go awry. *This will be the tricky part,* Sheridan thought, pulling open the door to reveal two annoyed sentries. He had not seen these two before, and wasn't sure if he had ever seen such an obvious example of complete opposites. One guard was short and heavy, his shape practically round, while the other was very tall and impossibly thin.

"It's time for your master to go to breakfast," said the rotund guard, peering past the mechanical man and into the room.

"It's terrible," Sheridan said, and he shook his head worriedly, releasing a whistle of steam from the valve at the side of his head. "No matter how I try to wake him, he won't get up. All he does is moan."

And as if on cue, Edgar began to moan from beneath the blankets, doing his best impression of Timothy in the grip of illness.

The tall, thin sentry shot a nervous glance at his partner and then peered deeper into the room, but he came no closer. "What's wrong with him?" he asked warily.

"I don't know," Sheridan replied, swiveling his head to look back at the heaped bedclothes. "But he seems very, very ill. Quite sick."

"Sick?" both guards repeated, taking a step back into the corridor.

"He has awful red spots on his face, his neck is swollen like a puff frog's, and I do believe his hair has begun to fall out," Sheridan told them, a tinge of panic in his metallic voice. This last he spoke in a whisper, as though he did not want the shape under the blankets to hear this unfortunate news.

Again Edgar began to moan, moving about under the blankets.

"I certainly hope it isn't . . . contagious," Sheridan added, bringing one of his segmented hands to his mouth.

"Con-contagious!" the tall guard stammered, stepping back even farther, covering his nose and mouth with his hand. His heavyset partner did the same, stumbling over his own feet.

"Well," Sheridan said sadly, "he's certainly in no condition to eat anything. If he had breakfast, he would only vomit it up, I should think. And if he is contagious . . . my, it might not be wise to parade him through the halls of SkyHaven."

The mechanical man stepped aside and lowered his head with a sigh. "But do as you must. Only please, if you cannot wake him and are forced to carry him, please be gentle with him. He's in a bad way."

The sentries stared at him for a moment, exchanged a quick look, and then both began to shake their heads.

"Probably best not to risk exposing everyone," the rotund sentry muttered.

"Right, right. Just as I was thinking," said the other. "Matter of fact, might be wiser all around to consider the boy quarantined until he's feeling better. Just to be sure. Bring him his food here."

Sheridan watched their conversation with fascination. He had never been fond of deceit, but observing its results turned out to be quite interesting. It was a good thing the sentries were unfamiliar with him and so could not tell that he was amused. At length, the two of them backed up one last step.

"You've already been exposed—," began the stout one.

"Well, he's metal, isn't he?" his tall comrade interrupted. "I don't suppose he can get sick."

The other nodded reasonably. "Right. In any case, you can see to the boy. We'll let Grandmaster Maddox know that he is unwell."

"Yes," Sheridan said, lacing his fingers together and glancing back at the moaning blankets in concern. "I think that's a wise decision."

The sentries continued to back away from the workshop door, as if they were expecting the mystery illness that had infected the boy to storm from the room and attack them. Then they nodded to each other and hurried down the corridor, in a rush to get as far away from the workshop as possible.

Sheridan slammed the door and leaned back against it, releasing a geyser of steam, the equivalent of a sigh. "We did it."

Edgar poked his head out from beneath the covers. "And it's about time, too," the bird croaked. "I thought I was going to suffocate under there. Caw! Caw!"

"I do hope this charade will provide Timothy and Ivar with enough time to complete their task," Sheridan said as he moved away from the door.

The familiar flew out from beneath the blankets to soar about the workshop and stretch his wings. "Don't you fret. They'll have enough time," he said as he touched down on the windowsill, ruffling his jet-black feathers. "Never underestimate the power of a contagious disease."

Caiaphas stirred the contents of the metal cauldron hanging over the blazing fire. The chunks of dried tree sap had been solid when he dropped them in, but were now melted to a golden, glutinous liquid, the thick aroma making the navigation mage feel lightheaded, as if he'd indulged in too much ale.

"How's the sap coming, Caiaphas?" Timothy asked from the other side of the room, where his latest invention was beginning to take form. He was glad of the navigation mage's help. His injured arm was still quite sore.

"I believe it's ready," Caiaphas replied, again peering in at the amber liquid.

They had begun construction of Timothy's latest creation almost immediately, moving all the items that would be needed for its fabrication to the solarium at the back of the Cade estate. The boy said that it would be messy work, and he did not want to cause any harm to the main body of the house.

The coachman was fascinated by the boy's activity as he darted about the room, assembling various aspects of the device. Timothy now stood within the framework of a sphere made from the flexible reeds of a marsh plant quite abundant on the island in the pocket dimension where he had grown up. The Asura, Ivar, was securing the joints with thick twine, also made from the leaves of a plant on Patience.

"The frame looks good," Timothy said. "Caiaphas, would you mind bringing the sap over here so we can begin to attach the outer skin?"

Staring at the bare skeleton of what Timothy had called his diving sphere, the navigation mage could not yet see how it would enable the boy and the Asura to travel beneath the ocean. What the boy had explained to him was nearly incomprehensible, but he had seen what Timothy was capable of, what he could create with his imagination and his hands, and so he did not doubt.

Sparks of icy blue leaped from the mage's fingertips. Using a spell similar to one that he wielded to lift his carriage into the sky, Caiaphas levitated the heavy cauldron across the room to Timothy.

The boy thanked him, then dipped a thick brush into the steaming liquid and used it to attach a patch of thin, transparent material to the framework. Timothy had told him that it was the skin of a whiskerfish, and Caiaphas marveled at the precise number of such fish that must have been caught in order to provide enough material for the boy's invention. In addition to his other skills, he was clearly a remarkable fisherman.

"When the sap dries, it'll create an airtight seal," Timothy explained, moving with deft speed. "The only water we want in here with us is what we let in through the valves for ballast."

"But are you certain you'll be all right?" Caiaphas asked.

Ivar was working with the fish skin as well. "The sphere is not so different from the huts my tribe once lived in," the Asura told Caiaphas as he laid the skin on the framework in long strips. He bonded one end of the pliable patch to another with the supremely sticky tree sap. "The floors were sometimes raised off the ground on stilts. The sap sealed the skin so tightly that it could hold the weight of a small family and their possessions. We will be quite safe."

Caiaphas watched them for a few minutes to see how it was done, then he, too, began to paste the skin to the frame. The three worked diligently, and soon enough the framework was nearly enclosed, an opening at the top of the sphere created to allow access to its hollow center.

They stopped for a brief rest, sharing a pitcher of water and some stale, yet tasty, biscuits they had found in the pantry.

"So, what do you think of it so far?" the boy asked proudly, sipping from a goblet as they studied the sphere.

The navigation mage lifted his veil to take a bite from his biscuit, his eyes upon the craft taking shape before them.

Ivar grunted in amusement. "He is speechless, Timothy," the Asura noted, peeling dried sap from his fingertips.

"It fascinates me, and yet I have no understanding of how it will work," Caiaphas admitted.

He could see that the boy was frustrated by his ignorance, but at the same time there was an element of excitement, a twinkle in his eyes.

"When this is done," Timothy said, directing their attention to his hollow creation, "a breathable environment will be created inside by a device that will remain on the surface of the water, pumping air down a long hose made of tubes from the Lemboo plant. The Lemboo tubes will be sealed together with the same sap we're using for the sphere." He moved to kneel beside another of his machines, placed safely in the corner. "This is our pump. It'll float along behind us at first, and then above us as we sink deeper."

On his hands and knees the boy crawled across the floor to a wooden crate filled with hollowed-out reeds about two feet in length. "And these are the Lemboo tubes we'll use for our hose," Timothy said, showing the flexibility of the plant by bending it in his hands. "We should have more than enough to reach Abaddon."

"If the sphere is filled with oxygen, how will you keep it submerged?"

"Two ways," Tim explained. "We'll both be weighted down, of course, but we'll also have tanks attached to the craft's side that we can fill and empty by manipulating these valves. Filling the tanks will make our density greater and cause the sphere to sink."

Caiaphas climbed to his feet and walked around the craft, once more inspecting their work. "So much more complicated than the reciting of a spell," he said, hands clasped behind his back.

"But at this point, our only option," Timothy replied.

* * *

There was a spell-key that would open the workshop door at SkyHaven, but Timothy had added his own locking mechanism, a metal bolt that slid into the frame, to keep unwanted visitors away. Leander knocked several times on the heavy wood.

"I'd think twice before going in there without some kind of protection, sir," said one of the sentries Grimshaw had put in place, a heavyset mage named Yarnill.

"If you ask me, the lad's extremely contagious," the other sentry added. "Protection is most definitely in order."

Leander despised having to deal with Grimshaw's lackeys. The two were practically cowering with fear in front of the workshop door. Leander had to hand it to Timothy, the boy certainly had come up with a clever scheme to mask his escape. Sheridan would put off discovery of the boy's absence for as long as possible.

"Wise advice, gentlemen," the Grandmaster said in his most authoritative tone. "Precautionary measures, then."

He pulled a spell of shielding from his vast memory of incantations and recited it, sketching at the air with his fingers to summon the magic he needed. An opaque veil of shimmering energy formed around the Grandmaster as he prepared to enter the supposedly disease-infested workroom. "I believe this will suffice," he said, and reached out to rap briskly upon the door.

The guards immediately stepped back, their hands covering their noses and mouths to keep any contagion from entering their systems.

"Perhaps it would be wise if you two were to leave the area," Leander suggested, as he heard the sound of movement from the other side of the door. "You can't be too careful."

"That's a good idea," said the extremely thin sentry, who turned and bolted down the hallway, the rotund Yarnill trailing close behind.

"It's just terrible! Terrible!" Sheridan wailed as he opened the door a crack. His circular eyes glowed like warm heatstones as he stuck his metal head out to examine the hallway.

"Oh, it's you, Master Maddox," Sheridan said. "Are you alone?"

"The guards couldn't get away from here fast enough," Leander replied, dropping the magical shield.

The metal man opened the door farther to allow him entrance. A low, painful-sounding moan filled the room, and the Grandmaster noticed a pile of bedclothes in the corner writhing, as if whoever was beneath them was in great discomfort.

"It's Master Maddox, Edgar," Sheridan called as he firmly closed the door.

The rook erupted from beneath the covers, fluttering his wings and ruffling his feathers. "So, how are we doing?" Edgar asked, his short, spindly legs giving him difficulty walking on the rumpled blankets. "Anybody suspicious yet?"

"Word of Timothy's illness is spreading through SkyHaven like hungry fire," the mage said, tugging at the end of his scruffy beard. "And I sent the resident physician away yesterday under the pretense that he'd not taken a holiday in quite some time. People are keeping their distance from this wing, never mind this workshop. They're terrified."

"Caw! Caw! Can't be too careful these days," Edgar crowed.

The Grandmaster walked toward the room's large windows and peered out at the early morning sky. It was breezy, wispy clouds being forced across the sky by a bullying wind.

"I hope and pray to the bright ones above that this ploy will allow Timothy and Ivar time to accomplish their task."

A high-pitched hissing sound drew his attention, and he turned to see Sheridan approaching, steam escaping the valve on the side of the mechanical man's head.

"Don't worry, Master Maddox. I'm sure that Timothy has more than enough time to secretly gain access to Abaddon, break Verlis free, escape the prison undetected, and accompany the Wurm back to Draconae to help his tribe." Sheridan paused, reviewing what he had just said and counting the number of tasks on the fingers of one metal hand.

"Oh, my," he fretted. "That's quite a list, isn't it?"

Edgar flew up from the blankets to land upon Leander's shoulder. "He'll pull it off," the bird said, but he did not sound completely confident. "Don't you think?" he asked the Grandmaster.

"Let's just hope we have enough time before Grimshaw becomes suspicious," Leander said, returning his gaze to the morning beyond the window.

A touch of gray now streaked the sky. It looked as though a storm was brewing, and Leander could not help but fear its coming.

* * *

Constable Grimshaw leaned back in the chair behind the desk in his office within the Parliament complex.

"I'm so glad you took the time to bring this information to my attention, Councillor Pepoy," he said, pyramiding his fingers beneath his chin, contemplating the news he had just heard.

Pepoy, a fussy gentleman, advanced in years, sipped from his cup of herb tea before placing it back down on the saucer balanced on his lap. "When Fitzroy went missing, I wasn't sure what to do," the councillor said with a shake of his head. "I'd always warned him that he could get into trouble or worse."

The old man had come about his friend, the latest mage to mysteriously disappear from the city of Arcanum.

"You did the right thing, sir," Grimshaw said, reaching for the carafe upon his desk. "More tea?" he asked.

Pepoy extended his cup so that the constable could pour for him.

"So, you are unsure of what your associate was investigating?" Grimshaw continued.

Pepoy took a careful sip from his refreshed cup. "That's correct, Constable. He had been working—along with some others—without Parliament's knowledge, for quite some time. I could make a list of who else was involved, if you'd like," the councillor volunteered. He leaned forward in his chair before Grimshaw's desk, as if concerned that even here, in the office of the foremost law officer in Sunderland, he might be overheard. He spoke in a conspiratorial whisper. "One of them was Argus Cade."

"The great Argus Cade, you say?" Grimshaw raised his eyebrows in mock surprise. "A pity about his son . . . and his *defect*."

The old man nodded in agreement. "Shameful. An embarrassment to all mages."

Grimshaw thought about the boy and how disruptive one chaotic force could be to the delicate balance of things. But that force of chaos had now been isolated, allowing him to continue with his task of restoring order unhindered.

"That list would be most helpful, Councillor," Grimshaw noted. "I will leave no stone unturned in my investigation of these disappearances."

Pepoy smiled, obviously proud of himself for having had secrets to share. "I'll compile it immediately," he said, placing his cup and saucer on the edge of the constable's desk. "And now I'll take my leave. I'm certain that one in your position has other matters to attend to."

Grimshaw rose from his chair. "My thanks to you again," he said as he took the man's dainty hand in his and squeezed. The constable watched with amusement as Pepoy winced. "And I would appreciate it if you would be so kind as to keep the subject of our meeting this morning confidential."

"Most certainly, Constable Grimshaw," Pepoy said, flexing the fingers on his smarting hand. "Your secrets are mine." And with that last statement, the councillor bowed at the waist and turned toward the door. "Good morn to you, sir," he said, and was gone.

A list of those who had been working in secret without Parliament's consent would be most helpful indeed, Grimshaw thought. He lifted the carafe of tea, pouring a cup for himself, a simple reward for a job well done. He began assessing what he would need to do once Pepoy's list was in his possession.

A patch of air above his desk began to shimmer and grow dark, and Grimshaw steadied himself. A passageway was opening from another place to admit a messenger. The constable sipped his tea, watching with a curious eye as the portal opened and a large mud toad, its flesh mottled and gray, crawled from the opening to squat on his desk. The flesh of its throat expanded and contracted as it stared at him with bulbous yellow eyes.

The creature slowly opened its mouth, wider and wider still, and a voice drifted from out of the open maw.

"A warning to you, Constable," said the voice, dry and brittle like ancient parchment. "A warning to you about the boy, Timothy Cade."

He sat down upon the edge of his desk, his hand coming up to smooth the curling ends of his mustache. "No worry there, I'm pleased to report," Grimshaw said with confidence. "He has been dealt with, and will interfere with us no longer."

The toad's mouth opened larger, its body seeming to swell until it would burst.

"So sure of yourself and your authority, are you, Grimshaw?" asked the voice. "Perhaps one should verify his facts before he is made the fool."

The constable sneered at the reptilian messenger. "I take insult at your implications. Timothy Cade has been placed under house arrest at SkyHaven, and has guards stationed out-side his door at all times. There are far more pressing matters to concern ourselves with at the moment. I've just received information that Fitzroy and Cade were not the only ones suspicious of your—"

"You try my patience, Constable," growled the voice from somewhere deep inside the toad. "You will go to SkyHaven at once. I sense that something there is amiss. The boy attempts to stir the ghosts of the past, to uncover truths long since bur-ied. Such a thing would interfere with my current plans. See that it does not."

And with that final command, the creature's mouth began to close, signifying that the discussion was at an end and there would be no opportunity for further argument.

"Very well," Constable Grimshaw said. He rose, bowed to the toad, and proceeded toward the door.

After all, his master had commanded him.

CHAPTER EIGHT

Timothy did not think he had ever been so aware of the passage of time. Every hour that passed was another span in which it seemed impossible that his absence from SkyHaven could go undiscovered. It was far too late for such concerns, however. He was committed to his plan. Regardless of what happened now, he was going to get Verlis out of Abaddon. The Parliament of Mages might have trouble telling the difference between right and wrong, but Timothy had no such difficulty.

Still, the young man was well aware that Leander had jeopardized everything that mattered to him in the world, and so he did his best to hurry. If he and Ivar were able to get back to SkyHaven without anyone the wiser, Timothy felt that it would be a miracle, the sort of magic that not even the most powerful mage could ever count on.

He stood now on the sandy shore of Hylairus, a tiny island

that was the sole bit of uninhabited land near their destination. Had they tried to reach Abaddon from the mainland, the air-circulating pump on the shore would certainly have been discovered, and he and Ivar might well have died beneath the ocean waves, not from drowning but from suffocation.

Caiaphas had flown them here in Leander's sky carriage—and it was not lost on Timothy that the navigation mage was also risking everything by aiding them. He was a good man, Caiaphas.

Even now, the navigation mage was waist deep in the water, holding the diving sphere steady while Ivar stood inside the contraption, setting the last of the posts in place. Timothy had been forced to break the invention down to transport it here, but once it had been built and the outer skin had been sealed, it was a simple matter to deconstruct and reconstruct its inner workings.

The sun shone warmly down upon them, but the breeze off the water was cool and Timothy shivered. He tilted his head to one side and studied the diving sphere. It was per-fectly round and, though the fish skin was yellowed, it was transparent enough that they would be able to see underwater. But they had to hurry, for the sunlight would only reach so far beneath the waves, and then they would have to rely upon the lights of Abaddon itself to guide them.

And if night fell while they were still deep in the ocean . . . well, Timothy did not want to think about that.

Caiaphas turned to him and nodded.

Timothy took a deep breath and strode into the surf. The

long tubes attached to either side of the sphere were floating on the waves, but they would not be for long. He tested the two slings that were draped across his shoulders—each of them weighted with half a dozen bags of sand—and found them secure.

As he walked toward the ladder that leaned against the sphere, Caiaphas gazed at him doubtfully.

"I mean no disrespect, Timothy," the mage said, his blue eyes gleaming in the sun, "but are you certain this will work?"

A flutter of trepidation went through the young man. He smiled as he considered lying. Then he shook his head. "Not at all. But it should."

"How will you seal yourself in? How will you keep the water out?"

Timothy glanced at the sun and saw that it had already slipped past the noontime position. He had little time, but he owed Caiaphas an explanation for all that the man had done. Patiently he waded nearer to the sphere and pointed at the round door built into its topside. He and Ivar had constructed it so that it was all sealed as tightly as the rest of the sphere.

"The pressure from the ocean will help keep it closed. There is a latch on the inside," he added, pointing to the metal clasp that would help pull the door tight against the frame of the sphere. Timothy had added a layer of the malleable, gummy wood from the swaying trees from Patience that Ivar called Wind Dancers. It was yet another precaution against the water.

"But we'll also be using a less permanent adhesive to glue

it closed from within," he told the navigation mage.

Caiaphas stared at the door a moment, and then a smile blossomed on his face. "You've really thought of everything, haven't you?"

Timothy gave a nervous laugh. "Well, when your life is in the balance, it just won't do to leave anything out."

Even with his features cloaked by the veil he wore, Caiaphas seemed grim as he turned to Timothy and extended his hand. "Good luck, young sir. I shall remain here and await your return."

That was it, then. Timothy heard the farewell in Caiaphas's tone and knew it was time to get on with it. He had been filled with righteous anger about the injustice that was being done to Verlis, and to him as well, but now that the moment had come to do the unthinkable, to lash out at all of the rules and customs of this world and the authority of Parliament, he hesitated. A tremor went through him. When he glanced at Caiaphas, he saw that the mage sensed his trepidation.

"Courage, young Master Cade," the man said, his eye shimmering with magic and kindness. "If you are half the boy Leander Maddox thinks you are, you will make short work of this adventure."

Timothy smiled and nodded. Then, without further comment, he climbed up the ladder and then down into the submersible sphere, and pulled the door closed above him while Caiaphas held it in place.

The submersible was cramped inside, crisscrossed with tubes that supported the framework of the sphere. Ivar had already taken his seat amid the support structure, and he nodded grimly to Timothy as the young man made his way to his own makeshift seat, in front of Ivar's place. There had been a time when Timothy had believed that his friend did not get nervous, but as he grew older he had come to realize that the Asura simply did not show such emotions on their faces. Timothy, at least, had been deep underwater before, with his diving apparatus so that he could breathe. Ivar had never ventured upon such a journey.

But there was only strength and confidence in the warrior's eyes.

Timothy smiled at him but said nothing as he took his seat. They often passed time this way, comfortable with each other. Ivar had taught him the value of silence.

Taking care not to rush, Timothy went over the controls he had set into the submersible. The long tanks on either side of the sphere were not merely for ballast—weight to help drag them under the water—but also for propulsion and navigation. There were pumps that Timothy could control with foot pedals attached to the inner structure of the submersible. These would draw water into the tanks. At his hands were levers that would vent the water out the rear of the tanks. His arm still ached a bit, but he was confident he could operate the craft.

Full tanks would pull them underwater. A constant combination of suction and vent would propel them forward. If Timothy cut off the suction but vented water, the submersible would rise. If he cut off the vent on one side and not the other, he could turn the sphere to the left or right, and thereby guide it wherever he needed to go.

Last, but most important, was the pump that would float on the ocean surface above them and pump air down to the sphere. As soon as they set out from the shore, Caiaphas would set it in the water. It would drag behind the submersible and then follow above them as they went deeper. He only hoped he had measured enough Lemboo tube for the depth of Abaddon. He had gauged it as best he could.

When he was satisfied that the controls were in working order, he glanced over his shoulder at Ivar.

"Here we go, old friend." Timothy grinned, his heart pounding. "Seal the door."

Ivar slipped from his seat and took up a small tub of adhesive sap, which he spread liberally all around the entrance, filling even the tiniest gap between the sphere and the door. When he was finished, he returned to his seat, and Timothy counted to one hundred in his mind. That was all the time it would take for the sap to take hold.

Through the strange yellow skin of the submersible, Timothy saw Caiaphas still holding them steady. The waves crashed upon the shore of that tiny island—a place that reminded him very much of Patience—and Timothy waved to the mage to set them free. Caiaphas gave the sphere a shove, and it slid out over the water, rocking on the waves. The coachman would be hurrying, even now, to set the pump into the water as well.

A moment later there came the hiss of the pump working, and fresh air filled the sphere.

Immediately Timothy began to pedal. He suctioned water into both ballast tanks, and the submersible became heavy in the water. When the tanks were only partially full, he began to vent water, and the submersible began to move out over the ocean.

"Twenty degrees east," Ivar instructed. He was navigating by the position of the sun in the sky, the island behind him, and by the dark outline of the very distant shore of the mainland. There was a compass, but they needed to confirm their heading first before they could be confident of their direction.

Timothy adjusted their angle, gauged that they were far enough out from the island shore, and stopped venting. He continued to pedal, water flooding in to fill both ballast tanks, and then they began to sink. The waves lapped higher on the outer skin of the sphere. Though there was plenty of air inside the submersible, still Timothy held his breath. He gazed in amazement as they went under, dragged by the ballast tanks and the sandbag weights they both wore.

The sunlight was diffused by the water, and the world underneath the ocean waves was a deep green-blue. They were rocked by the tidal flow. A school of tiny fish swam by, and then a long, flat eel paused a moment to regard them before hurrying on, slicing through the depths.

"Oh, my," Timothy whispered.

And in the gloom behind him, he heard Ivar reply, "Yes." That single word, more a whisper, was enough to tell him that the Asura was feeling all of the things that he himself felt. Timothy was at once terrified, as they continued to descend, the water flowing up around them, and exhilarated. He had built this thing! He had constructed something unimagined in this world. All of his life he had invented things, more out of necessity than out of a love for creation. But never had he been so thrilled with the result.

"Timothy," Ivar said, his voice still a hush.

"Yes?"

"We should not delay."

It took him a moment to hear the words. When he did, Timothy nodded, snapping himself out of the awed trance he had been in. He began to work the pedals and the levers, and the ballast tanks functioned perfectly, jets of ocean water shooting out from the rear of those chambers to propel them forward.

Ivar corrected his heading several times, and Timothy had to alter their course. The space within the submersible had always seemed narrow, but now it was more cramped than ever. He felt it begin to close around him. The deeper they went, the faster his pulse raced. His throat became dry. When he thought of Caiaphas back on the shore, he felt an urge to go back and join him. However, part of him was still fascinated by the undersea world around them, by long swaying reeds, plants that grew up from the sea bottom to be dozens, perhaps hundreds of feet high. Schools of cloudfish drifted by, their jellied bodies like ghosts, glowing with an ethereal light that was generated from within. Their long, poison tendrils hung down beneath them as though harmless, when they were anything but. It occurred to Timothy that he had met several mages that were much the same.

Over the course of long minutes, the sphere dropped deeper below the surface and forged through the water toward their destination. They left the sunlight far behind, and the gloom of the ocean enveloped them.

Once again Timothy held his breath. Only when his chest began to hurt did he inhale sharply. The ocean was growing darker around them, and he could barely see the controls in his hands. He could sense Ivar behind him, but wondered if he would be able to see his friend's face if he were to turn and look. His eyes darted from side to side, and he peered into the water, trying to see a fish, or any other sort of life that might be out there. And yet a part of him wanted to look away. A part of him was frightened by that endless, shadowy realm under the water, growing darker by the moment.

Intruders, Timothy thought. *We're intruders.* He shivered at the idea, but it clung, spiderlike, in his mind. He did not want to make a single noise, not even to breathe, though he had to. It felt to him as though something lurked out there in the deep ocean that might not want them here. It was not so foolish a thought, for he knew that there were such things as sea monsters, giant, hideous beasts that lived in the deep. But not in this part of the world. At least, not according to the books his father had taught him from.

Still, he did not feel that they belonged.

"It's . . . it isn't as fun as I thought it would be," he whispered, breaking the silence because he could no longer bear it, daring to make a noise because a whisper was better than a scream.

"Why would you think such a dangerous endeavor would be fun?" Ivar asked.

Timothy had no answer to that, so he gave none. He only held his breath and continued onward, the submersible gliding smoothly. More long minutes passed, and his hands and arms began to grow tired from working the ballast tanks to propel them. His muscles ached. He was thirsty.

The interior structure of the sphere creaked with the pressure of the ocean around them.

Only by summoning an image of the arrogant Constable Grimshaw into his mind could Timothy banish the anxiety that filled his heart. The man was hateful, and Timothy refused to allow him to succeed in his cruelty to Verlis. He himself had been treated like a criminal, not merely because he had challenged Parliament, but because they all knew what he was capable of. They all knew that he could move almost invisibly in their magical society, and it frightened them.

When he had first come to this world, they had treated him like a spy, and so he had become one. And now that they were treating him like a criminal, he was about to become one of those as well.

"There," Ivar whispered.

Timothy looked around. At first he saw nothing but the impenetrable darkness. After several moments, however, his eyes caught a flicker of light in the depths. He adjusted his course just slightly, and as he worked the controls, the lights of the undersea prison of Abaddon came into view.

* * *

Constable Grimshaw was not to be denied. He stormed along the main corridor of SkyHaven with two of his aides following in the thunder of his wake, and the Grandmaster's assistant, scurrying along beside him like some petulant child.

"Constable, this is very improper!" Carlyle whined. The skinny little man seemed as though he were about to throw a tantrum. "Very improper! If you will simply wait in the main hall, as I asked, Grandmaster Maddox will be informed of your presence and will join you there. I'm afraid I must protest! You cannot simply—"

With a thump of his boot upon the stone floor, Grimshaw spun on one heel and pointed a spindly finger at Carlyle. "Yessss!" he said, punctuating the word by poking the Grandmaster's assistant in the chest. "Yes, I can. I have been commissioned as special investigator for the Parliament of Mages. I wield the authority of all the guilds, including this one. As constable, I will follow my investigations wherever they may lead. At this moment, I wish to speak with the freak. And I have been told by the sentries I placed here that the Cade boy is ill—still in his workshop, though I find it curious that a sick young man would be in his workshop rather than his bed."

"Supposed to be contagious, Constable," one of his aides grunted.

Grimshaw ignored him. Instead he leaned in and glared at Carlyle. "I sense deception. I smell mendacity at work here. You, simpering lapdog that you are, will beg scraps from whatever master owns the table at which you sit. So feel free to run and tell *Professor* Maddox that I am here. But I will continue on course. I am quite familiar with the location of the room the boy has chosen for his . . . *workshop*."

He felt his own mouth turn up in a sneer of disgust at this final word. The idea of such a workshop was wretched, like animals mimicking mages. Without magic, the Cade boy was no better. An *abomination,* he had heard it suggested. And oh, how he agreed.

With that, Grimshaw turned, his cloak billowing out behind him, and strode toward the stairwell that curved down into the bowels of SkyHaven. His aides followed, but Carlyle scampered off to inform his master than they had an uninvited guest.

His footfalls were heavy on the steps that wound down into the heart of the floating fortress, but his heart leaped with the pleasure of thwarting the hopes of his enemies. When he reached the appropriate level of SkyHaven, Constable Grimshaw hurried down a long hall and at last rounded a corner, where he saw two of the guards he had set at this post snap to attention when they noticed his approach.

"The boy!" he snapped without preamble. "When was the last time you laid eyes on him?"

"Why, this morning," one of the guards said, brow furrowing in confusion as though the question had been difficult to answer. "He's ill, Constable. Deathly ill."

"Is he?" Grimshaw replied, wondering if the chill of his sarcasm was lost on the thick-headed guard. "And you saw him this morning?"

"Moaning, he was, under his bedclothes."

Grimshaw froze, glaring at the man. "*Under* his bedclothes?"

The guard, too stupid to understand the implications of this, nodded, eyes flashing with concern. He knew he was in trouble, but could not fathom why.

The constable glanced at the other guard. "Open it."

The guard hesitated. "Constable. Well, you see, he's contagious."

Grimshaw began to shudder with fury. His hands twitched and contorted almost into claws, and he raised them abruptly. Jets of oily black magic erupted from his fingers, coiled instantly around the throats of the two guards, strangling them.

They collapsed to the floor as he turned to his aides and gestured toward the door to the workshop. The nearest of them stepped forward and reached out a hand to the door. It shook in its frame, but did not open. Its spell should have opened for them, but something was blocking the way.

"Open it!" Grimshaw shouted.

The two aides drew back from the door and then slammed their shoulders into it. From within came the crack of splintering wood. Whatever had barred the door was breaking. He smiled grimly. They could have used a simple spell to blow the doors open, but he liked to have mages in his employ who were not afraid to get physical if such became necessary. That would be important when dealing with the Cade boy. The two mages in Grimshaw's service drew back once more.

"Constable Grimshaw!" a voice called, booming down the corridor.

Grimshaw glanced up to see Leander coming around the turn in the hall, even as the doors to the workshop gave way and swung open. Framed in the open door was the metal man that the Cade boy had constructed. It, too, was an abomination.

"I do not suppose you are very concerned with contagion," the metal man said, and then a long whistle of steam erupted from a pipe that jutted from the side of its head.

"Grimshaw!" Leander shouted again.

The burly, bearded mage stomped up to him, and Constable Grimshaw sneered at him.

"You'll pardon my eschewing some of the formal niceties in this visit, Professor Maddox," Grimshaw said. "I am in quite a hurry."

"I do not pardon your insulting behavior, Constable. There is protocol. There is common courtesy! And it is *Grandmaster* Maddox, if you please."

Grimshaw raised an eyebrow. "Is it?"

He followed his aides into the boy's workshop, stomach churning with disgust as he saw the various strange inventions that sat upon every table and shelf. The metal man said nothing more, only withdrew to a corner and stood silently, as though hoping they would see him as just another invention. Near the window was a heavy blanket, and standing upon the blanket was the black-feathered bird who had been Argus Cade's familiar. The rook stared at him with night-dark eyes.

"A surprise party?" the bird said. "For me? You shouldn't have, but . . . where's my gift?"

Grimshaw scowled and spat at the bird, which flapped its wings and jumped out of the way.

"Learn how to knock, jerk," the familiar muttered.

The constable shook his head, feeling both anger and exultation at the discovery that the boy was gone. He had been thwarted, yes. But only for the moment. In the end, the boy had only fed the flames of Parliament's suspicions about him.

Constable Grimshaw smiled and glanced at Leander, who did not even attempt to explain the boy's absence, or pretend that he was surprised to find Timothy Cade gone.

"Grandmaster, eh?" Grimshaw said. "Leader of the Order of Alhazred?" He laughed softly. "Perhaps, Professor, but not for long . . . not for very much longer at all."

For several dreadful minutes Timothy was forced to entertain the idea that he and Ivar might have failed, that they might have to return to the surface and leave Verlis imprisoned. Abaddon had several entrances, each of which was guarded only by a magical ward that would prevent any mage from entering without the proper spell-key.

Caiaphas had told them that each of these entrances led to a short tunnel, which would itself end in a large emergence chamber, where they might surface and find themselves in a pool inside the prison. Timothy knew some of this, having been to the prison before, but he had been so overwrought with concern for Verlis that he had not paid as much attention as he perhaps should have, and so Caiaphas's information had been quite welcome. There were very few visitors to Abaddon, the navigation mage had explained. And though he had himself used two of the entrances, he knew of a third which he believed was only ever used for the arrival of prisoners, never of visitors.

It was possible—and their only hope—that the prisoners' entrance would be largely ignored if there was no new captive set to be brought to the underwater prison. Logic was on their side—no one had ever escaped from Abaddon, and no one had ever entered the prison without authorization. Not ever. The magic spells that guarded the entrances were the most powerful that the joined skills and strength of the Parliament of Mages could weave. It was inconceivable to them that anyone should attempt what Timothy and Ivar were about to attempt, and so it was likely they could be taken by surprise.

Even so, there was always the chance that the prisoners' entrance would be monitored, that they would be discovered the instant they surfaced in the emergence chamber. But Timothy and Ivar had known the risk, known the odds against them, all along, and still had made the journey. They were not about to turn back now.

"Move slowly, Timothy," Ivar whispered. The yellow skin of the sphere glowed now with the illumination of the underwater prison, and when Timothy glanced at Ivar, the Asura had blended, his skin tone taking on the gleam of those lights. "Do not let your nervousness force your hand."

Timothy took a deep breath. "I won't."

His hands worked the levers slowly, and he vented a single spurt of water from each ballast tank. The submersible rose several inches and drifted forward. They had been at a complete standstill in the water. Now the sphere glided toward the prisoners' entrance to Abaddon. They passed beneath an overhang, into a dimly lit, unpleasant alcove in the lower portion of the prison.

"Now," Ivar said.

Timothy gnawed his lower lip, his breath coming in short gasps, and he let go of the levers and leaned forward. By stretching as far as his body would allow, he was able to place his hands on the inside wall of the sphere, the fish skin rough beneath his fingertips.

He closed his eyes.

The un-magician, they called him. At first it had seemed ridiculous. Magic did not work on him. But he was beginning to like the name, the word, for it seemed more appropriate now. With his eyes closed, he could feel an odd numbness in his fingers, in his skin, in the air around him. He had begun to notice this feeling whenever there was powerful magic nearby. And if he focused, he could make the feeling go away.

Through trial and error, he had learned what this meant.

When he forced that numbness away from him, he was expanding the null area that existed within him, the space in which magic would not function.

Now, as the submersible drifted forward, slowing down since he had stopped venting water from the ballast tanks, Timothy concentrated harder than he ever had. Lids closed, he could almost see in his mind's eye an image of that null field expanding. For just a moment, he felt something resisting that numbness, that un-magic, and then it gave way as simply as a bubble popping.

An opening appeared in the magical barrier that guarded the prison. The submersible slid through the prisoners' entrance and along a short tunnel, into the ominously silent belly of Abaddon.

CHAPTER NINE

Grimshaw snarled in frustration, his face flushing deep red. Dark magic danced upon his fingers, but his nostrils flared, and he lifted his chin as though he was disgusted at having to involve himself in matters he felt were beneath him. Leander watched him with a certain fascination, wondering what he might do next. He did not have to wait long to find out.

"Arrest *Professor* Maddox at once," the constable snapped, fixing Leander with a menacing stare, barely acknowledging the presence of Sheridan and Edgar.

The constable's deputies acted without hesitation. The pair murmured in unison what could only have been a spell of containment, and their hands began to glow as if suddenly white hot.

Leander reacted in kind. *How dare they treat me like some lowly criminal?* He had expected repercussions, but he would not be dealt with this way. The burly, shaggy mage summoned his own magic. "You dare conjure against *me* as though I'm some petty thief or gutter rat? In the home of *my* order?" the Grandmaster growled.

The air around him stirred with the arcane energies he was prepared to unleash, the power of the unnatural wind ruffling his hair and robes. The deputies cautiously stepped back, and he could see a touch of apprehension in their eyes.

"Just who do you think you are?"

"Master Maddox," Sheridan began, a puff of steam venting from his head.

Leander ignored the metal man's warning tone, ready to combat Grimshaw's thugs if necessary. The pair looked briefly to their master and then back to Leander. The magic that Leander commanded was an anxious predator, eager to leap forward, but he held it fast, the air about him snapping and sparking from the restraint.

"They are deputies in my service," Grimshaw declared, stepping forward to aid his men if they required it. "Servants of order who have sworn their allegiance to the centuries-old laws set forth by the Parliament of Mages—the laws you have broken, Professor."

Edgar cawed loudly and said nothing, though the bird seemed poised to attack if there was a battle to be fought.

Grimshaw raised his hands, mystical energies poised for release. "Stand down, Leander Maddox," he commanded, his tone leaving no doubt that he would unleash the full fury of his power if he was not obeyed.

Leander gritted his teeth, unwilling to give way, yet he was faced with a most precarious situation. He was infuriated by Parliament's inability to change—to see beyond their fears and prejudices—and here, standing before him, was the physical representation of that ignorance.

"I tell you, stand down," Grimshaw ordered. "Do not force our hand."

And with those words, Leander caught the slightest hint of a smile at the corner of the constable's mouth and the light of anticipation in his eyes. *You want this!* he realized. *Nothing would make you happier than to strike me down.*

Despite his better judgment, Leander could not bring himself to surrender. There was a moment in which the magics of the opposing forces in the room hummed and pulsed as if taunting each other, but still he and Grimshaw and the constable's deputies all held fast, neither side willing to make the first move. Leander had to wonder what Argus Cade would have done.

The sound of metal clanking upon the workroom's stone floor disrupted the tension momentarily. All eyes turned to find Sheridan approaching.

"Stand your ground, monstrosity!" Grimshaw bellowed. With a flick of his wrist, the constable sent a spark of oily black magic snaking out to touch the mechanical man, and Sheridan froze, paralyzed by magic.

"Please, Master Leander," the metal man pleaded. "Don't make a bad situation worse."

A streak of black feathers moved through the shadows, and

Edgar perched atop the head of the unmoving metal man. "Caw!" cried the rook. "Sheridan has a point. There's a time to fight. Now isn't it. You're not helping anyone that way."

He knew they were right. The immensity of destructive power present in the room at that moment was startling, and he shuddered with the thought of it unleashed. If this were to go on, it would help no one, Timothy least of all.

"Listen to your accomplices, Professor," Grimshaw prodded. "It appears that they are now the voices of reason."

Leander took a long breath and let it out slowly. His fury began to abate, and he lowered his defenses. The power that thrummed inside him receded to the vast reservoir of magical energies that powered the world, to be used, he hoped, for something more beneficial than the pursuit of violence.

"Constable," Leander said, "that is probably the first thing you've said that I agree with."

Abruptly released from Grimshaw's spell, Sheridan staggered closer as Edgar hopped down from atop his head to land on the mechanical man's shoulder. *Partners in crime,* the Grandmaster thought as they stood defenseless before the constable and his deputies.

"We surrender," Leander said, raising his hands, palms out to show that there was no longer any magic at his disposal.

"A wise decision," the constable sneered, the power he had amassed at his fingertips dispersing with a sputter and crackle. "But it doesn't change the fact that you cannot be trusted. *Incapacitate them.*"

Leander reacted, but too slowly. The beginnings of a spell

that would have shielded them was at the tip of the mage's tongue when he and his so-called accomplices were struck down by an attack from Grimshaw's deputies. Pain seared through Leander, and he was driven down into darkness.

Timothy had seen little of Terra, but already there were at least two locations in this world he never wanted to see again. One was the Tower of Strychnos, the headquarters of the guild, for his memories of the place were unsettling. The second, however, was far worse. If not for his loyalty to Verlis, if not for his promise, he would have been happy never to see Abaddon again.

Yet here he was.

The diving sphere bobbed in the docking berth as he and Ivar carefully peeled away the sap that affixed the craft's door. It came away from its frame with the faintest sucking sound, and the oppressive aroma of the prison facility wafted inside to welcome them. It was an odd stench—a stale smell, and something else more foul: a stink made from the fear and oppression of the poor souls forced to reside in this awful place.

Timothy could see Ivar's nose twitching. The Asura had an acute sense of smell. In this place the boy did not envy his friend. The dark patterns on the Asura's flesh grew more pronounced, angular and sharp, a sign that the warrior was preparing for the worst.

"The scent here is wrong," he said as he poked his head out of the sphere to investigate their surroundings. "There is much misery in this place."

Timothy emerged just behind his companion. "I'll agree with you on that," he said, looking around the docking bay. As Caiaphas had guessed, the prisoner transport had its own docking place, separate from where he and Leander had entered on their first visit. This room was much smaller and, luckily for them, unstaffed. There was no need to have any sentries on duty in this area, since no one could get in through the ocean-bottom entrance without the proper spell.

No one but Timothy Cade.

There wasn't a moment to spare. Here was a perfect opportunity to penetrate the main facility unnoticed. Timothy ducked back into the craft to retrieve his work belt from its place behind his seat and fastened it about his waist. The belt was made up of various pouches, each containing items that he thought might be helpful to him.

"Let's go." He jumped down to the stone dock. "The quicker we get this done, the quicker we can get out of here."

"Then let us use all our speed and wit. I do not like it here." Ivar hurried after him, one hand hovering by the knife that hung in its sheath at his side.

Abaddon made the Asura nervous, and Timothy could understand why. It was dark and oppressive, and it felt within that prison as though all the terrible weight of the sea were pressing in on the walls from outside, waiting to crush them and steal the air from their lungs. Ivar did not like enclosed spaces.

Timothy darted to a door, Ivar at his heels, and pressed his ear to the cool surface, listening for activity on the other side.

He heard nothing. "Let's see where this takes us," he whispered, placing his fingers in the crack between the door and frame.

Immediately the nullifying effect of his touch dispersed the magic that kept the door locked. It swung open easily. Cautiously the two moved swiftly into an even larger bay area.

"This looks familiar," the boy said. "I think we docked over there on my first visit." He pointed to an empty stall, its dark oily waters reflecting the faint light thrown from the ghostfire lamps adorning the walls. The spirit lights danced within their glass spheres.

"And . . . we exited through here."

They stopped before another, larger door and listened before prying it open. This door was heavier than the first, and Timothy appreciated his friend's assistance in sliding it aside.

"The place is kind of like a maze, but I think I remember the layout. Come on."

They left the bay, pressing close to the wall and sticking to the shadows. Ivar moved so silently that Timothy had to glance back from time to time to assure himself that his friend was still there. As they slunk down the long corridor he looked back once more and saw that Ivar's flesh was taking on the shade of the wall and the gloom around them. The Asura was blending into his environment. Timothy paused and stared, forcing his eyes to adjust so that he could see Ivar's silhouette. He didn't like not being able to hear or see his friend. It made him feel alone.

The idea of being alone in Abaddon at the bottom of the

ocean was not one he wanted to think about for an instant.

"I find the lack of life in this place unnerving," Ivar whispered as they stopped at yet another door. "Are there no guards?"

"I think they're just overconfident," Timothy replied, even as his touch neutralized the door's locking mechanism. "Given its location, and the incredibly powerful magic they used to build this place and to keep its prisoners captive, they'd never dream anyone would be able to break in. Come to think of it, I can't imagine they'd believe anyone would ever *try*."

The pair continued on, weaving down seemingly endless hallways, and passing through countless doors.

"Are you sure you know where we are going?" the Asura finally asked as they stepped through yet another doorway. "It all looks very much the same."

"I know exactly where we are." Timothy fixed his gaze upon the door at the end of this latest corridor. He recognized the large glass orb set into the door frame, the one that reminded him of an insect's eye. "That one will take us into—"

A sudden clanging reverberated through the stone hallway as the door before them began to open. Timothy's mind raced. There was no time to run for cover. A brief flash of an imagined future appeared in his head: Verlis in chains, and himself sharing a cell with the Wurm.

The door swung open, and a guard draped in a red uniform stepped into the hall even as Ivar grabbed Timothy firmly by the shoulder and yanked him backward, dragging him along the corridor to a bend in the wall. It was darker there, pooled in shadow, but certainly not enough to conceal them. Ivar shoved him flat against the cool, stone wall and then covered Timothy's body with his own. The boy was confused at first, but then realized what his friend was doing as he watched the surface of the Asura's flesh begin to change, blending with the shadows and the drab color of the wall.

This will never work! Timothy thought, fighting the panic surging up inside him. His heart hammered so loudly in his chest that he thought for certain it would give them away. He trembled. His throat went dry as he held his breath, willing himself thinner, flatter, as he listened fearfully to the guard's approaching footfalls.

The guard let loose a mournful howl, and Timothy was about to shout and try to attack, when he realized that the mage was yawning. He was tired, probably coming off a long, nighttime shift, Timothy thought. *Hoped.* Timothy closed his eyes tightly and felt Ivar's muscular body shielding him, conforming to him to block any view of him. The Asura was not breathing.

Then the guard was there, right next to them. Timothy could feel his presence. Again the man yawned, the soles of his boots clopping loudly on the stone floor. There was a moment that seemed to last for years, and then he was past them, stepping through a side door. And they were alone again.

Without a word, Ivar began to breathe again and stepped forward to allow Timothy to move away from the wall. It took the boy a few seconds before he dared to take a breath. Then the air rushed into his lungs, and he shook his head in awe.

"Thank you," he whispered, putting a firm hand atop Ivar's shoulder. "That was amazing. Now let's go get Verlis before we have any more surprises."

Ivar grunted in agreement as they continued along the corridor until they reached the door with the glass orb. This was not spell-glass, but the handmade variety. Most mages looked down upon anything crafted by hand rather than by magic, but not all of them felt that way. The Legion Nocturne, for instance, were powerful mages, but also worked with their hands. They lived in wilderness, hunted by hand, and were known as craftsmen. But Timothy had no idea whether there were mages who specialized in blown glass.

"I'm going to need help with this, I think," he whispered as he braced his feet and tried to slide the heavy metal door open. Then he paused and glanced back at Ivar. "I should warn you that what's behind this door is very disturbing."

Ivar obliged, the door resisting at first, but soon succumbing to their combined efforts. Quickly they stepped into the room, closing the door behind them, and found themselves in a vast chamber, hundreds of feet wide and equally deep. They stood on a catwalk, the air above and below them filled with honey-yellow spheres of magic, and within each one of them was a prisoner of Abaddon. A criminal. The worst of the worst.

But were they all? Timothy wondered about that. If Verlis was here only because Parliament felt threatened by him, how many others were in Abaddon because they had enemies in Parliament, or because their opinions were just a little too radical for their more conservative peers? It was a terrible thought, and once it entered his mind it was impossible for him to dismiss it.

"This is . . . terrible," the Asura warrior said, his eyes moving from one floating, petrified shape to the next. "I would rather be put to death than to suffer like this."

Timothy only nodded. He did not have words for the dreadful way this place made him feel.

"C'mon," he said, tearing his attention away from the prisoners of Abaddon, tugging on Ivar's arm. "Verlis is just beyond this door."

Timothy turned to the last obstruction and ran his hand along the smooth surface of the door. He could not imagine being a mage and trying to get in here without authorization. No door would have opened for him. And yet, as the unmagician, there wasn't a door that could keep him out. Even as he touched it, he could feel a flux in the air as the spell keeping the door closed was shattered. The boy grabbed the door handle and tried to slide it open.

It would not budge.

He frowned. Just a moment ago he had been thinking about how no door could keep him out. Now he felt foolish. What was this? Timothy studied it, wondering if there was some trick here, some trap, but no. It seemed this door was only heavier, sturdier than the others, as if they had wanted to take extra care to keep the prisoner within.

"I need your help again, Ivar." He grunted with exertion as he tried once more to open the door.

His friend did not respond. Worried, Timothy spun around to find the Asura frozen in his tracks on the catwalk, still staring wide-eyed at the mystical cages hanging weightless in the air around him like stars in a hideous sky.

"Ivar?" he whispered, almost afraid to break the warrior's intense focus.

The Asura's head whipped away from the nightmarish sight, and Timothy saw something in Ivar's eyes that he had never seen before.

Fear.

It was like looking into the eyes of a cornered animal. Timothy did not know much about the Asura's past, for the warrior did not talk of such things, but he remembered his father once mentioning that Ivar had been in captivity for some time before being brought to Patience. *Is he remembering that right now?* Timothy wondered. He sympathized, but they didn't have time for this. Every moment they spent lingering in one place increased the risk of discovery twofold. They had to get to Verlis, free him, and get out of this awful place as quickly as possible.

"Ivar, I need you," Timothy said, attempting to cut through the panic he saw in the warrior's eyes. "I need help." He gestured toward the barrier before him. "Remember, the quicker we're through here, the quicker we can get out. Please, Ivar."

With those words, the last of the Asura tribe took one final gaze at those hanging cages, and turned back to the boy, an eerie fire burning in his pitch-black eyes. "We must leave this place at once," he growled, charging the door, practically pushing the boy out of the way. "Not even a Wurm deserves punishment this foul." The patterns upon his flesh flowed and expanded across the muscular surface of his body as he exerted all his strength to slide the door open with a grinding rumble.

Timothy didn't waste any time, running past Ivar into the room, toward the platform upon which sat the metal, non-magical cage where the wardens of Abaddon had confined the Wurm.

"Verlis?" Timothy whispered as he approached the bars of the cell. The Wurm was lying on his side, his wrists, snout, and wings still shackled. Verlis was so still that for a moment Timothy feared the worst.

In utter silence, Ivar appeared at Timothy's side.

"He's so still," the boy noted. "Do you think he's . . . ?"

"The Wurm lives," Ivar said, scrutinizing the dragon's prone form.

Then there arose from within that cage a slow, soft rumbling growl that reminded Timothy of the approach of a summer thunderstorm.

"We've come to get you out," the boy said, moving to the cell's door, studying the lock. This was no magical contraption, but a sturdy metal thing. He had never seen anything like it, and it occurred to him that devising it must have forced the magicians who designed it to think as they had never thought before.

They would have had to think like Timothy.

It would have been his pleasure to dismantle it, to take it

apart and figure out how it worked. And he was confident he could have done it, given time. But there was none to be had.

"We don't have time for me to figure this out," Timothy said aloud. "I need to get this open fast, so subtlety is out of the question." He reached down to one of the pouches hanging from his belt and unhooked it, placing it carefully on the ground. He knelt on the floor and opened the satchel to reveal three teardrop-shaped pieces of fruit.

"This is not the time to think about your stomach, Timothy," Ivar said worriedly.

"I wouldn't want to eat these," the boy said as he gently lifted one of the fruits from the satchel. "It's just the hollowed-out shell of the Xiumi fruit." The boy loved the bitter flavor of Xiumi fruit. It had been a pleasure scooping it out of these shells, because from there it had ended up in his mouth. But now the shells served a much more important purpose. Slowly he brought one Xiumi shell toward the lock on the cell door.

"There's enough Hakka powder and coal in here to blast open this door."

The Asura stared as Timothy wedged the Xiumi shell between the door and its frame. "The fruit will explode?"

The boy laughed. "That's the plan." There was a strand of dry, woven tree vine that trailed from a small opening at the top of the shell. Timothy removed a pair of flint stones from another pouch on his work belt and rubbed them together near the end of that fuse. "When this burns, step back," he said, and a spark leaped from the stones to ignite the dried vine.

The two quickly retreated, watching as the sputtering

flame burned the length of the vine, finally making its way inside the shell. At first Timothy thought his plan had failed, but even as his brain was moving on to his backup plan, he was suddenly, explosively, proven wrong. He felt the blast in the hollow of his chest, as though an invisible hand had just shoved him, and it thumped loudly in the room, echoing in his ears.

Verlis's cage stood open. The door had been blown off its hinges and now lay bent and twisted on the platform.

"Maybe I used a little too much Hakka," Timothy said as he waved a hand before his face to clear the air of smoke.

Ivar had moved swiftly and was already inside the cage, squatting beside their ally. Timothy frowned, though, as a strange sound reached his ears. At first he thought it was just the fallout of the explosion, the strange ringing sound that filled his ears, but then realized it was something far more sinister.

"It's an alarm," he said breathlessly, entering the cell. "They know we're here."

Verlis's eyes opened, but there was a strange film over them, and the Wurm seemed unable to focus. He looked sleepy or drunk. It took Timothy only a moment to realize that the wardens had kept him sedated. Tranquilized. There were drugs in his system. That was going to complicate matters even further.

"Tim," the Wurm rasped, barely able to mumble through the metal muzzle over his snout. He lifted his shackled hands. "You came back."

"I promised," the boy said, as if that explained everything. And to him, it did.

Again Verlis shook his manacled wrists, but Timothy shook his head. "I know, you want me to try to use the Hakka powder to break them. But it's too dangerous. You'd probably lose your hands. We have to think of another way."

The alarm continued to echo ominously through the chamber.

"It is as you say, my young friend," Ivar said, placing a firm hand on his shoulder. "We have no time for subtlety."

The Asura was right. If they wanted any chance at all to escape, he needed to act at once. He went to the pouch and retrieved another of the explosive shells, removing the dried vine and emptying some of its powdered contents onto the floor. "Obviously, we're going to want a lot less of this."

He threaded the vine back inside the shell and stuck it the best he could between Verlis's wrist and the unyielding, metal restraint. "I know your hide is tough, but this is still likely to hurt you," he said, working the flint stones. "So I'll apologize in advance."

The Wurm only nodded and stared at the explosive shell. On the third try, the fuse caught fire, and Timothy and Ivar turned their backs, shielding their heads against the smaller detonation.

"Is he . . . ?" Ivar began as they squinted through the swirling smoke.

The sound of talons scraping metal echoed through the chamber. As the smoke cleared they saw that Verlis had risen to his feet and was tearing away the restraints that hindered his wings. Some of the scales at the Wurm's wrist had been badly singed by the blast, but the damage had been kept to a minimum. Timothy smiled, his chest swelling with pride and joy at his friend's release.

Verlis stretched his wings to their fullest expanse and then beat the air, fanning away the still drifting smoke. He then tore away the muzzle that restrained his snout, tossing the twisted metal to the floor.

"I am forever in your debt," the Wurm said, looking down on him with dark eyes, swaying from side to side under the influence of the sedatives.

"What are friends for?" Timothy asked, grinning, even as the clanging of Abaddon's alarm spurred them to move. "You ready to move?"

Verlis nodded, his monstrous face etched with grim determination. And then the Wurm pitched limply to one side, falling unconscious on the floor.

The alarm grew louder and faster in its insistent pealing, as if to echo the drumming of Timothy's heartbeat.

"We'll never be able to carry him to the diving sphere," he said, kneeling down beside Verlis and running a concerned hand along the rough scale of the Wurm's face.

Ivar turned to gaze toward the entrance to the chamber. "No need for further worry about reaching the sphere," the Asura said as the door slid open to admit a small cadre of Abaddon guards, their uniforms as red as blood. "I doubt that we will be leaving by those means."

The guards took up a position to block any escape, focus sticks sizzling with magic and aimed at the intruders. A moment later captain Simons strode into the chamber.

"Timothy Cade," she said, her eyes narrowing to slits that made her look unbearably cruel, "you will surrender immediately."

Ivar stood facing the guards and the captain, but Timothy was still on his knees, holding on to the fallen Wurm. He lowered his head as though in dismay and surrender, his face turned away from the guards. But his eyes were open and he stared at Verlis, willing him to awaken, trying by sheer force of will to shake the Wurm from his stupor.

"Verlis," he whispered. "This is it. I thought Ivar and I could get you out of here, but it looks like it was a three-person job. You're the third one. We got you out of the cage, but if you don't wake up and do something, we'll all be in Abaddon for the rest of our lives."

"Boy!" Captain Simons barked, her voice echoing throughout the chamber. "I am only going to give you one opportunity to do this painlessly."

"Verlis, please," Timothy hissed.

The dragon nodded his great, horned head and his eyes flickered open. An understanding passed between them, and Timothy stood, turning around to join Ivar at the edge of the cell's platform.

"Captain Simons," the boy said, speaking loudly, "it's a pleasure to see you again."

The captain strode closer, her focus stick lowered slightly.

"How did you get in here, boy? Who granted you access?"

"I got in here on my own," he explained.

She stopped before the raised platform, her guards following behind her. "Impossible," she snapped. "This facility is impregnable. To think that a mere boy could—"

Verlis surged up from where he lay, a deafening roar escaping his cavernous mouth as he unfurled his wings and began to beat them with great ferocity. The guards jumped back, focus sticks raised, but before they could fire, the Wurm belched liquid flame down among them, the searing heat causing them to panic.

Blasts of magical force crackled through the air, aimed at Verlis. The Wurm had surprised them, but it would be for nothing if they could not take advantage of the moment. In a matter of seconds the room would be overrun with prison security.

"Verlis," Timothy called as the Wurm let loose with another stream of orange fire. "We can't escape the way I intended. Magic is our only hope. Your magic."

An arc of crackling white power struck the Wurm in the shoulder, and Verlis roared in fury. The chamber was filling with thick, billowing black smoke from Verlis's fire breath, and the three companions had a moment—just a few heartbeats— to collect themselves.

"They're getting braver, Timothy," Ivar said, crouched in a battle stance but waiting to act until they had a plan.

Verlis furled his mighty wings, bringing them in closer to his body. "I will need a few moments to gather my strength."

"And you'll have them," Timothy said. He left Verlis to move closer to Ivar. Even without the smoke, it would have been difficult for their enemies to see the Asura there. Timothy did not have the same good fortune, but he was prepared to fight.

"Verlis needs some time. Let's see what we can do about giving it to him. Hold back, and wait for my signal." Timothy smiled and Ivar nodded in return. The boy leaped down off the platform, into the billowing smoke, and the warrior followed, his skin taking on the hue of black smoke. Through the obstructing haze they could hear the guards eagerly approaching.

They're afraid of us, Timothy thought, gathering up his courage. *Time to really show them what there is to fear.* And the boy charged at them with a ferocious cry filled with rage and desperation.

The guards clutched their focus sticks tightly. Captain Simons was shouting orders, but no one was listening any longer. Chaos had erupted. They opened fire on him with the magically charged weapons, multiple arcs of white magic, like lightning snaking through the air. But the attacks—the devastating energies summoned up by the guards and channeled through their weapons—dissipated inches away from him, not even singeing him.

The astonishment upon their faces, the confusion and fear, gave him more than a little pleasure. Magic made people arrogant, he had determined. And it was always entertaining to see what happened when the arrogant learned that magic could not solve everything. He advanced on the guards. Foolishly, they attacked again, as though somehow their previous attacks had gone awry.

"Try all you like," he told them as their magics failed miserably. "The results will always be the same. Didn't anyone tell you? I'm the un-magician."

Out of the corner of his eye he saw the slightest hint of movement, a distortion of air, something that an eye unfamiliar with the Asura warrior's abilities would fail to notice. Ivar was standing right in the midst of the guards, his presence hidden to them.

"Now, Ivar!" the boy shouted.

The guards were poorly trained in physical combat, depending too heavily on magic. Timothy and Ivar moved among them with swift brutality, using Asura fighting techniques that the guards simply could not counter. One after another, they were beaten and thrown or kicked to the ground. The guards were in total panic, some fleeing from the room, unable to comprehend a foe whom they could not defeat with magic.

Captain Simons had retreated to a corner of the chamber when the smoke had begun to clog the air. She kept a careful distance now, bellowing her commands across the room. Timothy grabbed a terrified guard by the front of his uniform, swept his legs out from underneath him, and brought him down hard to the floor. He chanced a quick look toward the platform where they had left Verlis.

The Wurm appeared to be in deep concentration, his

talons performing intricate gestures, as an incantation flowed from his mouth, accompanied by grunts and clicks of the tongue.

A guard who had mustered some courage tried to strike his head with a focus stick, but Timothy easily disarmed him, tossing the metal weapon away. The guard's courage evaporated and he fled, running from the room as if the devils of Harrdishak were chasing him.

"Timothy, I believe it is near time," Ivar said, gliding gracefully up alongside him. The Asura's color briefly returned to its natural state before shifting again to near invisibility.

Ivar was right. As he looked to the platform, Timothy saw that Verlis had conjured a swirling black hole in the air, and the portal was growing larger.

"Let's get out of here," Timothy said. He and Ivar sprinted to the platform. The portal was even larger now, and as the boy peered into its swirling innards, he realized that the sight he glimpsed on the other side was familiar.

Father's study?

"Quickly now," Verlis grunted with exertion. "I'm not sure how much longer I can hold it open."

"You first, Ivar," Timothy said.

The Asura turned to give Abaddon one final look. Face twisted with contempt, he spat on the floor, then leaped into the yawning hole to be swallowed up.

"Now, Timothy," the Wurm urged. "If you love the sky, go now!"

The boy could see that the doorway was indeed growing smaller.

"See you on the other side," he told the monstrous creature that he had learned to call friend.

Timothy Cade hurled himself into the swirling vortex.

CHAPTER TEN

Leander awakened in a dungeon chamber deep in the lower regions of SkyHaven, with Edgar and Sheridan watching over him, waiting for him to return to consciousness. The three of them were trapped within a shimmering, crackling cell made entirely of magic, a box created by a network of powerful spells to hold them imprisoned. He sat up, his body still aching from the manner in which Grimshaw's deputies had attacked him even though Leander had surrendered. The constable had commanded his men to attack regardless. The Grandmaster would not soon forget.

He said a silent prayer to the bright ones, wondering what had become of Timothy and if Grimshaw had managed to catch up to him. The worst part of being incarcerated here was that he had no way to find out if the boy had succeeded in breaking Verlis out of Abaddon. *How devastating it would be to have risked so much, and failed,* he thought, but quickly pushed such negativity from his mind. Timothy Cade was a remarkable boy, and if anyone in the whole of the world could accomplish such a feat, he was the one.

The walls of their cell hummed with the strength of their enchantment. Beyond that shimmering magic he could make out only the shadowy recesses of the dungeon.

Edgar waddled close to one wall of their cell and studied the red ripples of energy that ran across it. "Not to complain," the rook began, slowly stretching his neck toward the shimmering barrier, "but with you being the Grandmaster and all, I would have expected you to have enough power to counter this spell."

The wall sparked as the tip of his beak touched it and the bird fluttered back, his jet-black feathers practically standing on end.

"Don't you think we've exceeded our trouble quotient for today, Edgar?" Leander asked, sitting up and swinging his legs over the edge of the cot where the guards had left him. He folded his arms across his barrel chest.

Sheridan's release valve hissed as the mechanical man placed his hands on his hips. "Yes, unless you want the three of us to end up in Abaddon along with Verlis," he said, a hint of annoyance in his tinny voice. "Poor Timothy will have to rescue us as well."

The rook fluttered up from the floor to land atop Sheridan's head. "I just wanted to know if the option was there," Edgar squawked, beginning to groom himself with the side of his beak.

"Truthfully, I'm not certain I could escape," the mage admitted, combing his fingers through his thick, red beard. "But I don't think it would be wise even to attempt it. Any further action on our part would only sully what little credibility I still have with Parliament. I think it best that we bide our time until we learn of Timothy's fate. If he has been captured, rash action might become necessary. But perhaps he will succeed, and he is already on his way to Draconae. I have always wondered about the world of the Wurm. I wonder what marvels he will have to share with us upon his return."

"Do you honestly believe he will be allowed to reach Draconae?" asked a soft voice from the shadows of the dungeon, beyond their arcane cell.

Leander rose to his feet and peered through the magical barrier into the shadows. "Who's there?" he bellowed. "Show yourself at once."

Cassandra Nicodemus emerged from the gloom of the dungeon, her skin unusually pale, almost spectral, in the faint light. Her red hair framed her face, draping shadows across her eyes.

"I had hoped that the news of your arrest was nothing but a misunderstanding," the girl said with an air of disapproval.

Leander offered her a slight bow. "So sorry to have disappointed you."

"Caw! Come to gloat, have you?" Edgar crowed, flapping his wings, feathers ruffled in annoyance.

"You presume to know me, familiar," the girl said haughtily.

"But let me assure you that you do not. I am not your enemy."

"Then why have you come?" Leander asked. "To offer us our freedom? You'll forgive me if I am skeptical." Leander studied her, deeply curious. This girl was a mystery.

"Oh yes, that would be lovely." Sheridan perked up, his inner workings clicking and whirring excitedly.

Cassandra smoothed the front of her green silk cloak. "I am afraid that setting you free is not within my power at the moment," she said. "You have broken the law, Professor Maddox, and I'm sorry to say that you and your compatriots will remain imprisoned until the constable sees fit to arrange for your trial. Word has it that Parliament does not share our fascination with the son of Argus Cade."

"'*Our* fascination,'" Leander noted, sitting back down on the cot. "I wasn't aware that the boy had so captured *your* fancy," he said, a smile growing on his face.

The young woman appeared flustered. "I find him . . . interesting," Cassandra said, nervously twisting a lock of her hair and looking everywhere but at him, "and Parliament's fear of him completely unfounded."

Leander chuckled. Cassandra was flustered and he thought that it suited her, made her more like other girls her age. "Then if it is not to gawk at us fearsome lawbreakers, mistress, why exactly have you come?"

"Fearsome lawbreakers indeed," Edgar grumbled beneath his breath.

"Quiet, Edgar," Sheridan scolded. "There's no need to be rude."

The rook squawked and tilted his head to glare at the mechanical man. "Have you not noticed that we've been arrested?"

The girl scowled at the bird's derision, then returned her attention to the mage. "I come with information about Timothy."

Leander shot to his feet and approached the barrier that separated him from freedom. "What have you heard?" he asked eagerly. "Has he succeeded in releasing Verlis from Abaddon?"

Sheridan, with Edgar still perched on his head, moved closer, eager to share in the news of his creator's fate.

"Do . . . do you know if he is well?" the mechanical man asked haltingly, his timbre filled with concern. "I do so worry about him."

"Of course he's well," Edgar said, annoyed. "I'm his familiar. I'd know if anything serious had happened to him. I'd feel it in my bones."

Cassandra moved closer to the crimson barrier that separated them. "All I know is what I have overheard in the halls of SkyHaven," she said in an excited whisper. "And if the rumors are true, then what he has accomplished is momentous."

Leander experienced an odd mix of excitement and dread as he waited for Cassandra to continue.

"They say that he infiltrated Abaddon prison and has set the Wurm free. . . ."

The girl was nearly breathless, and Leander noticed a pink

flush upon her normally alabaster cheeks. *Ah, someone has been charmed by the boy's adventurous exploits,* he thought with amusement. *Timothy might have been so impressed by her that he failed to notice they are separated in age by only two or three years, but apparently Cassandra has not.*

"They escaped through a magical portal conjured by the beast."

"Caw! Caw! Caw!" Edgar cried excitedly, flying up from Sheridan's head and soaring about the confined space of the cell. "He did it! I knew he'd pull it off! Didn't doubt it for a moment."

"Edgar, please," Leander barked, not sharing in the bird's excitement. There was still too much they did not know, too many things that could still go horribly wrong. "Can you tell us anything more? Has the boy yet returned with his friend to Draconae?"

Edgar lit upon the Grandmaster's shoulder and folded his wings. "Good question," he said, anxiously leaning forward for the answer.

Cassandra shrugged lightly, a look of worry gracing her delicate features. "I know nothing, other than that Constable Grimshaw and his deputies are pursuing them. The rumors say that the constable was able to conjure a spell to track the Wurm's path."

"Blast!" the Grandmaster exclaimed, feeling ill. "Where to? Where have they gone if they are not yet in Draconae?"

"August Hill," Cassandra whispered. "To the home of Argus Cade."

Constable Arturo Grimshaw had spent most of his adult life seeking the perfection of order. He imagined that his obsession was likely a result of his upbringing. Though he walked among the wealthiest of mages now and received their respect, his parents had been simple people. Mages who were not from noble or wealthy families were required to choose a vocation in which to apprentice. Grimshaw's mother and father had met in a clothier where the most elegant uniforms, cloaks, and gowns of Arcanum's elite were designed and the fabric woven with magic. An honorable profession, and yet young Arturo's home life could best have been described as chaos.

Late that afternoon he sat within the constabulary transport as it sped across the sky toward August Hill, and a dark satisfaction settled heavily upon his heart. The transport dipped slightly forward and he knew they were nearing their destination. He tried to push thoughts of the past aside and studied the faces of those who accompanied him. Some of these men and women had been with him since he had first received his constable's rank; others he knew only from reports of their magical aptitude. They were his tools, his instruments of order. If only he had been in command of such implements in the days of his youth.

Mother and father imbibed, the juice of the vine helping them to relax after a long hard day at the clothier—or so they said. The drink seemed to release something trapped within the normally placid couple, something wild and turbulent. Many a night Arturo had gone to sleep hungry, forgotten by his parents, listening fearfully from his bed to the sounds of their raucous laughter as they drank themselves further and further into oblivion. He remembered how afraid he'd been, wishing that he had the power, the magic to make them right. To make them stop.

"We're approaching our destination, sir," the navigation mage called from his place atop the sleek, black transport, pulling the constable back to the present.

"Take us in," he ordered quickly.

But the memories of the past were not yet ready to release him fully. With a clawing dread deep in his belly, he remembered the night that an act of chaos took away all that defined his young existence. The investigating officials had said that it was an accident, the careless use of hungry fire. But Arturo knew otherwise, for it had been his first attempt at bringing order to his turbulent life.

From chaos there will come order, a voice had whispered from somewhere inside his head, and it had compelled him to act. His parents had been drunk again, quarrelling as they seemed to do night after night, and something snapped inside him. As he had lain in his bed, gazing up at the cracked and water-stained ceiling of his room, a calm silky voice that he had never heard before that night urged him to take action.

His thoughts still upon the past, Grimshaw gazed out the window at the darkened manse. They had arrived. He felt his officers' eyes upon him, and turned to look at the men and women awaiting his orders, waiting for him to take charge of the situation as he had done that night so long ago.

That night. Just a boy, younger than the Cade freak, he had lain in his bed, fighting the lure of sleep, waiting for his mother and father to succumb to the effects of the alcohol. When the house was finally silent, he had carefully crept out into the main room. Colorful reams of magically spun cloth lay strewn about, waiting to be fashioned into fabulous clothing for some socialite to wear to a gala ball. How his parents had yearned for an existence that would have found them invited to such events, but that was not the path their lives had taken.

He had found them slumped in their chairs, surrounded by their work, the stink of fermented grape wafting from their gaping mouths. They were silent, but he knew it was only a matter of time before the pandemonium that was their life would rise up again to claim them.

From chaos there shall come order, the voice whispered, and he had known what he had to do to carry out that edict of change. Beside each of his parents was a small lantern of hungry fire, the flame within its metal casing casting a light far superior to that of ghostfire for the purposes of their intricate work.

His thoughts were interrupted again by the voice of Hestia Trill, one of his deputies. "How shall we proceed, Constable Grimshaw?"

Grimshaw could not respond. He was trapped in his

memory. In his mind he could still see the way the hungry fire danced, eager to leave its confinement, ravenous for a taste of the magically woven cloth. As he had stood, watching everything he had ever known consumed in the growing flames, it would have been so easy to be caught up in the flow of madness. But the voice inside his head had not allowed it.

I have special plans for you, it had whispered, urging him from the burning home into the cold, dark night. *I shall make you an instrument of my return.*

"Sir?" urged a voice from somewhere nearby.

Grimshaw finally focused his eyes on the present and saw Deputy Denham standing before him, a look of concern upon his normally stoic features. Hestia was behind him, her features also etched with worry. They were frightened of him, these law mages. But they cared for him as well. It was a delicate but valuable balance.

"Yes, Deputy?"

"We've reached our destination, sir," Denham explained. "How shall we proceed?" he asked.

The constable considered the request, again glancing out the window. He saw the Cade estate and imagined it engulfed in flames.

"Move in, but use extreme caution," he ordered. "And, Deputy, if you are met with any resistance, kill them."

From chaos there shall come order.

"Kill them all."

* * *

"Verlis? Verlis, please try to stay with us. Time is short," Timothy said, gnawing on his lower lip as he watched the Wurm slip in and out of consciousness.

They had arrived at the home of the boy's father through the portal Verlis had conjured, completing the first phase of their mission by escaping Abaddon. Now they desperately needed to begin phase two, but in order to do that, Verlis had to conjure yet another portal, this one interdimensional. Without his full strength, such a spell might be impossible. Things did not look promising.

Ivar knelt beside the Wurm and placed a gentle hand on his armor-plated back. "Whatever the mages used to dull your senses," the Asura said, "you must overcome it. For our sake, and for the sake of your clan."

"Something in the food they fed me in that damnable place," Verlis hissed, his horned head seemingly too heavy to hold aloft. "Makes it difficult for me to stay awake."

"But you have to," Timothy urged. "You have to conjure the doorway that will take us to Draconae."

The Wurm's eyes began to close. "Perhaps if I had some time to rest," he grumbled, his large skull beginning to droop toward his chest.

"No!" Timothy cried, moving to stand before the dragon, grabbing hold of one of his horns. "Time is something we don't have."

Verlis opened his eyes to slits, the normally dark, piercing orbs clouded with a milky film.

"Constable Grimshaw and his deputies are sure to figure

out where we've gone. It can't be long before they're pounding on our door," he told Verlis. "What can we do to help you? Think, Verlis, think really hard, because my brain has just about had it for today."

The room was eerily silent except for the heavy, bellow-slike breathing of the Wurm. They were losing him again, and something told Timothy that it would probably be some time before they could wake him.

"Perhaps if he were to eat," Ivar suggested.

The logic seemed sound. After all, if they had been feeding him food spiked with drugs at Abaddon, maybe untainted sustenance would act as a purifier and move the poisons through the Wurm's system faster.

"What do you think, Verlis?" Timothy asked. "If you were to eat some untainted food, could it help?"

The dragon considered the idea. "Perhaps," he said weakly. "It has been a very long time since I consumed a proper meal."

"Excellent," Timothy said, trying to restrain his excitement. "What can we get for you? I think there's some bread and biscuits in the pantry, and some fruit preserves—"

"Volcanite," the Wurm whispered, slowly lifting his head.

Timothy was confused. "Volcanite?" he asked, looking to Ivar for clarification. "What's that?"

"It is the food of the Wurm," Ivar explained. "The common rock you know as heatstone."

"Heatstone?" Timothy said aloud. "Volcanite is heatstone?"

Ivar nodded as Timothy felt the world drop out from

beneath him. Back on the Island of Patience the black rock was found in great abundance, and he had used it to fuel his forge. But that was Patience, and he doubted there was time for a trip to the island.

"Heatstone," the boy said, sitting down hard on the floor beside the barely conscious Wurm. "All the things we brought over from Patience, and it had to be heatstone. It couldn't be Yaquis fronds, or whiskerfish skin; it had to be heatstone." He shook his head in disgust. "The one thing we didn't take with us."

Timothy felt himself slipping deeper and deeper into despair. If they couldn't come up with a way to make Verlis well enough to use his magic, they would never be able to reach Draconae, and everything they had accomplished so far would be for nothing.

"We have heatstone," Ivar said flatly.

"What did you say?" Timothy asked with surprise.

"We have heatstone," Ivar repeated, raising his arm to point in the direction of the solarium where they had built the diving sphere. "In that room. At least a barrel of it. Sheridan thought that it might be useful."

"Sheridan? Remind me to give him a new coat of polish!" Timothy jumped to his feet, suddenly optimistic.

Then a series of explosions rocked the Cade estate to its very foundation.

Dusk was falling across Arcanum. The homes on August Hill cast long shadows. The constable's deputies stood on the stone stairs leading up to the Cade house, their transport hovering in the air alongside the steep face of August Hill, which was nearly a cliff at this height. Powerful energies sparked from their hands as they attempted to breach the Cade estate's defenses, working in the shadow of the house.

In unison they raised their arms, casting spells that threw waves of destructive force at the facade of the esteemed residence, but all that raw power went to waste. The attack was harmlessly deflected by enchantments infused into the structure. Grimshaw had expected as much. Argus Cade had been a powerful mage and a gifted conjure-architect. Had the defenses of his home been anything less than formidable, the constable would have been greatly disappointed.

"Stand aside," he commanded, climbing the stone staircase.

"The shields are like nothing I've ever seen," Deputy Denham noted as the constable studied the structure, searching his vast memory for a spell that would be strong enough to counter the arcane artistry of Argus Cade.

"Understandable," the constable replied. "You're a law mage. Whereas I have studied many skills, many vocations. Conjure-architecture among them."

Grimshaw could almost sense his prey inside, the boy's horrific handicap a stain on the magical fabric of the world. And he was determined to remove that stain. The constable sang out his spell of deconstruction, the staggering energies unleashed from his hands assailing the barriers established by Argus Cade. At first the opposing force held, standing fast against his casting, but then, slowly, small cracks in the structure of the magic began to appear.

"Most impressive, sir," Denham said with a bow while the other deputies prepared to storm the house.

Grimshaw's hand slowly moved up to smooth the ends of his mustache, even as the large double doors exploded from their frame in jagged fragments. He smiled.

"Yes. Isn't it, though?"

The house shook as though a storm raged against its walls. Thunderous explosions reverberated through the halls as the defenses constructed by Timothy's father were torn away.

"We're running out of time," Timothy said nervously. "Does he look any better to you?" he asked Ivar as they watched Verlis slowly bring another jagged heatstone to his mouth. He and Ivar had managed to bring the heavy barrel of volcanite from the solarium into Argus's study and had fed their friend until he had the strength to do it himself.

"I could not say," the Asura replied with a sad shake of his head. "I have always found the look of the Wurm disturbing."

Another explosion rocked the house. Timothy glanced up in alarm and shot Ivar a nervous look. Ivar nodded. They both knew that time was running out.

The Wurm bit down on the black stone, producing a spray of sparks that rained upon the floor.

"What do you think, Verlis?" the boy asked. "Are you feeling up to it?"

The Wurm swallowed with a wet rasp and looked at the boy with hooded eyes that revealed nothing.

"Here," Timothy said anxiously, reaching into the barrel for another chunk of the stone. "This looks like a good piece. Eat up."

Verlis silently accepted the heatstone.

There came a clamor from the front of the house . . . but this time the thunderous noise was different. Closer. And it was followed by the pounding of booted feet. Timothy knitted his brows and glared at the closed, double doors of the study. They were inside now. There were intruders in his father's home—*his* home—and he felt his blood begin to boil.

"Not much longer now," Timothy said to Ivar.

The Asura's flesh had already begun to change, jagged patterns blooming upon the pale, exposed flesh of his face, chest, and arms—the markings of war.

"We will fight them?" he asked, reaching for the knife hanging at his side.

Timothy shrugged. "Don't really see the use now." He looked back to Verlis who now knelt, his great wings wrapped around his crouching form as if protecting him from the cold. The last of the heatstone lay in fragments on the floor. "He doesn't look better. He looks worse than ever."

He whipped around, ready for a fight, as angry fists began to pound on the study doors.

"Surrender!" a voice boomed from outside the doors.

"Give yourselves up, and we guarantee you will be treated fairly!"

"Why don't I believe that?" Timothy muttered. His gaze shifted from Ivar, who was crouched and prepared for battle, to the deathly still form of Verlis, enshrouded within his wings. The Wurm's scaly flesh had taken on a dull, grayish hue.

"Because you are not a fool," Ivar told him, freeing his knife from its sheath.

"I'm sorry, Verlis," Timothy said softly. "We tried, but it wasn't enough." He reached out to touch the Wurm's flesh and found it unusually hot.

The doors to the study exploded inward, sailing through the air to shatter against one of the bookcases across the room. Ancient texts spilled from the shelves and littered the floor like falling leaves.

The deputies swept into the room, their hands radiating crackling magic.

Ivar tensed, preparing to spring at the invaders, when Timothy reached out to grab hold of his muscular arm. The Asura looked at the boy, violence in his dark gaze.

"No," Timothy said flatly, shaking his head. "We're done. We've failed."

There was the slightest hint of resistance from the Asura, a moment when Timothy wasn't quite sure if his friend would submit, but then he felt the coiled muscles in Ivar's arm begin to relax, and the grave expression on his face receded, replaced by one of bitter resignation.

"If that is your wish," Ivar said quietly, returning the knife to its sheath.

The deputies encircled them, fear in their eyes. They knew that their magical powers would have no effect on Timothy, but still they had a job to do. Though he did not agree with the deputies' mission, the boy could feel nothing but respect for their courage.

"Timothy Cade, you are under arrest for crimes against the nation of Sunderland and the Parliament of Mages," proclaimed a particularly nervous law mage.

"You can relax," Timothy said calmly. "We won't be putting up any fight."

The deputies looked at one another with quick, nervous glances, none of them wanting to be the first to trust his statement.

"Are you sure about that, Timothy?"

The boy glanced at the ravaged doorway just in time to see Constable Grimshaw strolling casually into the study, hands clasped behind his back.

"Are you absolutely certain that you and the motley crew you call friends wouldn't care to resist us?" The constable stopped in the center of the room, his eyes darting about the study, as if searching for something. "My men were so looking forward to killing you," he said idly.

"Sorry to disappoint them," Timothy responded with equal vehemence.

"Oh, well," Grimshaw replied, and from behind his back he produced a pair of heavy manacles similar to those that had been used on Verlis. "I had these made especially for you." The constable tossed them to the floor in front of the boy. "I suggest you put them on at once."

Timothy stared at the chains coiled at his feet as if they were a poisonous serpent. Slowly he bent to pick up the restraints.

"Timothy, no," Ivar said, defiance in his guttural tone.

"That's enough out of you, savage," Grimshaw warned. "Go ahead, boy. Put them on."

"It's all right, Ivar," he said as he opened one of the manacles. They were much heavier than he imagined. "Maybe if I do as I'm told, they'll treat you and Verlis better." He looked at each of the deputies and then Grimshaw, hoping for some kind of confirmation.

"Of course. They will be treated the same as all criminals; fairly, humanely"—Grimshaw paused, his eyes twinkling maliciously—"before they are put to death."

Timothy felt as though he had been struck. "No," he cried, shaking the chains at the lawman. "You can't! What crime have they committed that was so terrible you would execute them for it?"

Grimshaw chuckled. "Escaping Abaddon, assaulting officers of Parliament. And if I were you, I would be more concerned about my own skin."

Timothy threw the chains to the floor, feeling both enraged and helpless. "You're a monster," he spat, scalding emotion filling his eyes.

Constable Grimshaw smiled cruelly as he motioned for

his deputies to retrieve the manacles. They converged on the boy. He fought hard, but these were not ordinary mages. In addition to magic, they had been trained in hand-to-hand combat, and their number soon overwhelmed him. He felt his urge to struggle bleeding away. Two more of the deputies had restrained Ivar, containing him in a sphere of crackling force.

This is it, Timothy thought as he felt the cold metal touch of the manacles.

They were preparing to put them on him when he noticed an odor. It was familiar, but he'd never smelled it quite so strong. It was the smell of the forge in his workshop, of heatstone brought to its highest temperature.

Volcanite, he thought, looking to where Verlis huddled, wrapped in his wings. Vapors had begun to drift upward from the now glistening flesh of the Wurm, and the pungent aroma of superheated rock filled the room. A slight tremble passed through Verlis's flesh. "Something's happening!" he called out, loudly enough that Ivar could hear from within the containment sphere that now imprisoned him.

Magic sizzled and danced along Grimshaw's fingers as he raised his hands. "The Wurm!" he bellowed to his officers. "Contain the—"

Verlis unfurled his wings and let loose a ferocious roar, his eyes blazing with such fury that even Timothy was terrified for a moment. The heatstone had done its work. The Wurm was healthy again. And enraged.

"Don't just stand there," Grimshaw barked, but his

deputies had frozen, stunned and terrified by the sudden turn of events.

The Wurm opened his jaws and everyone in the room could see the churning inferno deep in his throat. Smoke furled from his nostrils. Seething heat radiated from his flesh. All was silent in Argus Cade's study, except for the sound of liquid flame dripping from the corners of Verlis's vast, razor-toothed maw, sizzling and hissing as it landed on the floor.

Drip, *hssssssss,* drip, *hssssssssssss,* drip, *hssssssssssssssssss* . . .

A tension built in the air and time seemed to stand still. Timothy was reminded of the anticipation he felt when he lit one of his own explosive devices, and the deceptively prolonged wait as the fuse burned down to detonate the deadly mixture within.

"Kill it," Grimshaw commanded, his voice cutting through the palpable silence. "Kill the beast and be done with it!"

And that was when Verlis exploded.

The great Wurm's roar was deafening, his wings expanding to pound the air. Plumes of liquid fire erupted from his gaping mouth, scattering the constable's men. Tim watched as the glowing bubble that encased Ivar dissipated now that its conjurors were seeking cover from the dragon's wrath and could no longer focus on it. His concern for his father's house was quickly relieved as he witnessed enchantments instilled in the walls cancel out the raging blaze before it could do any serious damage.

"Come to me!" Verlis roared over the beating of his wings.

Timothy and Ivar ran to the Wurm as the constable's voice shrieked above the confusion.

"Kill them! Kill them all!"

The air was filled with blasts of deadly magic, and although the boy had nothing to fear from the bolts of hazardous energy, he worried for the safety of his friends. The Wurm beat his wings, creating gale force winds that helped to keep their attackers at bay.

"Grab hold of me," Verlis growled, and Timothy and Ivar did as they were told.

The constable and his deputies were almost upon them, enchantments that were surely meant to murder crackling at the tips of their fingers.

"Hold tight," the dragon roared.

Verlis tensed his powerful legs, then sprang from the floor, his wings lifting them into the air with incredible speed and taking them up through the ceiling with a thunderous crash. But the dragon did not stop there, continuing on his destructive path, breaking up through the next section of ceiling, and the next, and the next after that. Argus Cade had put wards in place to protect his house from fire and from attack, but there were no spells in place to prevent their escape. Timothy's father had never imagined anything would have to crash *out* of his home.

Timothy could hear the cries of dismay from the soldiers somewhere far below them, the sounds of angry voices growing smaller and more distant as Verlis propelled them through the roof of the old house, escaping into the open air.

Clutching the dragon's waist for dear life, Timothy opened his eyes to see that they soared far above August Hill, the fabulous city of Arcanum spreading out below to the emerald green ocean. If he hadn't been so frightened he would have thought this to be one of the most breathtaking sights he had ever seen.

Ivar wore a similar look of sheer wonder, the patterns on his flesh expanding and changing at a breakneck pace as Verlis continued to flap his leathery wings, taking them higher and higher still.

"Where are we going?" Timothy yelled, hoping to be heard over the rushing air, fearful that the dragon would take them up farther into the frigid, near airless atmosphere.

"Take your hands from me," Verlis instructed.

Timothy glanced down. "I don't think so."

"You must in order for the spell to work," said the Wurm. "Hold fast to Ivar."

Carefully Timothy did as Verlis asked, moving his grip from the Wurm. He started to slip, but Ivar grabbed hold of him with one hand, while with the other he clung tightly to the Wurm's scaly torso.

The Wurm extended his arms, his talons moving about precisely in the air above him. Timothy heard the start of a spell, a magical incantation spoken in the guttural tongue of the Wurm race, and watched in wonder as a black rip in the very fabric of the sky tore open above them. Then he knew where they were going.

"I take you now to the land of my people," he heard Verlis bellow. What had first appeared as a tear in the sky above their heads was now more a yawning black mouth, opening wide to swallow them whole.

Draconae, Timothy thought, holding tightly to Ivar. *We're finally going to Draconae.*

CHAPTER ELEVEN

Constable Grimshaw let loose a roar of frustration. His body shook with his anger, and it took him several seconds to settle down and remember that he was not alone. His deputies surrounded him, scattered around the foyer of the Cade estate, obviously at a total loss as to what to do with themselves now that the boy, the savage, and the filthy Wurm had escaped. The mages who served Grimshaw fretted in awkward silence, looking everywhere but at their master, shifting from one foot to the other, apparently unable to decide what to do with their hands.

"Go," he said through gritted teeth. With one hand he waved them away. "Search the entire house. If you find wards that are too powerful for you to break, call for me. Look for any hint as to where the criminals might have gone. It's likely they'll try to go to the Wurm's dimension, but we may be able to stop them before they do."

They responded instantly, disappearing into the depths of the home that had been built so long ago by Argus Cade. Grimshaw was confident they would rather be anywhere other than in his presence. Nor did he want them nearby. He tried to cultivate a calm, confident persona, but he felt ready to explode. It would be best if his subordinates did not witness any more of this. The boy had beaten him, for the moment, and the constable did not like being bested . . . but it was particularly infuriating when it happened in front of others.

He was humiliated.

It occurred to him that the deputy constables who were there at the house with him, who had witnessed his embarrassment and loss of control, might be better turned to other duties. Far from Arcanum and the Parliament. Far from anyone who might hear of the scene that had just unfolded. After all, Constable Grimshaw's reputation was at stake.

The more he thought about it, the more he thought perhaps even that was not enough. Perhaps it would be best if his deputies were to be eliminated in a more permanent fashion. Grimshaw was going to have to give the idea some serious consideration.

While the deputies were searching through the house, the constable wandered about the foyer, his cloak swishing behind him and his boots clicking on the floor. He frowned deeply as he studied the alterations that the Cade boy had made to this part of his ancestral home. There were sconces on the walls that had been rigged to burn with hungry fire rather than magical ghostfire. Dangerous, but the boy was clearly unafraid of the voracious nature of such flames.

Grimshaw sniffed, attempting to dismiss from his mind the thoughts that were rising there. He was beginning to think that he had underestimated Timothy Cade, that the boy was an adversary who could prove to be a very long-term thorn in his side. All along, the constable had assumed that the defeat and destruction of Nicodemus had been a fluke, that the boy had gotten lucky.

Now he wasn't so sure.

He listened for a moment to the sounds of his deputies moving through the house, their footfalls echoing down from the upper floors, and he nodded in satisfaction. If there was anything to be found—

A low hiss interrupted his thoughts. Grimshaw turned toward the familiar sound and saw the ripple in the air that signified the passage from one dimensional space to another. With a sneer he raised both hands, bruise-purple light flickering from his fingers as he prepared to execute Timothy Cade and his allies.

But it was not the boy returning. He realized this the moment he saw a form beginning to coalesce on the third step of the grand staircase in the foyer. A moment later the transition was complete. There, upon that step, was a hugely fat mud toad, its yellow eyes shining sickly.

Grimshaw's upper lip curled as though he had just sipped curdled milk, and he reached up and tugged at one end of his mustache. He was loyal to his master, but he despised the toad. It stank like rotting vegetables, and though it had no voice of its own, there was something about its features that suggested it disdained him.

Him!

If it had not been his master's familiar, Grimshaw would have cast a hex upon it that would have turned it inside out.

Now the mud toad's mouth opened, and a single, long croak escaped from its foul innards. And then another voice echoed from its throat: the voice of his master.

"Argus Cade was a clever mage, Constable Grimshaw," came the voice from inside the toad. "He was suspicious, and I believe that are many things he learned, or at least was curious about, before his death. His study is on the third floor. Go there and search every crevice, every nook. If he kept records or journals, they may be magically hidden, and they may contain secrets I would not like to have discovered.

"Go. Search."

This was punctuated by a loud croak from the toad that sounded more like a belch, and then, with that hiss of dislocation, the air shimmered and the toad disappeared.

"Damned toad," Grimshaw muttered as he stormed up the stairs, his cloak flapping in his wake.

Moments later he found Argus Cade's study. There was a ward at the entrance, but Constable Grimshaw had not achieved success in his field of expertise without becoming a master of shattering such wards. It was among his specialties, along with torture, interrogation, and immobilization.

His arms ached as a result of the spell required to break into the deceased mage's private sanctum, but it was an almost pleasant feeling. Grimshaw stood in the center of the room, with his arms crossed, surveying the shelves that were empty save for a few old, yellowed manuscripts, three tiny bottles of tincture, and a display case that appeared ancient enough to date back to the days of the Wizards of Old. Magical archaeology had been one of Argus Cade's passions. There were indentations in the fabric inside the case that indicated there had been talismans or artifacts of some kind within, before the study had been cleared out.

Grimshaw frowned. *Maddox*. The Order of Alhazred's current Grandmaster—a situation that was about to change—had been Argus Cade's primary apprentice and acolyte. Someone had cleaned out Cade's study, packed away his belongings, and organized his manuscripts, and Grimshaw felt certain the job had fallen to Maddox. But if the professor had found anything suspicious, surely it would have come to light by now.

Perhaps he had not looked hard enough.

Another of Constable Grimshaw's skills was in the magic of discovery.

With a deep sigh he threw his head back and stretched his arms out. A low chant began in his chest and rose up into his throat. He huffed air out of his lungs, grunting the words to the chant that were painful to utter. An icy chill gripped him and fingers of cold ran up and down his spine and up the back of his neck. His hands felt frozen, as though they might shatter like icicles at any moment.

The constable shuddered, and then he doubled over in pain. Gritting his teeth to avoid crying out, he held the spell inside him for a moment, and then he stood up straight. His wrists twisted with a flourish. He exhaled a plume of icy blue breath that crystallized in the air. It joined with a draft of cold air that swept off his hands and began to scour the study like the north wind itself, whipping through the room and across shelves, searching for a cache.

On the far side of the study, above a high-backed chair and a lamp of ghostfire, there was a mirror whose silvery spell-glass shimmered, awaiting a mage whose reflection it could provide. But the mirror was more than that. As the frigid air and icy crystals of Grimshaw's spell struck it, it froze instantly. The surface turned white and translucent, and then it simply shattered. Shards of ice showered down upon the ghostfire lamp and the high-backed chair, revealing a niche in the wall, and a set of thin books bound in leather.

Grimshaw grinned and strode across the room to pluck one of the books from its hiding place. He opened it and found within that the writing was as crude as the manufacture of the books themselves. Argus Cade, an archmage, had written the words with his own hand rather than through magic, and the books themselves had been crafted by hand. Why the mage had gone to such lengths he could not understand . . . and then the constable realized why the old man had done such a thing.

The boy. The boy could not have read the journals if they had been magical devices. If the words had been written with a spell, they would have disappeared the moment Timothy Cade touched them. Argus had written these journals for his son.

A broad smile formed upon Constable Grimshaw's face, and he grabbed the rest of the journals, slipping them into a magical pocket inside his cloak, where he could have hid the entire house if he'd had a mind to. If his master's secrets had been in jeopardy from the existence of these journals, Grimshaw had just ensured that they would not be a problem in the future. His master would be pleased.

But that was not the reason for Grimshaw's smile. His mood was considerably improved by the knowledge that these were the personal communications of Argus Cade to his freakish offspring, and now the boy would never see them.

Perhaps the day had not been a complete waste after all.

In fact, even the boy's escape was not of enormous concern. After all, Grimshaw still had Leander Maddox in custody, along with Timothy's familiar and that ridiculous metal man.

The boy would be back.

And Constable Grimshaw would be waiting.

Timothy's only experience with traveling between dimensions had been through the door that separated the Island of Patience from his ancestral home. But his father had been a powerful mage and had carefully constructed that passageway—a passageway that he hoped Constable Grimshaw would not discover. It was a well-traveled path between worlds, and perhaps because of that, passing through it caused no discomfort whatsoever, only a momentary feeling of disorientation.

Once, while he was growing up on Patience, Timothy had been climbing a Yaquis tree and fallen from its upper branches.

The impact when he struck the ground had cracked several of his ribs and stolen the breath from his body. He had lain there, unable to breathe, trying to gasp for air, his eyes bulging out, and had been certain that he was about to die.

Traveling through dimensions using the spell Verlis had cast to bring them to Draconae was much like that experience.

They tore through the fabric of reality on Draconae, intruding into that world with enough force to create a loud noise, almost an explosion of air. Ivar fell to his knees, breathing deeply as though to avoid throwing up. Timothy wished he was that fortunate. For his part, he went down on his face, jittering as though he had been struck by lightning, and barely managed to roll over and stare up at his friends. His hands flailed as he gestured to them, trying to indicate to them that he could not breathe. His face felt warm. Blackness began to seep in around the corners of his eyes and his chest felt as though Verlis were sitting on it.

He began to think the blackness would claim him, then Ivar knelt beside him. The Asura had recovered almost immediately, and now he lay one hand on Timothy's chest and bent to stare into his eyes.

"Calm," he whispered.

Timothy felt a peacefulness spreading through him. For a moment he was frightened, thinking that this was his body's surrender to death. Then he found himself able to inhale, and he drew in a long, grateful breath of the air of Draconae.

And he began to choke.

It was several anxious moments before he had steadied his breathing and gotten the coughing and choking under control. The air was thick with the smell of smoke and burnt things. As he got up on his knees at last, Timothy frowned, wondering why Verlis had not been there to help him recover from the dimensional jump.

Then, as he rose, Timothy saw the reason.

They were on a steep mountainside. A tiny stream ran down from much higher up the mountain. In the distance were thickly forested areas, with dark-hued trees whose leaves were the color of drying blood. Built into the mountainside were shadowy openings, the mouths of caves, but Timothy could not tell if they were natural or if they had been dug into the stone and soil.

All around them was a circle of devastation. The ground was charred black from fire. In some places embers still burned and smoke rose in swirling eddies. The dead husks of trees, now just withered fingers pointing accusations at the golden sky, dotted the blackened landscape.

Verlis stood, wings folded tightly against his back, and stared up the ravaged mountainside. The Wurm shook his massive head from side to side, as though by simply denying it he could erase the horror that was laid out before them. Suddenly he let out a hitching gasp, and his wings spread. With three sharp beats of those broad wings he flew like a dagger through the air above the burnt ground and landed among a group of squat, twisted tree husks. Their charred branches jutted in all directions.

Then he saw the dead trees for what they were. Timothy hissed air in through his teeth and hugged himself.

Ivar moved to stand beside him, one gentle hand resting on the boy's shoulder.

"It's terrible," Timothy whispered.

The Asura nodded grimly, and uttered one, simple word. "Wurm."

Long ago Ivar's tribe had been mortal enemies of the Wurm. Though they would eventually both become the victims of the cruelty and prejudice of mages, at that time, their hatred for each other had been even greater than the mages' hatred of both of their tribes. In his childhood Ivar must have seen the results of an attack by the Wurm. But Timothy never had. He wished he could make the memory leave his mind.

For the small cluster of twisted, gnarled, blackened trees that Verlis had landed in were not trees at all. They were the charred bodies of members of his tribe, Wurm who were probably his friends, perhaps even his kin. The vestiges of their wings and their bones jutted upward like those dead trees.

There was a civil war here on Draconae. But from the look of it, Timothy was wondering if it wasn't already over.

Slowly he walked across that ravaged landscape and joined Verlis. The Wurm furled his wings against his back again. When he glanced up from the corpses, there were tears of liquid fire sliding down his leathery face. Plumes of flame shot from his nostrils.

"One of them is Gavlor, the brother of my father. The others . . . the others are burned so badly I cannot identify them. My family was encamped here. My mate. Our children. All of my compatriots. All of those who wished to live in peace, to avoid the hateful, spiteful philosophies of Raptus and those like him. That was all we wanted. Peace."

Timothy nodded, but found himself unable to speak any words of comfort. In his heart he felt the weight of terrible guilt. If Verlis had not helped him to defeat Nicodemus, he would never have been captured. If they had been able to come back to Draconae sooner, this horror might have been avoided.

"Friend Verlis," Ivar began softly, "I grieve for your kin. But there are few dead here. The others of your clan might yet live. There may still be a chance that they could be saved."

"Or their remains might be in the caves," Verlis said bitterly, snorting fire.

Timothy went to him and reached up to put a hand on the Wurm's leathery shoulder. "We'll help you look."

"No," Verlis said, shaking off the boy's touch. "They are my tribe. The task is mine."

With a shuddering breath, Timothy nodded. He bit his lip to keep from speaking again. Verlis's tone was clear. Timothy blamed himself for delaying their return, and Verlis blamed him as well. He wanted to say how sorry he was, but now was not the time.

The Wurm turned from them and started up the mountainside toward the mouth of the nearest cave. Ivar came up beside Timothy again.

"It is not your fault," the Asura said, his voice low. "You

cannot be blamed for the crimes of others."

He was right, but it did not make Timothy feel any better.

The two of them watched Verlis walk toward the cave. So focused were they on their friend that they did not see what emerged from the cave. Instead they only saw the way Verlis reacted. The Wurm froze for a moment, then his wings spread out wide, and he rose, wings beating the air, bellowing fire.

Only then did they see the figure of another Wurm emerging from the mouth of the cave. The creature was taller than Verlis and clad in armor the same blood red as the leaves of the trees. In one hand it held a long chain, at the end of which was a metal ball with spikes jutting from it. The other hand was alight with a burning yellow sphere of magic.

Timothy and Ivar were in motion at the same time. The two of them were running to aid Verlis.

The rest of it happened so fast they barely had time to react. Wurm flew down from the sky, some of them armored. Others spilled from the caves up the mountainside, armed with vicious bladed weapons, with swords and maces and axes. Timothy and Ivar paused only a moment, and then they heard the beating of heavy wings above them and glanced upward to see a legion of Wurm descending from the yellow sky, claws reaching for them, fire hissing from their open jaws.

They never had a chance.

Heat seared Timothy Cade's left cheek and the back of his left hand. He woke up hissing through his teeth from the pain, but when he put his palms on the ground to push himself up, they were scalded as well. Timothy put his hands on his lap and sat, not letting his bare skin touch the floor now, and surveyed his surroundings.

It was a cave, but he immediately sensed that this was not one of the caves he had seen upon arriving in Draconae. The air was so dry that his lips where chapped, and when he breathed in, his lungs were stung by the heat. Jets of steam blew up through cracks in the stone floor at various points in the cave, and the floor nearly glowed with the heat coming from somewhere below.

Where his flesh had touched the ground while he had been lying unconscious, his skin was burned. He winced as he reached up and touched the left side of his face. Painful, but not much real damage. He hoped.

Even now, the heat radiated up from beneath him, and he could not sit on the stone any longer. He stood, shaky on his feet at first, but then regained his equilibrium. The soles of his boots protected his feet, but the temperature inside the cave was lethally hot. He felt as though he were being cooked, and the cave were one big oven.

With his unburned hand Timothy pushed his hair away from his eyes and stepped carefully, exploring the cave. It was not large, but he appeared to be its only occupant. A frown creased his forehead. This made no sense at all. He had not really expected to ever wake up at all after the Wurm had attacked him, Ivar, and Verlis in such numbers and with such savagery. They had fought and he had been pummeled. Slipping into unconsciousness, Timothy had believed that they were all about to die.

Yet here he was. Stiff, bruised, scratched, and with new burns from the floor of the cave. Otherwise, he was unharmed. There was no sign of Ivar or Verlis, but Timothy had to hope that if the Wurm had taken him prisoner, that his friends were also prisoners. He tried not to remember the grisly image of the charred corpses of the Wurm on that mountainside.

"Hello?" Timothy called into the recesses of the cave. Only the hiss of steam and the echo of his own voice replied.

He retraced his steps, careful not to put his hands on the walls. They were likely as hot as the floor. His chest burned inside, and his throat felt scorched, as though he himself were a Wurm and at any moment might exhale an inferno of liquid flame instead of breath.

Alone, he thought. *You're alone.* But this was not the first time that Timothy Cade had found himself alone in a world that was alien to him, and he did not have it within his character to surrender to fear. Somewhere nearby, perhaps in caves much like this one, his friends still lived. He felt sure of it.

It was simple enough to find the entrance to the cave. But through that opening his gaze beheld a hellish panorama, a vision of darkness and fire and terror. Timothy shuddered and tried to swallow back the dread that rose up within him.

"Oh," he whispered softly, not even aware he had spoken.

The cave he was in was one of hundreds that riddled the inner walls of the throat of a terrible volcano, as if the entire thing were a beehive. The Wurm kingdom was alive with motion. The descendants of dragons circled and soared and glided all through the vast open space, traveling between the cave mouths or up and over the rim and out into the dark night of Draconae. Some of them were spitting fire, though for no apparent reason. Timothy guessed it might be some form of communication—some system of signals. Far below, hot, molten lava boiled, casting a reddish-orange glow upward, illuminating the extraordinary city of the Wurm. Though there were stars and a single, silver moon in the night sky, visible above the rim of the volcano, the glow of the lava overpowered the celestial light.

The caves were of varying sizes, and many were surrounded by ornate formations of dried lava that seemed to have been sculpted into aesthetically pleasing shapes. There were cracks in the volcano walls of the lower parts of the city, and fire belched up from those cracks in spurts that shot hundreds of feet into the air.

"Beautiful, isn't it?"

"Aaah!" he barked as he flinched and looked straight upward, searching for the source of the voice.

His boot slipped on the ledge, superheated stone giving way, and he could feel his balance shifting. Timothy flailed his arms, trying to keep from going over the edge, but it was no use. He felt the heat from below blast upward, baking his skin, and he caught a single glimpse down at the boiling lava, knowing that it would melt even his bones.

A powerful claw clamped his shoulder, caught him in mid-air, and Timothy was dangling there, a fiery death waiting below. He looked up into the face of his rescuer, a hideous Wurm with a single deep scar running from its forehead down across one grotesquely empty eye socket and out to one nostril. Tiny jets of flame erupted from its nostrils, one of them wider than the other, where the scar cut through its snout. The Wurm wore no armor, but a jagged insignia had been branded into the leathery hide of its chest.

"I would suggest that you watch your step, boy, but I imagine even your kind are not so stupid that you have not realized this already."

As the Wurm set him down again inside the cave, Timothy marveled at the creature. It appeared cruel, but its voice was warm, even kind, with a dry humor to it that made him confused. They had been attacked and captured.

"You're . . . you're being nice to me. You saved my life."

The Wurm snorted, and Timothy had to back up a step to avoid being singed. "Do not waste the breath to thank me, young mage. I am your guard. Raptus would not be pleased with me if I were to allow you to die while in my care."

Timothy frowned. He did not like the sound of that. But at least the Wurm was willing to speak to him.

"You're to keep me prisoner, then. What's your name?"

"You may call me Hannuk, young mage."

Young mage, Timothy thought. Obviously, the Wurm did not know yet that he had no magic. And he decided he would keep that fact to himself for now.

"And there is no door on my cell because—"

Hannuk interrupted him with a laugh. "Because you have

no wings. You are welcome to attempt an escape, but I wish you would not. As I said, Raptus would not be pleased if you fell to your death, and no other outcome of an escape attempt is likely. Your hands are too soft, your muscles too weak. And a spell has been cast upon you so that you cannot use magic here."

Timothy was only barely able to prevent himself from smiling at that. "And what of my friends. What happened to them?"

Only now, as Timothy mentioned Verlis and Ivar, did he see the glint of cruelty in Hannuk's eyes. The Wurm's entire demeanor seemed to change. He glanced out at the kingdom that sprawled over the inner circumference of the volcano's throat.

"The Asura has been put to work. His kind are good workers if they can be broken. If they cannot, they make excellent meals for our spawn. Oh, I remember the rich flavor of Asura meat. We thought they were all dead, slain by the scheming mages. It is a pleasant surprise to find one alive. They are a delicacy. No child of this new generation of Wurm has ever tasted the flesh of an Asura. If it comes to that, and he fails to prove himself a capable slave, they will be fighting for a scrap of him."

He remembers, Timothy thought. He knew that Wurm could live hundreds of years, but Verlis had been only a child when his people had been banished to Draconae and Timothy had never met another Wurm. This one was old and battle scarred, but still strong, still powerful. And yet he remembered the time when the Asura and the Wurm had been engaged in constant tribal warfare, before the mages began to persecute both races.

"As for the traitor . . . he is being questioned."

Timothy felt every muscle in his body stiffen. His jaws clamped down and he breathed through his nose to keep from screaming and panicking. If Ivar did not cooperate with them, the Wurm would *eat* him! And Verlis . . . Timothy could only imagine the torture that might be used to question him.

"And me? What about me?"

Hannuk snorted fire again. "For now . . . you are here."

"But Raptus wants me alive?"

"You have many questions, young mage," Hannuk muttered. With a hiss of liquid fire that drooled to the ground and burned there in a small pool, he turned and launched himself away from the cave. His wings beat the air several times, and he circled around to come to a stop once more above the entrance to the cave.

Timothy hesitated only a moment. He needed to know what was going on here. There might be some bit of information that would help him stay alive, that would help him save his friends. He moved carefully to the cave opening, trying not to look down at the churning lake of burning lava below.

Hannuk raised one thick brow and glared down at him.

"Is Raptus the king?"

"We have no king," Hannuk spat dismissively. "Raptus is our leader. Our general."

Timothy paused. He had to learn more. Hannuk seemed

to like to talk, but obviously had decided the less said to his captive the better. He tried to think of a way to get the Wurm to speak. After a moment, a tiny smile twitched at the edges of his mouth.

"Why?"

Hannuk sneered. "What do you mean, 'why'?"

"Why is he the leader? Why is Raptus the general? Why him and not someone else?"

Hannuk grunted in frustration. His wings unfurled, and then he pinned them back again. His shoulders rose and fell with a sigh, and he glared down at Timothy. "Had I known you were going to be so talkative, I would have let you drop and burn."

"But Raptus wouldn't have liked that."

The upper part of Hannuk's snout curled into a sneer. "No. No, he would not. In answer to your question, Raptus is leader because he has vision. He is general because we will all follow. We know what he has suffered because of your kind, your monstrous, traitorous kind, and we know that with him in command, you will all be made to suffer for our pain."

Timothy shook his head. Despite the torturous heat and the knowledge that these creatures would never set him free, he felt some compassion for them.

"I'm sorry," he said.

Hannuk flinched.

"I am. Truly. I grew up away from mages, from my world. I know very little about the past. Most people on my world—

the younger people especially—know only what's been taught to them. They see you as monsters."

The Wurm grunted. "*We* are monsters? We made no war on mages until they began to attack our settlements, all driven by the demon Alhazred, Prince of Lies. He showed us what to expect of mages—betrayal and treachery."

Timothy frowned. "You speak of betrayal and treachery. What do you mean? Alhazred and the Parliament were stupid and brutal. But treacherous?"

Fumes drifted from Hannuk's nostrils as he considered Timothy's words.

"Look, if I'm going to be your prisoner," Timothy prodded him, "if my friends and I are doing to die for the crimes of others . . . I think it's only fair of me to ask what those crimes were. The mages were your enemies. I understand that. But betrayal . . . I don't understand."

Hannuk stared at him for a long time before at last he spoke, his voice no longer friendly. Now he seemed only cold and distant. The heat shimmered in the air, but there was ice in the Wurm's eyes.

Hannuk began, his words dripping with venom. He told the story of his own experiences in the months leading up to the banishment of the Wurm to Draconae and revealed things Timothy could have never even dreamed of.

Timothy knew that the Parliament had banished the Wurm out of hatred, but had never known the extent of their betrayal—the secret truth behind the mages' war against the Wurm and the destruction of the Asura. As Hannuk concluded, Timothy could only stare at him, horrified.

"One of the original peacemakers, one of the ambassadors who met with the Parliament of Mages that day, was Tarqilae, father to Raptus. Thanks to the wounds he received in that struggle, Tarqilae did not live long after the banishment. He was the one who called this place Draconae, the land of dragons, harkening back to the primitive beasts all Wurm are descended from. The general never saw his father's eyes; the ambassador was dead before he was born. Tarqilae was the first Wurm to die on the soil of Draconae, and his son was the first to be born here. Raptus was raised with hatred for the mages in his heart."

Hannuk's snout contorted into what might have been a smile, his scar stretching obscenely. "He will use all of the resources of Draconae to find a way back to your world, young mage. And we will destroy you all."

Timothy shook his head. "But not all Wurm believe in Raptus's vision. Verlis and his tribe, his clan, they wanted peace. They only wanted to make the most of their lives here. Why did you have to destroy them? Couldn't Raptus have just gone ahead with his plans without them?"

"You are a mage. It is no surprise that you do not understand. They are traitors. If they will not support the general, then they are betrayers to all of Draconae, to our entire race. As traitors, they must die."

Timothy felt an aching sadness fill his heart, overpowering even the searing heat and his fear.

"They must die, and yet here I am, a mage, and you're going to keep me alive."

Hannuk tucked his wings in tightly to his body and bent down so he could curl his head into the cave and peer into Timothy's face. Merriment seemed to dance in his eyes. The flickering flames from his nostrils rose a bit higher.

"You misunderstand, young mage," Hannuk growled. "I am to keep you alive, yes. I am to keep you from killing yourself while trying to escape. But that is only so that Raptus will not be robbed of the pleasure of tearing your heart out with his own talons in a public execution, so that all the Wurm of Draconae can watch, and cheer.

"It will be excellent for morale."

CHAPTER TWELVE

It was a long and terrible night. Timothy did not sleep. Several times he began to nod off, but the moment one of his bare hands or his face would touch the floor of the cave, he would hiss in pain and sit up again. At best he had perhaps an hour's rest, propped up carefully with his legs beneath him, his back against the wall, and his hands on his lap.

Morning came far too soon.

Sometime during the night Hannuk had brought him a tall stone jar filled with water to keep him from dehydrating completely. There was only a small gulp of it remaining when the red glow outside the cave began to lighten to a golden orange.

Whatever star served as the sun for this world had risen.

He raised the stone jar to drink the last of the water, and when he lowered it, Hannuk stood just inside the cave entrance, silhouetted by the golden orange glow from outside. Two other Wurm came in behind him, both of them in the same dark red armor he had seen on the warriors that had attacked them the day before.

Half a dozen witty barbs came into Timothy's head, but his mouth would form none of them. He gnawed his lower lip and could only watch as Hannuk stood aside to allow the Wurm warriors to approach. He let his limbs hang loosely and lowered his head as if in surrender to his fate. But Timothy had spent years being trained to fight by an Asura warrior. He would not surrender without a battle. As a tiny child he had sparred in combat with a full-grown Asura, and learned that greater size could be turned against an opponent. The moment one of the Wurm reached for him, he acted.

Timothy grabbed the wrist of the nearest Wurm and hauled the monster down toward him, at the same time bringing up his knee with every ounce of strength his tired muscles could summon. He slammed his knee into the creature's jaw, then drove his knuckles into a pressure point at the Wurm's temple. Its snout hung slack, and a snarl came from the fiery bellows of its gullet. Then it collapsed on the floor beside him.

The second warrior lunged at him, but there was no room for it to fly. Timothy batted its hands away, spun sideways, and shot a hard kick at its head that made a loud cracking noise as it connected. Flaming spittle shot from its nostrils, and Timothy darted past the Wurm, grabbed hold of its wings, and began to shove it toward the open mouth of the cave. Even with his training, he knew that his chances of surviving the next few seconds were ridiculously slim, but they were going to execute him anyway. He at least had to attempt an escape. The Wurm tried to get its footing back, but Timothy had it off balance. He would shove it out into the air over the volcano. It would have to fly to save its own life. If he could just get to the rim . . . or a place from which he could climb to the rim—

Hannuk grabbed him by the hair and hauled him backward. Timothy cried out in pain as the Wurm slammed him to the searing stone floor.

"I told you," the Wurm grunted, "my assignment was to keep you alive. And I mean to do so. If you are broken and bleeding when you are presented for your execution, Raptus will not mind."

Timothy froze. He felt the heat from the Wurm's breath and pressed his eyes shut. Fear and sadness filled him, but he refused to let the monsters see it. When he had gotten control of himself again, he slid backward, ignoring the scorching heat of the floor on his palms, and sat up. Hannuk moved out of his way, and Timothy rose to his feet. The warriors who had come to take him were wary now, and enraged, but Timothy could see in their manner that they would not damage him. Raptus was the one to decide his fate.

"The time has come," Hannuk said, and then he gestured for the warriors to take him.

The armor-clad Wurm each took one of his arms and shuffled him to the mouth of the cave, to the ledge overlooking the roiling lava below. Timothy glanced up at the golden sun, and then he felt the forward momentum, the second of free fall as they launched themselves out of the cave. There was a jarring tug as they spread their wings, and then they were flying upward with him.

A roaring cheer echoed off the interior walls of the volcano's throat. Gushing jets of fire blew out from nearly every cave, and then the Wurm showed themselves, crawling out across the rocky walls and, clinging by their talons, watching the spectacle of the boy whom their leader was about to slaughter. There was a low, humming sound, and it took Timothy several seconds to realize it was a sort of chuffing, grunting noise that came from the throats of all of the Wurm, a sound of their pleasure.

Level with the rim, in the center of the space above the volcano's fiery heart, a cluster of armored Wurm hovered like carrion birds, beating their wings and swaying in the updraft from the inferno below. Some of them had swords, others the spiked ball-and-chain combinations he had seen the day before. Several had no weapons at all. One that Timothy could see had glistening green-black energy spilling from her eyes and pooling around her fingers in midair. The female Wurm were just as hideous as the males and, if anything, they looked more dangerous. Their talons were longer, their snouts thinner, but with fangs that jutted downward over their lower jaws.

At the center of this group, though slightly higher in the sky, a single Wurm beat his wings, hands crossed in front of him as though he were completely at peace. Twin jets of dancing fire swirled upward from his nostrils in long plumes with every breath he took. Though he was clad in the same blood-red armor as the other warriors, there were black stripes on his chest plate that looked like claw marks, and his head was covered almost entirely by a black helmet, horns jutting up through holes.

Raptus, Timothy thought. It had to be him.

The young man expected some kind of great speech. He thought that Raptus would address his people, the way the leader of the mages would have done. But the Wurm were not mages. Their customs were not the same. Raptus only waited patiently while the two warriors beat their wings and carried Timothy up toward the cluster of Draconae's leaders.

They brought him before Raptus. Two additional warriors flew up below him, each of them grabbing one of his legs so that four of the monsters held him, one by each of his limbs. They pulled his arms and legs out straight so that he was completely exposed, completely vulnerable. Timothy could barely breathe for the fear in him. His eyes burned with tears that demanded to be shed, but he denied them. He would not cry. They were the villains here, and he had done nothing wrong.

Quickly he surveyed the walls of the volcano, searching the cave openings and the ledges. He thought he could see Ivar far below near the mouth of a cave. It was not difficult to identify him, as the Asura was the only other creature in the Wurm city who did not have wings. Ivar was in chains.

From off to his left there came a roar of pain and misery. Timothy hung his head to the left, twisting around enough so that he could see Verlis. He was also in chains, hanging upside down from an outcropping in the wall, dangled above the boiling lava by his bonds. His wings had been pinned together with black spikes that pierced them.

Timothy felt as though he might vomit.

Then the four warriors who held him pinned in midair pulled on his arms and legs again, and pain wracked his body. He let out a shout and snapped his head around to glare at Raptus.

The Wurm general only watched him with the same passive expression he had shown all along. Another twin spurt of liquid flames danced up from his nostrils with a long exhalation. The black metal helmet Raptus wore had slits for his eyes, but Timothy could see only darkness within, as though there were no eyes there at all, and it made his legs weak.

He was going to die.

"No," he whispered.

Raptus snickered. "You spoke? Your last thought, then?"

His voice was low and rough, like stones grinding together. Timothy only stared at him. Raptus nodded and then he raised both hands. The Wurm had been cheering for his execution, but now they fell silent. Their leader, their general, lowered his left hand but kept the other raised. His talons shone in the light of this world's golden sun. Timothy tried to picture his father's face. Tried to comfort himself with the knowledge that he would soon see his father again. He only prayed that his spirit could travel between dimensions, that his ghost could join his father's, regardless of what world he was on when he lost his life.

Raptus swooped from the sky, darting downward.

Timothy blinked, following his path. The general flew at blinding speed around the circumference of the volcano. He dove toward the bottom of the city, then circled on his way back up. Raptus was not cheered by his fellow Wurm. All of the citizens of Draconae's city were silent, as though it were part of a ritual. And perhaps it was. They watched him circle, whirling up and up and up. He passed the place where the warriors held Timothy and continued upward as though blown by the updraft of the volcano. Finally, when he soared up above the rim, Raptus stopped, stretched out his wings, held out the talons of his right hand, and swooped down toward Timothy.

At first Timothy flinched, turning his eyes away, knowing those talons were going to pierce his chest and tear out his heart.

But then he realized he had to look. He would not turn away from his death.

Raptus sliced the sky, dropping toward him.

Timothy's anger boiled over.

"You have no right!" he screamed. "What have I done? Only a savage takes innocent lives!"

The general's wings spread, tipped up, and he stopped himself only inches from Timothy. The boy could feel the heat of his fiery breath, and it stank like a garbage pit. Now he could see the eyes beneath that black metal helmet, and he understood why he had not been able to before. They were even blacker than the metal. Blacker than the blackest heart. Dark with hatred.

"Innocent?" Raptus growled, his wings beating slowly to keep himself aloft.

He darted backward, stretched out his arms, and addressed the city around him, all the creatures who thrived in the volcano's throat. "Innocent?" he screamed.

The roar that shattered the silence of Draconae was deafening. Timothy gritted his teeth and refused to let himself be cowed by it. If he was going to die, it would not be in silence. It would not be in surrender.

"If I am not innocent," he called, "then before you execute me, at least tell me my crime."

At this, Raptus seemed almost to forget the city around him, to forget the Wurm that were his followers, his soldiers. He flew nearer to Timothy again. Hunched over in the sky, as though prepared to rip into the boy at any moment, smoke curling from his maw, the general glared furiously at him.

"Your crime is that you are a mage. You are a traitor, like all of them before you."

Timothy shook his head. "Not all. Alhazred and his lackeys twisted the truth and manipulated the mages. He used you, and when he couldn't use you anymore, he used Parliament. What they did was wrong. Horrible. But you can't blame an entire race for the actions of a few. The Parliament of Mages represents all the mages of the world, or most of them. But that doesn't mean the whole world knew what Alhazred was doing—how he planned to double-cross your people. The history of Terra isn't written that way. I don't think even the Parliament knew. Not most of them, anyway. You can't blame all mages for the actions of one evil man and his followers."

The Wurm tilted his head to one side, and for several moments he only stared at Timothy. And then Raptus began to laugh, a terrible sound that spilled liquid fire out of his jaws, drizzling it down into the long throat of the volcano, where it would merge with the molten lava far below.

"You are a liar. And even if you spoke the truth, it would not matter. The world was taken from us. We will take it back. And every mage shall bear the punishment for what we have suffered."

Timothy swallowed, his throat ragged and scorched from the heat. But he had one last gambit. "All right," he said. "If that is what you have to do. Even so, you cannot punish me for the crimes of mages."

"Why not?" Raptus scoffed. "Because you are a boy? Your age means nothing." He raised his talons and with a subtle change in the angle of his beating wings, moved closer.

"No," Timothy said. "Because I'm not a mage."

Raptus paused and stared at him.

"I have no magic at all. None. I can't cast spells. I can't touch magic and it can't touch me."

"You lie," Raptus snarled.

Timothy shook his head slowly, his arms and legs still held

taut by the warriors who carried him aloft. "Test me. Attack me with magic. Cast a spell on me."

Baring his yellowed fangs, Raptus gestured toward the female Wurm Timothy had noticed before, the sorceress whose green-black magic was pouring out of her as fluidly as the fire spilled from the others. She nodded to her commander and raised a single finger. A tendril of sparking, snaking energy arced through the air toward him and struck his chest.

Green-black light spread across his shirt for a moment and then was gone.

The sorceress Wurm's jagged brows knitted together, and now she brought both hands up. With her talons contorting, she seemed to sculpt the air into a sphere of crackling power. With a flick of her wrist she sent it surging toward him, growing. Timothy could feel the tug of its presence, as though it were creating its own well of gravity as it passed through the air.

The destructive sphere evaporated just before it reached him. Timothy heard a grunt of relief from both of the warriors who held his arms. They had been in mortal peril a moment ago, and he had saved them from severe injury, possibly even from death.

"You're welcome," he muttered.

Raptus held up a hand, and the sorceress lowered her head and glided away on her wings to a perch upon the wall. The spell had drained her, apparently, and she needed to rest.

Then the general stared at him, black eyes glaring from beneath his helmet.

"It isn't only that the magic cannot touch you. Your presence disrupts it."

"I am not a mage," Timothy insisted.

"Perhaps not. But you came here with Verlis, himself a traitor, and a filthy Asura. Mage or not, you have declared yourself an enemy of Draconae."

Timothy had no answer to that. He might have said he was an enemy only of the citizens of Draconae who wanted bloodshed and violence, and a friend to those who wanted peace. But that would not have kept him alive. Not for another moment. There was a time for valor and dignity and a time for using his head. Something was going on in Raptus's mind. The general might still consider him an enemy, but Timothy's words and his invulnerability to magic certainly had made Raptus hesitate.

At length the general pointed at the warriors who held Timothy. "Bring him. Follow me."

Timothy felt a surge of relief begin to rise in him, but it receded an instant later as Raptus flew down to look him in the eye once more.

"You live for now. I think I may be able to make use of you. And if I am mistaken, I will simply execute you tomorrow, instead of today. I was so looking forward to holding your little black heart in my hand." Raptus nodded to himself, smoke pluming from his nostrils. "Perhaps tomorrow I will have the pleasure."

CHAPTER THIRTEEN

I var held his breath as he watched Timothy being brought before Raptus for execution. If he had had more time he would have been able to help, but it was too late for that. There was not enough time, and Timothy was too far away. The Wurm held him high up in the air, almost to the rim of the volcano. His young friend would have to rely upon his own wiles and upon luck. Fortunately Timothy had a great deal of both, a fact proven when Raptus apparently abandoned plans to execute the boy. Ivar watched in fascination as the commander of this Wurm city led the way, flying up and over the rim, out of the volcano. Perhaps a dozen of his warriors followed, two of them carrying Timothy with them, his legs dangling beneath him.

Time, Ivar thought with a satisfied nod. The boy had just bought them some time. But he did not know how much, and so he could not waste another moment.

Since he had been taken captive by the Wurm, Ivar had been tortured and chained with heavy metal bonds. He had been forced to work, mining heatstone from a quarry that had been tunneled into the side of the volcano wall. Hours of this labor had passed, and he was tired and sore, but he barely noticed his own discomfort. His attention, throughout his brief time in slavery, had been spent observing. He had taken note of every aspect of the Wurm city that his eyes could see, including the comings and goings of their warrior class. Not all of the dragon-kin were warriors. There were families here. Teachers. Laborers. Artists. All of the Wurm had some innate magic, but those who had studied and honed their skills were the city's sorcerers. And then there were warriors. All of the Wurm were dangerous, but not all of them were used to combat. Most would have learned in their lives to rely upon the warrior class to do their fighting for them.

Ivar was pleased.

Now that Timothy had been removed from the situation, it also made his own course of action much clearer. With the boy in a cave under guard, and Verlis hanging from the outcropping far above, bound and motionless, the Asura had had difficulty devising a course of action that would allow them all to emerge alive.

But with Timothy gone, the course was clear.

Ivar had been marched out to a wide ledge deep in the volcano to watch the spectacle of his friend's execution. Now that Timothy's life had been spared, the trio of Wurm that had alighted upon the ledge grumbled to one another in disappointment and took flight, soaring on the scorching air that vented upward from the churning, molten lava below. That left only a single Wurm, the one who was in charge of supervising the mining operation—the very same Wurm who had already tortured Ivar dozens of times.

The heat from the volcano made it nearly impossible to breathe. Ivar ignored the discomfort, the pain and tightness in his chest, and turned back toward the tunnel where he had left his quarrying tools. The ledge was rough beneath his bare feet and had his skin not been far harder and thicker than a mage's, the heat would have burned him horribly. His senses were attuned to everything around him, the eddying of the blistering breeze that wafted up from the volcano, the location of the dozens of Wurm that darted across the air above him, and—more importantly than anything else—the grim lumbering presence of the Wurm behind him. The creature snickered derisively as it noticed that he was returning to his work.

"All the stories I've ever heard about the Asura talked of your tribe as fierce warriors, as proud and dangerous and clever. As always with legends, the reality seems a pale shade of the whispers."

Ivar paused and turned slowly to gaze at the ugly, monstrous visage of his captor. It amused him to think that the Asura were legends to this generation of Wurm. Though many of the older creatures would still remember the conflict with the Asura, it was so long ago that they had obviously allowed themselves to think the tribe's reputation had been exaggerated. Clearly they did not consider Ivar a threat. He was in the bowels of the Wurm city, surrounded by sheer rock walls, and he had no wings. He had shackles on his arms, but there was a long chain between his wrists so that he could still work. Where could he go? One warrior. The last of his kind.

He did not respond to his captor's antagonism.

"Get back to work," the Wurm snarled, and raised the whip. It came whistling down toward his face.

Ivar reached up and snatched the end of the whip out of the air. He leaped at the Wurm, ignoring the astonishment etched upon its features, and slipped the whip around its neck. With a snap of his wrists, Ivar wrapped his chains around the Wurm. In a single, swift move, he dislocated both of his thumbs and tugged his hands free of the shackles. Then he pulled the chain tighter, snapped the shackles together, and trapped the creature's wings against its back. It would not last, but it would take several seconds at least for the Wurm to free its wings from the chains.

Silently Ivar shoved the creature off the ledge. It tumbled end over end, struggling against the chains as it fell into the molten, churning lava below. Wurm were fire beasts. Their hides were thick and difficult to burn. They had furnaces in their bellies. But even that heat was nothing compared to the heart of the volcano. The Wurm would not resurface.

"No more work," Ivar muttered.

Free of his bonds, he ran with uncanny speed to the

tunnel entrance, but he did not go inside. Instead he stood for a moment against the volcano wall, and his skin changed pigment, the color matching the black glass sheen of the volcano's throat. Then he dug his fingers into the rock, pressed his body against it, and used his feet to search for the tiniest crack, the smallest bit of leverage.

Then he was climbing.

For long minutes he clambered up the inner wall of the volcano, completely unnoticed. The heat was terrible at first, searing his flesh, but it diminished as he climbed higher. He was more than halfway to the outcropping where Verlis dangled in chains out over the abyss, when an alarm was raised far below. Ivar paused and glanced down. Several Wurm, including two warriors, had alighted upon the ledge where the heatstone quarry tunnel was. His absence—and that of the guard he had killed—had been discovered.

It occurred to him that it would be far easier to escape undetected if he left Verlis where he was. But regardless of the fact that he was a Wurm, Verlis was his ally. To leave him behind, even if it meant sacrificing Ivar's own survival and the possibility of rescuing Timothy, would be dishonorable and undignified.

The Wurm began to hunt for Ivar. Warriors and guards and even some of the ordinary citizens of the city joined the search. They started from the heatstone quarry, thinking the Asura could not have gotten far. Ivar's ears were quite sensitive, and so he even overheard one warrior calling to another that he had probably fallen into the volcano.

Invisible against the wall, he continued to climb. Several times Wurm flew by so close that he could have spit on them as they passed. When this happened he grew still and waited until they were gone so that his motion did not give him away. He knew that the creatures had a powerful sense of smell, and that if they came close enough they would scent him. Thus far he had been saved by the fact that there was only updraft here, and none of them had come in directly above him. As he climbed, Ivar moved from side to side to avoid being immediately below any of the cave openings.

Swords were drawn. Shouts of rage and disgust were raised. Ivar ignored them and continued to climb.

Every muscle in his body hurt. The tips of his fingers were scraped raw, and he hoped they would not begin to bleed badly, for that would make climbing very slippery. His toes found purchase wherever they could. He stretched his legs far out to either side, contorting his whole body however it was necessary to continue upward. And soon enough he found himself just below the outcropping where Verlis was imprisoned.

His ally hung upside down, chained, wings pinned back and together. Verlis had his eyes closed, but Ivar sensed he was awake. The Asura warrior climbed onto the top of the outcropping that jutted from the volcano wall. Still blending the color of his flesh with that of the rock, he crawled slowly to the farthest tip of rock and then hung his head over the side.

"What, precisely, were you waiting for?" Verlis asked, his voice a low growl.

A slow smile crept across Ivar's features. "The moment when it seemed least likely one of us would die. You knew I would come?"

The Wurm opened his eyes. A small puff of smoke rose from his nostrils. He looked absurd, hanging upside down with his legs wrapped in chains. "I caught your scent while you were climbing. You do smell quite badly, you know."

Ivar raised an eyebrow. "After your experience in Abaddon and now here on Draconae, I would have thought you would be more interested in your freedom."

Verlis did not react. He knew Ivar would not leave him there, so the threat was hollow. The Wurm only grunted. "In addition to your personal stink, there is one other, small thing that concerns me."

The Asura reached down and ran his fingers along the chains. Before he released Verlis, he wanted to free the Wurm's wings. It was the simple matter of releasing a catch on the clamp of black spikes that had pinned his wings together. A device for the torture and imprisonment of their own kind, invented by Wurm. Ivar was horrified.

When he unlatched it and Verlis's wings were free, the Wurm sighed with relief, moving only a little in the coil of chains that held him aloft.

"What is it that disturbs you?" Ivar asked, his hands now moving again along the chains, searching for the place where they would be locked together. It took him only a moment, and then he began working his fingers over each link, searching for a weak one.

"I can also smell your blood."

Ivar froze. His brow creased in a frown.

"They whipped you, did they not? Your back will be striped with bloody wounds. Even if you managed to get all the way up here without them noticing the splashes of blood that would not blend, the way your skin does, into your surroundings, they must have smelled it."

For the first time since childhood, the Asura warrior felt like a fool. He was on his belly on the outcropping, his arms wrapped around it, fingers tugging on the chain, trying to break Verlis free. Now he raised his eyes and gazed down past his captive ally.

He counted seventeen Wurm in a rough semicircle just below him. There would be others above. They had swinging maces and swords, and in their midst were a pair of sorcerers whose magic shimmered around them.

Ivar knew they were going to die, and yet his only concern was for Timothy.

His fingers found the weak link, and he twisted it sideways. The chain snapped. Verlis shrugged out of it, the metal bonds falling away toward the volcanic maelstrom far below. He spun into the air, wings spreading, and caught an updraft. With a roar, he beat his wings and hovered there, facing his enemies. Ivar stood up on the outcropping and let his flesh return to its natural color. The time for battle had come. If he was to die by the side of his ally, Ivar would do so proudly, as the last of the Asura.

One of the Wurm warriors shouted a command and each of them opened their jaws and let loose a short blast of liquid fire, not an attack so much as an intimidation.

A chorus of roaring replied, but it was not from below. It was from above. Far above.

Ivar glanced up and saw Wurm darting through the air, streaking downward, soaring on the superheated drafts into the throat of the volcano. None of them wore armor, but they did carry weapons. For a moment he presumed these were only reinforcements. But then the new arrivals began to attack Raptus's warriors, swords and spears flashing in the golden glow of the sun above, and the red glow of the volcano below.

Verlis roared something in the ancient language of the Dragons of Old, and Ivar, whose people had known the Wurm as enemies for ages, understood. Upon their arrival, they had found Verlis's settlement destroyed, but only a few corpses. The others had not been captured or destroyed; they had escaped. This was Verlis's clan, his family.

With a grin, the Asura leaped off the outcropping, landing on the back of the nearest Wurm. It tried to knock him off, but he broke the monster's wrist and stole his ball-and-chain mace. Then Ivar began to swing the spiked ball over his head, letting loose the ululating battle cry of the Asura.

The volcano city existed in the midst of an oasis of lush vegetation that was supported by the warmth of the volcano itself. But a short flight from the base of the volcano, the vegetation was smaller, grayer, and then finally died out entirely, giving way to frozen tundra. Timothy saw all of this as the Wurm flew with him over that inhospitable landscape. In the distance he could see that the tundra became a mountainous region of ice and snow. *The barrens,* he heard the Wurm call it in hushed and reverent tones. They were creatures of fire. They would not venture very far into the barrens.

Though the land was composed of such different environments, it all bordered a roaring, frigid ocean. The waves churned and leaped far higher than anything he had seen, either on the Island of Patience or in the harbor of Arcanum. At the edge of the frozen tundra, a high cliff fell away in a steep drop down to the ocean.

As his Wurm guards carried him toward that place, Timothy stared, transfixed with horror, at the transparent, shimmering wall of energy that rose from the cliff's edge so far up into the sky that the top of it could not be seen. On the cliff there were two small buildings that looked as if they were made of heatstone. These were clearly meant as shelters for the Wurm who were posted out here. Working out here. From a distance, he could easily make out a team of eight or nine Wurm on the cliff. Several seemed only to be observing, but the others were all sorcerers. They were arranged on the bluff overlooking the crashing waves so that they could all face the shimmering magical barrier before them.

Not just a barrier. But *the* barrier. He was sure that was

what it was. The one that the mages put between their own world and Draconae, to keep the Wurm from ever returning. Raptus had his sorcerers stationed here, on the cliff, attempting to breach it, to get back through into the world of their birth. Timothy tried to imagine how long they had been at it, how many years they had spent attempting to get home to take their revenge, and the thought chilled him.

"Oh, no," he whispered to himself.

He knew where this was going.

Up ahead, he saw Raptus dip his wings and swoop down toward the cliff. The warriors that were his personal guard followed. Then the Wurm that were carrying Timothy followed, and he had to hold his breath as the ground rushed up toward them, the wind whipping at his face. His stomach lurched and he nearly vomited. And then they were on the ground.

The warriors yanked him upright. Raptus roared a command at the sorcerers and they backed away, staring at their general, and then at Timothy himself. The ocean crashed far below. The cold wind swept around Timothy. The wall of magic, the barrier the mages had built, rose as high as he could see.

Raptus strode toward him, slightly hunched. Timothy stared at the black helmet, at those black eyes, as the general bent to stare at him. Raptus clutched Timothy's face in one hand, talons digging into the boy's throat and cheeks, drawing blood.

"You are a fascinating creature. Unique, to my knowledge.

There are many ways you might be useful to me. If not, I could simply kill you."

Timothy swallowed hard, trying not to inhale the general's stinking breath. His eyes watered. His face and throat stung where the talons cut him.

Raptus released him and stepped back. He gestured toward the barrier. "Your touch disrupts the presence of magic, unravels spells. So be it. Touch the wall. Push through it. Open the door."

Open the door. . . .

Not on your life.

Timothy shook his head. "I've never tried to disrupt anything this powerful before. It . . . it probably won't work. It could kill me."

He was lying. But he would have said anything at all just then to avoid doing Raptus's bidding.

"Not so confident now?" the general sneered. A snort of fire came from his snout. Then he reached out and grabbed Timothy by the hair. He hauled the boy off his feet. "Do it!"

Raptus dropped him and Timothy collapsed to the ground. He took his time rising, first to his knees and then to his feet. He felt sick to his stomach thinking about the Wurm attacking Arcanum unannounced. There were Wurm who were adept sorcerers, but even the warriors—even the least creature among them—had some magic. And they were savage. Fierce. The Wurm might eventually be stopped, even destroyed, but first there would be a massacre.

For a long moment he stared at the transparent wall, and

at the ocean beyond. Then he turned and faced Raptus, standing as straight and tall as he could manage, still barely more than half the general's height.

Timothy shook his head slowly. "No."

Raptus snorted, his jaws opening and closing as though he were ravenously hungry. Those black eyes stared out from inside that helmet.

"If you refuse, we will force you."

"If you force me, I'll fight to my death. Then what good will I be to you?"

Raptus snarled and beat his wings. He darted back and forth in the air in such a fashion that it reminded Timothy of the way his father had sometimes paced. Several moments went by. The warriors alternately watched their general, their captive, and the shimmering barrier that kept them from sating their bloodthirsty vengeance.

When at last Raptus landed, Timothy knew what his reply was going to be. The general gestured toward him again.

"Push him through. Try not to hurt him. But if he dies fighting, that is preferable to never knowing whether or not his power would end our banishment. Take him."

Timothy Cade had been trained in armed and unarmed combat by the last of the Asura. The Wurm could not have known this. When the first of them reached for him, he fought back. He dodged, letting the Wurm's left arm slide beneath his right, and then he twisted, snapping bone. When a second lunged for him, Timothy slashed his fingers across the air and tore at his eyes, blinding the Wurm. Several of them raised their weapons, but they would not use them, not after Raptus's caution.

He punched another Wurm, then took the sword right from the creature's grasp.

They moved in around him and Timothy turned around and around, trying to keep them all in sight as they circled, closing in.

"Raptus!" one of the warriors barked. "Look!"

Dozens of Wurm were flying toward them from the volcano at blinding speed. Beyond them, many, many more were spilling out of the volcano's gullet in pursuit. In the front of the oncoming group, Timothy saw a Wurm carrying a person—Verlis and Ivar!

"The rebels!" Raptus roared in fury. He began barking orders, pointing into the sky as Verlis and Ivar led the others—Verlis's clan, Timothy assumed, miraculously alive—toward the cliff. Toward those shelters and the shimmering magical barrier. Toward Timothy himself.

They outnumbered Raptus and the few warriors he had with him by far. Even with the sorcerers, who were now being summoned from their shelters, Verlis and his clan had a superior force. But the rest of the Wurm city, Raptus's followers, were in pursuit, and Verlis and his clan had less than a minute's lead on them.

Timothy had only one course of action.

Sword in hand, he took advantage of the moment of distraction, of the chaos as Raptus's warriors prepared to repel an attack. He darted past the Wurm nearest to him and ran right at Raptus. The general was staring into the sky, ordering his warriors to take flight, to combat the rebels.

Timothy gripped the sword in both hands and ran him through. The general roared in pain, but Timothy did not attempt to stab him again, or to see what result his attack had wrought. He turned and ran with every bit of speed he could muster. Around him the Wurm were taking flight, most of them not even noticing that Raptus had been wounded, their attention fixed upon the attackers flying in from above and the commands that Raptus had issued only a moment earlier.

The boy ran below them as they took off, ducking under clawed feet and wings. As fast as his legs could pump, he sprinted back toward the volcano, toward Verlis and his rebellious clan. He did not even look back, focusing only on Verlis and Ivar.

Above him, the Wurm were clashing now. Weapons clanged. Battle cries split the sky. Spells crackled and sparked in the air, knocking Wurm down, causing them to crash into the ground or the magical barrier. Past them all he saw the citizens of the Wurm city giving chase. Verlis's clan could defeat Raptus, destroying him forever, just by over-whelming his forces here. But there was no time. Raptus's reinforcements would be there all too soon.

Verlis must know that, he thought. *Ivar must know.*

Timothy realized that they did not hope to win. They were not battling for victory, but for him.

And then Verlis dropped down out of the sky with a female Wurm beside him. Ivar shouted something Timothy could barely hear and did not understand, and then the female Wurm picked the boy up and they were flying, soaring away from the battlefield at a speed that stole his breath away. Timothy twisted around, trying to see what was happening. As they gained more distance, the air became colder, even frigid, and he shivered. Verlis and Ivar were right beside the Wurm that carried Timothy. She was strong—perhaps even stronger than Verlis.

Behind them came the rest of Verlis's clan. Raptus's warriors—those who were not already dead or dying—were giving chase. Those from the volcano had nearly arrived at the site of the melee, and now there were not a dozen, but hundreds of Wurm pursuing the group that gathered around Verlis in the air now. His clan. Thirty of them. Perhaps a handful more than that. Nothing in comparison to the others.

They were headed straight toward the barrens.

The air grew ever more frigid, a bizarre counterpoint to the scorching air inside the volcano. They had passed beyond the tundra into the barrens and were flying over mountain crags covered with ice and snow. He kept craning his neck to look behind, and at first it seemed that Raptus's warriors would catch up to them.

The cold felt like daggers in his skin. Every exposed bit of his flesh started to grow numb. The Wurm flew more slowly, their flesh getting gray. Some of them looked frightened.

The next time Timothy looked around, Raptus's warriors had turned back, given up the pursuit.

But Verlis and his clan, carrying Ivar and Timothy, kept on flying, up into the frozen mountains of the barrens of Draconae, where nothing awaited them but an icy death.

CHAPTER FOURTEEN

Timothy, Ivar, and the Wurm took refuge in the shadow of a steep cliff. They were in a valley of sorts, but the wind was blowing at such an angle that the mountain took the brunt of it. Still, with the ice and snow it was very cold. Ivar did not seem terribly bothered by it, despite the fact he wore very little, but even in his thick shirt, Timothy shivered and his teeth chattered, and he knew that this cold, endured for too long, could kill him. The Wurm, though, were even worse off than he was. Their skin had quickly become mottled and gray and their eyes had clouded over.

In spite of the obvious truth—that the cold was devastating to them—Verlis and his clan seemed in no hurry to depart. Light snow fell from the sky. The ice cracked and shifted beneath them. The wind howled off the edge of the cliff high above, but might shift direction at any moment. Yet the Wurm were too busy arguing to even notice.

"What are they waiting for? We can't just sit here. We'll all die!" Timothy said, glancing at Ivar.

The Asura warrior crouched in the snow with his back to the cliff face. He was not far from Timothy, but he seemed intent only upon the arguing Wurm. The boy would have liked to move closer, to share Ivar's natural warmth, but he could tell from his friend's stance that Ivar did not want to be disturbed. He was obviously on edge, alert, as though he expected an attack. That made no sense, of course. They had eluded Raptus and his followers. Their enemy now was the weather.

Ivar did not respond to his comment, except to raise a single eyebrow. Timothy did not understand. He focused his attention again on the Wurm who were scattered in a rough circle a short distance away. They were spread out across the plateau beneath the cliff, the ugliest most monstrous creatures Timothy had ever seen. And yet he was not going to make the same mistake Parliament had. Despite their appearances, these were rational, thinking creatures, no better or worse than a mage, or himself, for that matter.

Whatever I am.

The Wurm hopped around on the snow, their wings spreading and then wrapping around them again. They snapped their jaws closed in a series of clicks, and they made certain grunts and gestures and snorts of fire that he could only assume were some form of communication among their kind. Like Verlis, the clan all seemed to be able to speak the tongue of mages, but Timothy realized now that it was not their native language. Verlis was arguing furiously about something, and only occasionally would his gaze shift toward Timothy and Ivar.

But they were all weakening, slowed by the cold. From time to time one or more would stand back from the others and let loose a long blast of fire that would warm the place where they gathered. Timothy could barely feel the heat from where he stood, and he longed for it.

He wrapped his hands in the bottom of his shirt, and then he could take no more. Cautiously, not wishing to interfere or offend, he approached the Wurm nearest to him. Throughout the argument, the one among the clan who had not seemed to move at all was the female who had scooped Timothy off the battlefield, who had saved his life. During their escape, he had learned that her name was Cythra, and that she was Verlis's wife. Now, as he moved nearer to her, it occurred to him that she was not so much standing around as she was standing between himself and Ivar and the other Wurm. He furrowed his brow at this realization.

"Cythra," he said quietly, the howl of the wind high above drowning out any chance the others would have of hearing him. His teeth chattered and he hugged himself. The cold had started to work frozen fingers into his head, and it ached.

"You should stand back, Timothy Cade." Her eyes were kind, but also hard, and her expression was grim. Something was happening here. Whatever it was, it had Cythra and Verlis very worried.

"I think I've done enough standing back," the boy replied

with far more confidence than he felt. "Verlis is my friend. He risked a lot for me, and I've done the same for him. What is it, Cythra?"

The massive female Wurm turned to look down at him, her yellow eyes narrowing. She looked at him as though for the first time, and a low snarl came from her throat and twin jets of fire seethed above her nostrils. Still, he had the idea she was amused.

"You are quite like your father," Cythra said.

Timothy did not understand. He shook his head. "I'm nothing like my father. He was a great mage. A great man."

Cythra bent low and he could feel the heat emanating from her. It warmed his face. Her massive jaws were close enough that she could have bitten off his head. With one long talon she tapped his chest. "Greatness is in here. Magic, too, the kind that matters."

Then a low, rumbling sound came from her throat, and she glanced over at her husband and the rest of the clan for a moment, as though contemplating what she would say next. After a moment her gaze locked on Timothy's again.

"Your father taught Verlis to cast the spell that let him break through to the mages' world a long time ago. It was a . . . safety measure. Verlis has only performed the spell twice. Once to travel to your world, and the second time to come home, with you and the Asura by his side. He never dared use the spell otherwise, for fear that Raptus would discover it. One day the tyrant will succeed in his efforts to shatter the barrier between worlds, and then the blood of mages will run, and their flesh will burn, and there is no knowing what will come of it. But we would not hasten that day by letting Raptus know that this spell exists, or how it is done.

"And we had no real reason to use the spell. Though we were banished here, Draconae became our world. We were content with it. Even when Raptus and the others began to rise to power and the violence began, even when civil war erupted, we still hoped to remain here, to combat their terrible philosophy and make this a world of peace and prosperity. We never imagined wanting to return to the world of the mages, and even if we had, we know we are not welcome there. We know they think of us as monsters, as unclean things to be destroyed."

Timothy nodded. "Trust me. I know exactly how you feel."

"Now we have no choice," Cythra said, her gaze drifting back toward the others. "It has come to this. We must flee to the world of mages, or Raptus will slaughter us all. He has not pursued us into these frozen barrens because he expects us to die here."

Timothy followed her gaze and watched the gesturing and listened to the snorting and gnashing of jaws and guttural words that made up the argument among the clan.

"So, that's what the fight is about? Some of them don't want to go, and Verlis is trying to convince them they don't have a choice?"

Cythra turned to look at him. At first she seemed confused. Then, when she understood, she shook her head slowly. "Oh, no, Timothy Cade. None of us is so foolish to think we can remain here. They are arguing because, though your Asura friend has been Verlis's ally and helped saved his life, all Wurm are natural enemies to his tribe. Aside from Verlis and me, all of our clan want to kill him before we slip between worlds."

Timothy's throat went dry and his eyes widened. "But— Ivar has saved—"

"Yes, yes," Cythra interrupted, her wings twitching upward. "Agreed. Verlis is honorable, not to worry. He would sooner give his own life than see harm come to the Asura. It is only that it will take some time before the others are willing to realize exactly how sincere he is in his conviction. Then it will pass."

Timothy looked over at Ivar, whose eyes darted back and forth. He was watching the debating Wurm intently, and for the first time Timothy realized that with the Asura and the Wurm being ancient enemies, Ivar must understand their strange language. He knew exactly what they were saying. Which explained, as far as Timothy was concerned, why he looked as though he were preparing to fight off an attack.

"Well, they'd better come to that conclusion pretty fast," Timothy replied, worriedly watching the arguing Wurm and shivering with the cold. "Or we'll all freeze, and then Ivar will probably be the only one of us to make it out of here. The rest of us will be dead."

It was late afternoon, and though the spell-glass window at the apex of the Xerxis showed a clear, bright sky beyond, the light did not reach down into the shadows of the parliamentary chamber. Only the flickering ghostfire lamps shed light upon those proceedings, and that light seemed gloomy indeed.

Leander wished that it was night, and that through that small window he could see Terra's moons. He often wished upon Hito, the cold, icy moon that was the smallest and most distant. But wishes so rarely came true. He stood in the center of the parliamentary chamber and gazed around at the assembled grandmasters of all of the world's magical guilds. Many times he had addressed such a gathering, both as a professor from the University of Saint Germain and as a respected apprentice to the late, venerable mage Argus Cade. More recently he had addressed the Parliament as the Grandmaster of the Order of Alhazred.

Never in his life would he have imagined that one day he would stand before them as a prisoner, and address them in his own defense.

A short distance away Edgar ruffled his black feathers, perched on Sheridan's cold metal shoulder. Leander had been firm with Edgar, insisting that the often disrespectful bird remain silent during the proceedings. Sheridan did not have to be cautioned. Leander knew the mechanical man would say nothing for fear of making things worse for Timothy, and for Leander himself. It sickened the mage to see Sheridan held there by a pair of Constable Grimshaw's deputies, for he was not a prisoner so much as he was considered evidence in the case, an example of Timothy's unnatural tendencies. Or so Grimshaw and many others would have Parliament believe.

Grimshaw himself stood by the door, as though he were afraid Leander might try to escape. His deputies stood around the circular chamber at the base of each set of stairs that led up into the gallery where the members of Parliament were seated.

In the chair that was assigned to the Grandmaster of the Order of Alhazred, Cassandra Nicodemus sat, intent upon every word spoken in that chamber. The young woman was eerily beautiful and grimly serious, and though she was the granddaughter of one of the most despicable mages the world had ever seen, Leander had no reason to think of her as his enemy. He did not blame her for challenging him for the role of grandmaster. In truth, he wanted to believe her motives were pure, that she felt the title and position were her right and due, and not that she was anything at all like her grand-father.

Perhaps he was a fool. If so, he would confess to that crime when the time came.

Just as he had confessed to other crimes today.

The tribunal had begun hours earlier, conducted by Alethea Borgia, the Voice of Parliament. But though Alethea was the Voice, Grimshaw had done most of the talking. As his accuser, the constable had brought forth witnesses—his deputies, as well as several Alhazred mages, and Leander's aide, Carlyle—to corroborate Grimshaw's version of events at SkyHaven. Leander had denied nothing.

Now a silence descended upon the chamber, a silence that seemed to echo up to the peak of the Xerxis. The Voice strode around the floor, pausing in front of each section of the gallery to regard the gathered grandmasters gravely. The Cuzcotec Grandmaster actually chuckled when she passed. The elegant, sensual Drayaidi, Mistress Selkie, shook her head in sadness. Lord Foxheart of the Malleus Guild bared his sharp teeth and nodded in approval of the proceedings. Leander noticed that Siberus, the aged Grandmaster of the Order of the Winter Star, remained completely still. Siberus had not so much as whispered to any of the others seated around him throughout the proceedings.

At length the Voice returned to the center of the chamber and paused to gaze at Leander. There was an extraordinary elegance to her aging face, and her gray hair gave her a regal air that caused him to nod once, deferring to her. Whatever else happened, he had far too much respect for Alethea to challenge her authority. She drew a long breath and looked at him with kind and gentle eyes.

Then her expression hardened and she turned away.

"You have heard the accusations against Professor Maddox," the Voice declared. "You have heard the testimony of the witnesses. And you will note that Professor Maddox has yet to refute any of their statements. As is our custom, Professor Maddox will now be afforded an opportunity to speak in his own defense."

Alethea bowed her head to the assemblage and then stepped to one side. All eyes were on Leander. He could feel the weight of their anger, their curiosity, and their expectation. He cast a long look at Sheridan and Edgar and took a moment to wonder, for perhaps the thousandth time that day, what had become of Timothy.

Leander frowned. Even with all of the members of Parliament staring at him, he could feel the glare of Constable Grimshaw. He glanced at the man, saw the smug satisfaction and disdain upon his features, and Leander Maddox grew angry.

"Members of Parliament. Masters. Venerated friends," he began. "My fate is in your hands. I confess that I wish I had greater hope that you would treat it with fairness and great deliberation, but I do not."

The Parliament gasped at this insult to their integrity. Leander did not care. He scanned the chamber, defiantly meeting the eyes of as many of them as he could.

"Your treatment of Verlis the Wurm was rash. To condemn one creature because of the behavior of others of its kind is the worst kind of prejudice. It is blind and foolish and dark at heart. Never would I have thought such a collection of sages and scholars as sits within these walls would fall victim to such stupidity. And it only grew. The Parliament is filled with such hatred and fear that you have given absolute authority to a man filled with more sadistic cruelty and venom than I have seen in any mage since the fall of Nicodemus."

A wave of hushed whispering went through the chamber. Shocked expressions turned nervous, and many glanced over at Constable Grimshaw. Leander did not bother to look at the man.

"You forget yourself, Professor," Grimshaw said from the

doorway, his voice cutting through the room. "Those words will not go without response."

Leander shook his head. "I am the only mage in this room who has not forgotten himself. And you will shut your mouth now, Constable. Unless the Parliament wishes to completely abandon the entire history of its protocol and procedures because you frighten them too much, it is my time to speak."

Leander glanced over at the Voice. Alethea nodded for him to continue.

"Argus Cade was the greatest among you. His son has no magic, but in his heart and mind he is much like his father. He is kindhearted and strong willed, courageous and clever. But he is *different*. For that, you think him a freak or an abomination. A danger. An enemy.

"An enemy! A boy not yet old enough to grow a beard, and you hate and fear him. You disrespect the memory of Argus Cade, and you dishonor yourselves with your ignorant treatment of the boy. You hand over his fate to Grimshaw. You will not listen to reason when he speaks it, asking about the Wurm. The Wurm who was integral to the defeat of Grandmaster Nicodemus. Who had proven himself our ally."

Leander shifted his gaze so that he was looking directly at Cassandra. Her expression was unreadable.

"When it became clear to me that he intended to free Verlis, I knew immediately that I had no choice but to aid him in his escape from SkyHaven. Did I try to hide his absence for as long as possible? Certainly, I did. And before you determine my fate—a decision I trust will be made with the same fear and prejudice and hatred that has ruled this chamber of late—I want to tell you why.

"I gave my loyalty to Timothy Cade because he earned it. I gave him my help because though he was ignoring the commands of Parliament, his decisions were honorable.

"And yours have not been."

With a roar, Lord Romulus stood, his fur cloak flapping. "How dare you, Maddox? You'll face the executioner for such talk."

Leander only smiled and chuckled softly. "Honestly, my lord, I expect nothing less. What else would you do but kill or banish or imprison all that you do not understand, all that you fear? If that is to be my fate, then so be it. As I stand here today I find there is far less shame in being your prisoner than there would be in being your colleague."

Leander clapped his hands twice, the symbolic end to his defense—though he had hardly defended himself—and took one step back. He was meant to bow his head, as custom demanded, but he did not bother. Alethea stared at him for a long moment, taken by surprise at this abrupt end to his speech. At length she looked to Grimshaw.

"Constable, you have the final word."

With a sneer Grimshaw strode to the center of the chamber. His cloak flowed like shadows behind him. The ghostfire light shimmered on his face. He came face-to-face with Leander, then glanced at the Voice before turning around and gesturing to the assembled guild masters with a flourish of both hands.

"You have heard him damn himself with his own words. There is little more I could add, save that the Wurm, Verlis, and the boy, Timothy Cade, are not to be pitied. They are dangerous, and their ingenuity in escaping Abaddon has proved that the honorable members of Parliament were correct in distrusting them. There was suspicion that they were plotting against Parliament, and there can be no doubt that they have revealed themselves as the adversaries of honor and decency and the rightful rule of the Parliament of Mages. As your servant, I have done my duty to the best of my ability. For myself, I can only say that I hope you will take Lord Romulus's suggestion, and execute him."

Grimshaw paused. Slowly now, he stared up into the gallery, his gaze sweeping the entire Parliament. There was menace and dark promise in his eyes.

"Professor Maddox is highly regarded as a lecturer at university. He is well spoken and passionate. Yet the truth here is as clear as the law. And the law is irrefutable. Why, even to suggest otherwise would be no less treason than the actions of Professor Maddox."

Leander gaped at Grimshaw. The man had just threatened the members of Parliament with imprisonment should they disagree with him. It was outrageous, and yet from the continued hush in the room, he could tell that the guild masters took the implications of Grimshaw's warning quite seriously indeed.

Only Alethea Borgia replied. She crossed her arms and studied Grimshaw closely. "Constable, are you presuming to tell this Parliament how to conduct its business?"

Grimshaw bowed deeply. "Not at all, Madame Voice. I am confident that the members of Parliament are more than familiar with the law."

For a long moment, not even the Voice spoke. Leander knew that he could not change his fate. He glanced over at Sheridan and nodded to the mechanical man, and to Edgar, proud of the bird for having remained quiet. He suspected the Parliament would let the bird live, but Sheridan would surely be dismantled. Destroyed. For that, Leander was truly sorry. But he was certain they would not have argued with him if he had been able to tell them earlier what he planned to say to the Parliament. At the same time he felt Edgar's and Sheridan's approval, he sensed the disdain and the fear from the mages gathered in the room.

"All right," Alethea said at last. "All right. The time for words has passed. Now is the time for judgment. Is Professor Leander Maddox guilty or innocent?"

Leander felt his throat go dry. His heart pounded in his chest. He did not understand why, for though some foolish hope still flickered in the back of his mind, he knew what the outcome would be. He glanced around the room. In their seats, each of the members of Parliament held out a hand, and from each palm there sprang a crackling ball of flame. Red for guilty. Blue for innocent. As commanded by the Voice, none of them spoke, but the flame of judgment was statement enough.

There was not a single blue flame.

"And what of his sentence? Is Professor Maddox to be executed?"

Every hand closed, snuffing out the red flames. Leander's gaze darted about the room, trying to see who would be the first to judge him. After several moments a single red flame ignited in the open palm of Mistress Belladonna of the Order of Strychnos. Several other reds quickly followed.

And then a blue.

A red.

Three more blues in quick succession.

A tiny spark of hope sprang into Leander's heart. Two thirds of the Parliament had to vote for his execution in order for the sentence to be carried out. The alternative—imprisonment in Abaddon—was probably not much better than being executed, but he would certainly choose life over death, regardless of the circumstances.

One by one Parliament voted. Leander did his best to calculate the votes quickly in his mind. Many of them wanted him executed. Too many. In the end it came down to a single vote. One mage. A red flame would mean his death, a blue flame would give him his life. Leander stared into the gallery at the one mage whose palm was still closed.

Cassandra Nicodemus.

She clutched her fist tightly and grimaced as she stared at him, hesitating.

The building shook with a sudden impact. A rush of air swept through the chamber, and Leander looked up. Roaring fire, Wurm burst through the spell-glass windows in the spire of the Xerxis. Their own magic had shattered the spell-glass. There were only a few of them at first, but dark wings blocked out the daylight, and he could see there were many more behind them.

Parliament erupted in chaos. Mages shouted in anger and fear and began to scatter from their seats in the gallery. Ghostfire lamps were broken, the souls that provided illumination dissipating, drifting into the afterlife.

Wurm opened their jaws and seared the air above the Parliament with liquid fire. Mages threw up their hands and began summoning spells. Magical energy arced through the chamber. A female Wurm was struck, and her wings furled and withered as though they had been crippled by age. She fell.

"Stay together!" Lord Romulus shouted. "Stand your ground!"

"Yes!" Constable Grimshaw said. "Fight them! This is the boy's doing! The traitor!"

But Grimshaw did not fight the Wurm. He did not raise his arms to cast a single spell in their direction. Instead he rushed at Leander and, with a flick of his wrist, produced a long, ridged dagger that glittered with dark purple light.

"Traitor!" he shouted, and he raised the blade.

If Cassandra Nicodemus had opened her hand to reveal a red flame, Leander might have accepted that dagger as his fate and his due. But he had yet to see what her judgment would be, and so he stepped back to defend himself. Even with the Wurm descending, with mages shouting and fighting, and some fleeing for the door, he mustered all the magic in him and gritted his teeth as golden light spilled from his fingers, streaking the air. Grimshaw raised the dagger in both hands. Leander hoped that his magic was more powerful than the constable's.

Alethea Borgia, the Voice of Parliament, shouted for Grimshaw to halt and ran toward them, summoning a spell of her own. But she was too late.

Leander never let loose his magic.

With a snarl Verlis darted down from the heights of the chamber, grabbed Grimshaw with a single talon, and then bit his arm off all the way to the elbow. Verlis dropped him then, and Grimshaw hit the floor with a scream of pain. The Wurm spit out his forearm, and it hit the ground not far from the constable, cursed dagger still clutched in dead fingers.

Leander spun, the magic still spilling from his hands. Alethea was right behind him, and when he faced her, she shook her head firmly.

"Do nothing, Professor. Nothing. We shall see what comes."

And she was right. For even as Leander turned around in a circle to see that the Wurm had alighted in force upon the ground, three dozen strong, and were in a standoff with the gathered mages—a moment that could erupt into all-out war in an eyeblink should any Wurm or mage make a wrong move—he heard the cry of the rook.

"Caw, caw! Tim! It's about time, kid! You had us worried!" Edgar called.

Leander looked up to see a pair of Wurm gliding down to the main floor of the parliamentary chamber, one carrying Ivar of the Asura, and the other carrying Timothy Cade himself.

"Grandmasters, listen to me!" the boy shouted, his voice echoing through the chamber. "The Wurm are not here to fight, but if they are attacked they *will* defend themselves. Don't let your hatred make you do something stupid."

"Timothy, thank goodness!" Sheridan said, and a blast of steam burst from the valve on the side of the mechanical man's head. It whistled such a high note that it sounded almost like music to Leander.

Alethea crouched beside Constable Grimshaw, using her magic to staunch the flow of blood. She was not a Healer, had not studied those skills, and though she could not restore his arm, she would be able to keep him from dying from his wound. It was a disturbing sight, and yet Leander paid little attention to it.

Ivar dropped from several feet up and landed in a crouch. He ran to Leander's side and then turned, as though to stop anyone who might dare try to attack him now. Timothy was set down lightly, and the boy rushed to Leander and threw his arms around the mage's middle.

"I was so worried about you!" Timothy said.

"*You* were worried about *me*?" Leander shook his head in amazement. "It's wonderful to see you. And your timing is impeccable."

One of the members of Parliament pushed past the others,

climbed over a row of seats, and clambered down the stairs. The Wurm in the center of the chamber blocked his view at first, so Leander could not see who it was. But he knew that voice.

"This is an outrage!" Lord Romulus bellowed. "Proof of Grimshaw's every word!"

Romulus tried to push through the Wurm and one of them spit a thin stream of flame at him. It set his fur cloak alight. Lord Romulus tore it off as black smoke rose from the cloak; he threw it aside and raised his hands, black light dancing on his fingers.

Leander stiffened. Surprise had caused the grandmasters to hesitate, and then Timothy's words had given them pause just seconds before an all-out battle would have erupted in the chamber. The Wurm were hated—the enemy, as far as most of them were concerned. But as long as the fire-breathers did not attack Parliament, the mages might hold back, knowing the slaughter that would otherwise ensue. Or if Romulus made a fight of it, the stalemate would be over. It would be a massacre, leaving very few alive inside that chamber.

Timothy's smile disappeared. He shook his head and walked up behind the Wurm. They moved out of his way as though he commanded them, and Leander could not help but be impressed that they trusted him so completely. When they had moved aside, that left Timothy face-to-face with Lord Romulus.

"Is there a problem?" the boy asked.

The mere question made Romulus shake with fury. "Your insolence will be the death of you, boy."

"Maybe," Timothy said. "But not today."

He reached out swiftly and tapped Romulus on the chest. The black fire disappeared from his fingers, and it seemed to Leander that Lord Romulus shrank a little bit. The warrior mage's eyes bulged and his mouth dropped open.

"My magic. What have you done?"

Timothy shrugged. "You'll get it back in a minute or two. If you behave."

A ripple of fear went through the room. All along they had been inventing reasons to be afraid of Timothy Cade. Now, Leander saw, he had finally given them one. The boy turned and addressed the room.

"Grimshaw was attacked because he was trying to kill Leander. I told you before that these Wurm are not here to hurt you," he said. "They are here for your help."

This time it was Cassandra Nicodemus who spoke. "Help? Why would we help them? Wasn't one Wurm bad enough? Now you have brought us dozens of them."

Her fist, Leander saw, was still tightly closed. Her voice was firm, but filled with a nobility that could not be denied. Her eyes sparkled, and there was no mistaking the effect her beauty had on Timothy. Though, if Leander was not mistaken, there was something else in the look that the two exchanged, as though they shared some secret.

Timothy studied her, and then he regarded the entire assemblage once more.

"Many of you are not old enough, or have not been members of Parliament long enough, to know the true history of the conflict between the Wurm and the mages. But some of you are. Some of you were probably in this very chamber when it was decided that the Wurm would be driven from their homes, many of them murdered.

"But you all know that piece of history. And because you know a piece, you think you know it *all*. But you don't. Or, at least, most of you don't."

"Go on, then, boy," Lord Romulus scoffed. "Tell us this secret history."

Timothy nodded. "Secret history. Yes, that's exactly what it is. And, yes, I will." He scanned the faces in the room and saw that he had their complete attention. Timothy wondered if some of them had always suspected there was more to be told, if they had sensed it.

"To those of you who were in Parliament in the days before the Asura were slaughtered and the Wurm driven out—in the days when Alhazred was in power—I ask this. Did you ever hear of mages being attacked by Wurm or by Asura before Alhazred began to warn you about their savagery? About the threat they posed to your society?"

"There were villages burned to the ground! Mages and their children slaughtered!" snarled the Cuzcotec Grandmaster.

"Yes," Timothy agreed. "But that was afterward, wasn't it?" He glanced around again. "Wasn't it? The Wurm and the Asura were bent on destroying each other's tribes, and they paid little attention to mages. When they made new settlements in areas that mages claimed as their own, they did so without violence."

"That's not true. They were barbaric—"

"No," Timothy interrupted. "No, they weren't. That was only what Alhazred wanted Parliament to believe. He manipulated it all. Filled this hall with panic, with stories of creatures he painted as monsters. He *lied*."

There were angry shouts and low mutterings, and some of the mages moved as if to attack. The Wurm hissed and beat their wings to remind them of the bloody consequences of an all-out battle in the Xerxis.

"Why?" Alethea Borgia asked.

"Don't listen! He lies!" cried Lord Foxheart.

"Why would he do such a thing? Alhazred was one of the greatest mages who ever lived," Alethea went on.

"I know." Timothy sighed, but he stood up straighter. "But it wasn't enough for him to be one of the greatest. He wanted to be *the* greatest. Alhazred saw the Parliament coming together, and he wanted to control it. Wanted to control all of it. His successor, Nicodemus, was much the same, wasn't he? Trying to gather the power to take over. Well, Alhazred was sneakier about it. The Asura and the Wurm he gave to the guilds as a common enemy. Fear of these strange races helped to solidify the alliance that the Parliament represented. It united the guilds. And Alhazred presented himself as the only one with a plan to deal with this seeming threat."

The Cuzcotec Grandmaster stepped forward and spread his hands wide, appealing to the other grandmasters. "This is absurd. Parliament would never have ceded power to one mage. Even if Alhazred had such ambition, it would never have worked."

"That's true," Timothy agreed. "It didn't work, thanks to my father. Argus Cade was the voice of reason. He was the conscience of this chamber. But when Alhazred saw that his plan wasn't going to work, he came up with another plan. He nurtured the hatred of the Asura, and the fear of them, and plotted the series of attacks that wiped out the entire species. All except for one, Ivar, whom my father saved."

Timothy paused. He glanced at Leander, then around the room, and finally looked at Alethea again. "Alhazred went to the ambassadors of the Wurm then, including Tarqilae, and told them that he had destroyed the Asura in a gesture of good faith, and he proposed an alliance."

The effect of his words was immediate. Gasps filled the room, and the mages began to glance around at one another, some in suspicion, some in defiance, and others in disbelief.

"Alhazred presented himself as sympathetic to the Wurm. He wanted to help the Wurm attack Arcanum, to destroy the Xerxis and as many members of Parliament as possible. He would lead a counterattack on the Wurm, but it would all be for show. All of the guilds would have rallied behind him then, given him whatever power he wanted as long as he could protect them from the Wurm. And in exchange, Alhazred would leave the Wurm in peace in their jungles and mountains.

"I've been called an abomination. Ivar is considered a savage. The Wurm are called monsters. I can't think of better words to describe Alhazred. It is terrible enough that Parliament was so easily manipulated, that such wise mages were so eager to wage war on a race of beings just because they looked different. Just because they weren't like you. And before any of you who weren't around in those days try to claim innocence, I'll remind you that it's exactly the same thing that you all did to me, not very long ago."

The uproar in the chamber was deafening, all denying the things Timothy had said about them, and about Alhazred.

Lord Romulus took a step toward him. Leander tensed, because while most mages would be helpless without their magic, Romulus led one of the few guilds that did not rely entirely on their magical power. Timothy had been trained by Ivar, but Romulus could probably still kill the boy with his bare hands.

"You are a liar! A criminal! A traitor!"

"If so, then I hope my cell in Abaddon is big enough to fit all of us, because I'm no worse a criminal or a traitor than any of you."

"Filth!" Romulus shouted, and before Timothy could react, he struck the boy across the face.

Timothy could have fought him then. Instead he stood, all eyes upon him, and faced Lord Romulus. Wurm had started to move on the warrior mage, but Timothy gestured for them to stay back. He stared boldly up at Lord Romulus, but the mage was taken aback by his lack of reaction and did not strike him again.

"I'm not lying."

Alethea stepped toward him. Constable Grimshaw lay unconscious on the floor behind her, but he still breathed. He still lived. There was a terrible dread in Alethea's eyes. "How have you come by this knowledge? If these are secrets, where did you learn them?"

Timothy smiled. "From a Wurm named Hannuk, who was one of the ambassadors who dealt with Alhazred directly."

"From a Wurm?" Romulus roared. "From a Wurm, and we're to believe such lies? You are all that I said, boy, but you are also a fool!"

"I can prove they aren't lies," he said, and the room fell silent again, though he had not shouted. The grandmasters watched him expectantly. He turned to Alethea. "When I was studying the customs of Parliament, I read that the Voice has access to spells that can compel the truth."

The Voice nodded. "Within the Xerxis, yes. But magic won't work on you, Timothy. And even if it did, this is hearsay from a Wurm!"

"I don't mean for you to cast the spell on me," he replied. Then his eyes scanned the mages who were gathered on one side of the room. He saw a familiar cloak, night black and sparkling with the glitter of stars. "You see, Alhazred had followers. Conspirators who worked with him. If you want to find out if what I say is true, then the Voice should simply ask someone who was close to Alhazred at that time. Ask Lord Siberus of the Order of the Winter Star."

Silence reigned for several heartbeats. The rest of the mages retreated from Lord Siberus as though he had been stricken with the plague and might infect them. Even those who were Timothy's most vocal critics gazed at Siberus with suspicion.

The ancient mage only gazed at them, eyes glowing yellow in the shadows of the hood that hid his face. "Alethea," he said, his voice as icy as the winter star that was the symbol of his order, "you cannot possibly believe this. Alhazred was one of the founders of this Parliament. And this boy . . . he is less than nothing."

The Wurm started to fume, smoke and fire drifting from their nostrils. They beat their wings, and some of them moved closer to the mages. Verlis and Cythra forced them back with commands issued in grunts and clicks.

Alethea Borgia raised her hands. When she began to speak, the room thrummed with her words, the air vibrated, and it sounded as though every mage in the Xerxis were speaking through her.

"I am the Voice of the Parliament of Mages. Grandmasters, open your hearts to me so that we may see into the heart of another."

Then she looked at Lord Siberus, and in that same voice that was many voices, she asked him: "Grandmaster Siberus, does the boy speak true?"

Siberus began to shake. His head whipped back and forth, as though he were attempting to defy the Voice. Then he fell to his knees, head bowed in defeat.

"Yes," he hissed. "The boy speaks true."

The outcry was deafening. It was a full minute before Timothy could draw their attention again.

"Listen to me!" he shouted. And at last they did. "You were wrong about the Wurm," Timothy told them, speaking softly.

"Wrong about Verlis. Wrong about me." He pointed to his friends. "You're wrong about Sheridan and Ivar, and certainly wrong about Edgar and about Leander. There's no mage more loyal to the Parliament, and more a credit to his guild, than Leander Maddox.

"But none of that matters anymore. You see, the Wurm were banished to a world they named Draconae. They have thrived there. Built armies. And in all the time they have been there, they've been feeding on their hatred of the people who betrayed them. Mages." The boy pointed one finger and waved it around the room. "You. For what you did—and they blame you, no matter how Alhazred manipulated you—they want to kill you all. You. Your families. Your guilds. They want to kill every mage in the world. They're led by a Wurm called Raptus."

This news was met with more gasps of horror and mutterings of disbelief.

Now Timothy nodded toward the Wurm who gathered in that very room. "Verlis and his clan were the only ones to oppose Raptus. They wanted peace. For that, Raptus tormented them. Attacked them. Killed and tortured many of them, including Verlis's parents. I brought them all back here, to ask the Parliament of Mages to put aside the past, and to give them sanctuary."

At last, despite their fear, the mages in the room reacted. There were boos and hisses, shouted curses, and even laughter. But after Timothy's revelations and Siberus's confession, not all of the grandmasters reacted this way. Most of them only listened.

"Even if all you say is true, you've said yourself they want to kill us. Why should we trust them? Why help them?" Cassandra Nicodemus asked, moving closer to Timothy, studying his face. For a moment it was as though the two of them were alone there at the center of the room.

Timothy looked at her gravely.

"You have to," he said. "Cassandra, you have to. Raptus is not some stupid beast. He's vicious, and very smart. And he has sorcerers who have been working for ages to tear down the dimensional barrier that keeps them on Draconae. I got a close look at what they're doing. I don't think it's going to be long before they figure out how to get through."

Timothy nodded toward Verlis again. "If the Wurm of Draconae do get through, with Raptus leading them, then my friends here are the only hope you've got."

Alethea came to the center of the chamber. Constable Grimshaw lay on the floor behind her, only beginning to stir to wakefulness again. But Alethea seemed to have forgotten the constable. Her focus was on Verlis.

"You, Verlis. Wurm. You would do this? You and your clan would pledge to aid us against others of your kind in exchange for safe haven here?"

The Wurm snorted smoke and fire. Their wings flapped slowly as they all gazed about at one another. Verlis snapped his jaws shut with a clack. One by one, all of the others did the same. When they were through, Verlis turned to look at Alethea.

"We swear it. On the hearts of the Dragons of Old, we

swear it. But will you swear? On the souls of the Wizards of Old, Voice of Parliament, will you swear it?"

Leander held his breath as Alethea looked first at him, then at Timothy, and then around the chamber at the guild masters who huddled there, unsure what was going to happen next. They were afraid and ashamed and angry, all at the same time.

Cassandra was still face-to-face with Timothy. She studied him for a long moment. Then Cassandra, this girl who held Leander's life in the palm of her hand, opened her fist.

Blue fire danced on her palm.

Leander's life was spared.

Alethea nodded at her, and then the Voice addressed Verlis again.

"We shall see," the Voice declared. "A vote will be taken, and we shall see."

"What?" a shrill voice shrieked. "How can you? How dare you? This is war! These monsters have attacked the Xerxis! They are vermin! They must be exterminated. Do something!" Grimshaw shouted to Lord Romulus as he tried to struggle to his feet, clutching the white stump where his arm had once been. "All of you! You must do something!"

Timothy raised an eyebrow and glanced at Leander. He looked at Alethea for a moment. There was a confidence in his gaze that Leander had never seen there before, and it reminded him powerfully of the boy's father. Alethea had cared deeply for Argus Cade, and Leander had no doubt that she saw it too.

The un-magician strode over to Grimshaw and reached out toward him. The constable flinched at Timothy's gesture.

Bright silver energy began to crackle in Grimshaw's one remaining hand and to spark in his eyes.

"Don't you dare!" he commanded.

Timothy shrugged. "I only wanted to give you a word of advice. You might want to keep quiet now. You've had your say. And if you don't want to hold your tongue, well"—he glanced over at Verlis—"I'd guess the Wurm are probably still very, very hungry."

EPILOGUE

T he Cade estate was filled with the sounds of the
Wurm.

Timothy and Leander stood in the foyer of the
great old home and listened: the pounding beat of leathery
wings; the heavy tread of clawed feet on the floors above; the
roars, clicks, and clacks of their ancient language. The Wurm
had been introduced to their temporary residence two days
prior and were still acclimating themselves to their new surroundings. They had been a great deal of help in repairing the
damage Verlis had done while escaping from Grimshaw with
Timothy and Ivar, not to mention cleaning up the mess
Grimshaw's deputies had left behind. There were a great many
of them, but it was an enormous house, with rooms and entire
wings Timothy had yet to even begin to explore.

"It's quite noisy today," Leander said, flinching as one of
the new residents glided down from the second floor, a

shrieking roar exploding from its cavernous mouth while two smaller Wurm doggedly pursued it.

The larger beast flew twice around the chandelier hanging above the foyer, then dropped down to skate mere inches above the floor before rocketing skyward, heading back from whence he came. The smaller Wurm did their best to keep up, roaring their excitement as they continued the chase.

"I didn't notice," Timothy said, and he smiled as the two walked deeper into the house. "How are things at Parliament?" he asked the mage, frowning deeply.

The mage shrugged. "They are as they've always been, Timothy. Afraid. Afraid of you, the Wurm, even me. Afraid that the fragile world they've built for themselves will come crashing down around them. There are changes in the wind, and even the most stubborn of them can see that."

Begrudgingly Parliament had decided to allow Verlis and his clan to stay on Terra, not that they really had much of a choice. Just the thought of an invasion led by the fearsome Raptus was enough to cause even the most stubborn of grandmasters to reconsider their position on the Wurm. If an attack was indeed inevitable, and instinct told Timothy that it was, Parliament needed to be prepared. The clan's offer of support was but the first step in a long and arduous journey for both the mages and the Wurm. Mages had betrayed their species horribly in the past. A trust had to be built if the two were ever to exist together. Now the threat of war provided the proper incentive.

The boy and his mentor walked down the hallway toward

Argus Cade's study. "I think you'll be pleased at how far Verlis's kin have come in just a short while," Timothy said.

The sound of Sheridan's metallic voice could be heard drifting out from the room. They stopped in the doorway to see the mechanical man standing at the front of the study, Wurm of all sizes sitting on the floor, listening to his every word with rapt attention.

"Yes, I would love a cup of brew," Sheridan said, lifting a delicate cup from a saucer and pretending to drink. He then bowed his metal head toward his audience, urging them on.

"Yes, I would love a cup of brew," they repeated, some of the Wurm pretending to drink from an imaginary cup.

Sheridan's head swiveled away from his students as he noticed Timothy and Leander standing in the doorway.

"If you will pardon me," he said to the gathered Wurm, setting his cup and saucer down and clomping across the room, short bursts of steam escaping from the valve at the side of his head.

"If you will pardon me," the dragons repeated in unison.

"Good morning to you, sirs." Sheridan bowed. "My pupils are making great progress today."

Leander chuckled. "You are doing a remarkable job, Sheridan," he said, patting the mechanical man's shoulder. "They'll be speaking Terran better than Verlis in no time. Carry on." He motioned for the mechanical man to return to his duties.

"Very good," said Sheridan, and he bowed again, waddling back to his class.

"It appears they are adjusting well," Leander said as he and Timothy left the study. "Parliament will be pleased with the positive progress."

Timothy was glad. Anything to get on Parliament's good side would be a step in the right direction. By disobeying their laws—freeing Verlis from Abaddon and traveling to Draconae—Timothy had greatly strained his already fragile relationship with the mages who comprised Parliament, but he hoped that the damage was not irreparable.

"Has anything been decided . . . about your penance?" Timothy asked Leander, still bearing the guilt of what his actions had done to the Grandmaster's standing within the Parliament of Mages.

Though Leander had been found guilty of his crimes, he had yet to be sentenced. Apparently there was great debate about how serious his punishment should be.

"Nothing official yet," he said, resignation and sadness in his tone. "Most of my duties as Grandmaster have been given over to Cassandra, and my presence at parliamentary gatherings will no longer be necessary, unless requested. What more can they do?" he asked, hands clasped behind his back as they walked. "Although some feel that being given the responsibility of monitoring the activities of our Wurm friends here is penance enough." The large man chuckled.

"I'm sure it's only a matter of time before they decide my fate," he continued, "but right now, they are distracted, the winds of change and all." The mage waved his hand in the air.

Timothy felt horrible, and had ever since his return with

the Wurm. "I've been nothing but trouble since you found me," he said, hanging his head sadly. Maybe this was what his father had feared all along, the reason he had hidden the boy away. "I guess you wish you'd never stepped through that door to Patience."

"I'll hear none of that talk," Leander responded, slipping an arm about Tim's shoulder and giving him a reassuring squeeze. "What has happened, has happened. There is nothing that any of us can do to change it."

"But since I've been around, everything's been thrown into turmoil. Maybe it would have been better if I had just stayed where you found me."

Leander stopped in the doorway to the solarium and turned to the boy, placing a large hand beneath his lowered chin, lifting his face so their eyes could meet. "If you had not come, would we ever have learned of Nicodemus's evil? Or of the potential for a Wurm attack? No, I think it is good that you have come to live with us, and besides, think how boring my life would be otherwise. With your father gone, there would have been no one to get me into trouble."

They both laughed as they stepped into the solarium. The room was filled with boxes, each packed to the brim with heatstone from Patience, brought to feed the dragon residents. Edgar was flapping about the room, having been placed in charge of coordinating the collection of the stones.

"That's it, boys," the rook croaked, directing five Wurm, each of them carrying a large, heavy crate of heatstone with ease. "Set 'em down wherever you see an open space."

The bird fluttered to land upon one of the rock stacks and craned his head as he noticed Timothy and Leander. "This should keep their bellies full for a few more weeks," he squawked, "or at least until Parliament figures out what to do with 'em."

Although the Cade estate was fine for now, it was far too small for the Wurm to live comfortably. Parliament, however, had yet to decide upon a more permanent location for Verlis's clan.

"There has been talk of a volcanic island off the Trindian coast," Leander said.

"Yeah, well, I suppose Parliament's got bigger things to worry about," Edgar said, and the room became eerily silent, all of their thoughts likely dwelling on the same thing.

The threat of Raptus.

"Do you really think he'll be able to get through the barrier?" the familiar asked.

Leander looked at Timothy, and the strange sense of intuition returned, warning of a danger yet to come.

"If there's a way, I think he'll find it," the boy replied, remembering the cold hatred in the Wurm general's dark eyes. "We have to be ready."

Timothy turned, walking toward the spell-glass windows that separated the solarium from the back of the estate. The spell-glass blinked from existence as he neared it, allowing him to pass.

Leander followed him outside, onto a broad stone patio with a view of distant towns and of the steep, rough face of

August Hill. In the sky the Wurm honed their aerial combat skills, flames shooting from their mouths. On the broad expanse of the patio, Ivar trained others of the draconian clan in the deadly fighting techniques of the Asura. Even so, the wind was cool and gentle, and despite the preparations for war, it was almost peaceful.

Almost.

Verlis stood side by side with the Asura, a sight that most of the older Wurm would never have thought possible, while Ivar demonstrated that skill and swiftness could overcome size and strength, and even magic.

"I pray to the bright ones that Raptus never succeeds in breaking free and all this is for naught," Leander said grimly as he watched the Wurm and the last of the Asura prepare for future combat.

"So do I," Timothy agreed, watching the Wurm in flight above them. "But if prayers fail us, and Raptus does break through, we'll be ready for him."

"I hope you're right," Leander said, turning away to return to the great old house.

Timothy stayed on the patio, thinking about what the future held—for him and his friends, for the Parliament of Mages, for all the world of Terra—and he was afraid.

Very afraid indeed.

It was long after dark in the city of Arcanum and the shadows were deep.

Councillor Pepoy squinted through the crack of the slightly

open door, the expression on his pinched features showing annoyance, and perhaps the slightest hint of fear, that he had been pulled from his bed at this late hour.

"Constable Grimshaw?" he whispered in surprise, his bony hand clutching the top of his silken dressing gown. The fussy older man allowed the door to open wider. "Please, do come in."

Grimshaw entered, the inside of the councillor's abode stiflingly warm, a noticeable contrast to the evening's damp chill, although he wasn't sure which one he preferred.

"If I'd known you were planning to stop by, I would have had some refreshment to offer, but as you can see I've already retired for the evening," the councillor said. "Here, let me take your cloak."

"No concern, Councillor," the constable said as he stood in the entryway, shrugging off his cape as a serpent would slough its old skin. "This is not a social call." Grimshaw turned to face the man. "I've come for the list you promised me."

Pepoy's eyes widened with shock.

Since the loss of his lower arm to the Wurm's bite, the constable had grown used to the startled stares.

"Attractive, isn't it?" he said, raising the stump, the sleeve of his uniform pinned back with a simple placement spell. "Just another example of the chaos I'm attempting to squelch."

The old councillor brought an age-spotted hand to his mouth. "Oh, my," he murmured. "I had heard that you were injured, but I didn't realize. . . . Was reattachment not a possibility?" he questioned.

The constable gazed down at the space his lower arm had once occupied. He could still feel its presence, as if the ghost of his arm were haunting him. "The acidity of the beast's saliva, you see . . . the damage was too extensive."

"My condolences," Pepoy whispered.

"Accepted with heartfelt appreciation," the constable said, clamping down tightly on the rage that simmered within him. "But the list of names you promised to provide would prove far more valuable to me than your sympathies."

"Certainly," the old mage muttered nervously, moving around the constable, his eyes looking everywhere but where the arm used to be. "I'll get it for you now."

The fussy old man entered a room to the right of the entryway, and Grimshaw followed. Lamps of ghostfire came to life as Pepoy hung the constable's cloak, and he moved around his desk, searching for the requested list. The surface was cluttered, chaotic, and the foul mood that Grimshaw had been in since his arm was taken from him grew all the more intense.

"I completed it earlier this evening," the old man was saying as he carefully moved about pieces of parchment, as if to disturb their placement would be to throw off some intricate cosmic balance. "Ah, here it is." He pulled a long sheet of yellowed paper from beneath a stack of others very much like it.

"And this list comprises all the mages who were working outside the authorization of Parliament?" Grimshaw asked, anxious to be finished with this task, so that he could move on to more important matters. "All of the . . . rebels."

He tasted the word. It was sweet.

Pepoy studied the list, as if he were seeing it for the very first time. "Yes, this is all of them," he said, his eyes moving down the page. "I find it very unnerving that most of those who make up this list have either passed from life, or have mysteriously gone missing." He lowered the parchment to fix the constable in a fearful gaze.

Grimshaw snatched the list from the old man's trembling hand.

There were thirteen names. Eleven of them, including Argus Cade, bore an intricate star symbol beside them, indicating that they had died or disappeared.

"Very good, Pepoy," Constable Grimshaw purred, reading the names of the two remaining mages and committing them to memory. "This is all of them?"

The old man nodded. "Fitzroy was quite excited, and a tad arrogant, if I might say so, to be meeting with mages of such caliber," the councillor explained, referring to the close friend whose disappearance had led Pepoy to seek out the aid of the constable. The constable, among whose duties was the investigation of those very disappearances. "He was very specific as to whom he had become acquainted with."

"Excellent, this should make my job much easier."

The councillor smiled, nervously playing with the collar of his dressing gown. "I'm so glad that I could be of assistance," he fawned. "So I would imagine you will be placing the final two mages under your watchful eye?" the aged man pried. "To protect them from the dangerous threat that stalks our fair city?"

Grimshaw looked up from the list as it suddenly burst into flames in his hand. "Oh yes, I'll surely be protecting them," he said, the burning parchment dissolving to nothing before it even had a chance to land on the floor. "I'll be protecting them just as diligently as I protected the others on your list."

And then he smiled, even though he knew he shouldn't have, and by the look that blossomed on the face of the old man, the expression must have been something to behold.

"I . . . I don't think I understand," Pepoy stammered nervously, twisting his nightclothes in his hands.

"But given time, you might," Grimshaw growled, extending his arm and opening his fingers wide. "Which is why you must be dealt with, just as the remaining two enemies on the list will be."

"Constable Grimshaw, please," the councillor yelped, his face twisted in a mask of fear. "I haven't the slightest idea what you are talking about. I've done nothing—"

Five tendrils of crackling black energy erupted from Grimshaw's outstretched hand to strike the old man in the center of his chest, cutting off his panicked speech and hurling him against the wall of the office.

"Hush now," Grimshaw said, manipulating his fingers so that the ebony magic at his command could perform its function.

The old man opened his mouth in a silent scream, but the constable's black sorcery had stolen the councillor's voice away.

"Feel pride in knowing that your sacrifice this night will

bring my master's plans that much closer to fruition."

Pepoy's body had begun to wither. Held aloft by the five spears of magic trailing from Grimshaw's fingertips, his body shriveled with a sound very much like the rustling of autumn leaves.

Flesh and bone became dust, and the councillor's clothes fell to the office floor in a lonely heap. Grimshaw retracted his voracious power, the crackling energies returning to spin upon his fingertips. He retrieved his cloak from the rack and, with just the one, deft hand—the one that had just committed the act of murder—he draped the cloak over his shoulders and attached the clasp about his throat.

It was time for him to be on his way. He glanced once at the pile of cloth on the floor, which had begun to burn with an eerie green light. Soon that, too, would be gone, not a trace of the fussy old man to be found.

Just like all of the others.

Catch a sneak peek at the next
Magic Zero adventure,

GHOSTFIRE

Anticipation crackled in the air. His expectations were so high that it tingled upon his skin like magic.

Or, at least, the way Timothy Cade imagined that magic would feel. Yet in this world where everything and everyone was connected by magic, Timothy was a blank space. Magic could not touch him, and he could not wield it. He was uniquely alone, cut off in a way that no one else could ever understand, and so he had to create his own kind of magic.

That was the source of his excitement today. He felt jittery, and his stomach fluttered, and he felt a prickling all over his face and hands and the back of his neck, and wondered if this was what it felt like to be in tune with the magical current that ran through the world. In his heart he suspected that even this wonderful feeling could not compare with the sensation of magic that would always be denied him.

But even so, he could not erase the grin on his face. If this was all the magic he would ever have in his life, Timothy would still consider himself lucky. It would do. It would most certainly do.

On that crisp, cool morning, Timothy and several of his friends had gathered in an open, grassy knoll behind the servants' entrance to SkyHaven's kitchen. SkyHaven was a magnificent estate, an island fortress that floated hundreds of feet above the ocean, just a short distance from the shores of Arcanum. High above the water, the wind could blow quite cold, and so the boy raised the collar of his tunic and renewed his focus upon the task at hand. His friends had come to see him test his latest invention.

Timothy called it the Burrower, and he had built it to drill into the earth. The original design had occurred to him in a dream, back in the time when he had lived on the Island of Patience. He had woken and quickly sketched out a rough design, thinking that if he could only get the parts together, it would allow him to build an underground workshop that would be a safer refuge when the tropical storms swept across the island in the spring.

Now, that dream had gone from rough sketch to reality. Or, almost. The vehicle he stood before now was the prototype for a much larger digging machine that he would build if this version proved successful. It was a boxy-looking thing, about the size of a sky carriage, with a studded, conical nose that would twist to tear into the ground and funnel the disturbed soil toward the back of the Burrower. It had one seat behind a thick shield of metal to protect the driver from flying debris as the cone spun, digging into the earth. There was a small window at the center of the metal shield so that the driver could monitor the progress of the dig. The window was made of a transparent and quite durable material called vitreous that he concocted by mixing together the gummy saps of two of the land's most prevalent plants. The vitreous would not shatter. The Burrower's power source was located behind the seat, a steam engine also of Timothy's design, and powered by the burning of the heatstone Vulcanite. The entire craft rested on a six-wheeled chassis.

Timothy walked around the Burrower and made yet another final inspection, feeling the expectant eyes of his audience upon him. He had been readying the craft for its trial run for nearly an hour.

"Are we going to do this today, or should we come back later this week?" a grating voice squawked, and Timothy turned to glare at Edgar. The black-feathered bird was his familiar—his animal companion—as well as his friend.

"Caw! Caw!" Edgar squawked, waiting for Timothy to speak. Taunting him in the way the rook always did. Timothy smiled. The bird could always get a smile out of him.

Three of Timothy's other friends were also there for the test run of the Burrower. Edgar flew in a circle and came to a fluttering stop on the shoulder of Sheridan, a steam-powered mechanical man Timothy had built while growing up on the island. His other companion during those years had been his mentor and teacher, Ivar, the last surviving warrior of the Asura tribe. Last but not least, there was Verlis, a new arrival to Timothy's company of odd comrades. Verlis was a Wurm, a race descended from the Dragons of Old, and his presence in the world of Terra was the subject of much debate. But for the moment, not one of his friends was focused on anything other than the success or failure of his latest endeavor. Their attention was making him nervous. Timothy could tell by their expressions that they shared Edgar's impatience.

"You *know* how I am about testing my inventions," he said. "I have to be absolutely certain that everything will function properly before I give it a try."

"Oh, we know. We're just getting bored waiting for you to start her up," Edgar squawked, feathers ruffling.

A blast of steam erupted from a valve at the side of Sheridan's head, and the mechanical man reached up to take a swipe at Edgar. The bird's talons clicked and clacked upon the metal as he evaded Sheridan's attempts to silence him.

"Keep quiet, you!" Sheridan scolded. "Timothy can take as long as he likes. 'Better safe than sorry,' that's what I always say."

Over the years Sheridan had become so much more than one of Timothy's inventions. As far as the boy was concerned, he was as much flesh and blood as any of his other companions, even though made of metal and powered by steam.

"Thanks, Sheridan," Timothy called. "It's nice to know that *somebody* understands."

Edgar flapped his wings, taking to the air, flying in a circle around the gathering. "You've been over the thing ten times already," the bird complained. "It's time to give it a go."

Timothy looked back to the Burrower and thought of all the things he'd like to check one more time, just to be safe.

"My friend," came a rough, deep voice. The boy turned to see Verlis unfurling his large, leathery wings. "The bird is correct. There is still much to be done to prepare for the expedition to Tora'nah," the Wurm reminded him. "I mean no disrespect, but time is of the essence."

Timothy nodded. It was true enough, but he was still reluctant to go ahead until he was absolutely certain he had done everything possible to ensure a safe trial of the Burrower. He did not want to waste his friends' time, but he had to be sure. Too much depended on the success of this latest invention. For the first time since he had come to live in this world, the Parliament of Mages—the ruling body of Terra—had asked for his help. Many of them were still suspicious of him because he had no magic. They called him the Un-Magician . . . and many other things, far less kind. Abomination. Freak. And worse. But now the Parliament had asked him to help them prepare to defend all of Terra against the threat of an impending invasion. The Wurm had been banished years ago to an alternate dimension, and now, led by a cruel, vengeful commander called Raptus, they intended to return to Terra and make war.

With the safety of every man, woman, and child hanging in the balance, Timothy could not say no, regardless of how he felt about Parliament. He needed the Burrower to work properly. He didn't want to fail the Parliament. He didn't want to fail this world.

Frustrated by Edgar's attitude, he turned his back on his

friends and continued his examination of the craft. There could be no room for error. Timothy concentrated on the Burrower's engine, flipping open the door to the compartment that contained the craft's power source. The Vulcanite rocks glowed white-hot, heating the large, metal container of water that would create the steam necessary to fuel the Burrower.

"Timothy?" said a soft voice, like the whispering of the wind, very close by his ear. He jumped, startled. He hadn't heard Ivar's approach, but that shouldn't have been a surprise. The last of the Asura was the stealthiest being Timothy had ever encountered. It was natural for him to move about unheard.

"Is there something wrong with the machine?" The Asura leaned closer, looking for signs of trouble.

So far, Timothy had found nothing out of order. "No. But you can never be too careful with these things."

"Then you expect to find something wrong?" Ivar asked, eyeing the Burrower calmly before turning his gaze upon the boy.

Timothy shook his head. "No, but it's just that . . . this has to work right. There is too much at stake for it to fail."

"And if there is nothing wrong," Ivar said, cocking his head and raising an eyebrow, "it will work."

The boy took a deep breath and let it out in a sigh. He stared at the beautiful black patterns that shifted and moved across the surface of Ivar's flesh. They were tribal markings of a people who no longer existed. The Asura could control the pigment of their skin so that they could change their color to blend in with almost any environment, becoming nearly invisible. But at rest, those tribal markings were always there. Something about them had always calmed the boy.

"But what if it *doesn't* work?" Timothy asked quietly.

The Asura shrugged. "Then we will fix it so it does." He bowed his head slightly to indicate that he had spoken his mind and that, for now, the conversation was done. Ivar turned to walk back to join the others who had gathered to watch.

"Thank you," Timothy called after him. Ivar had always tried to instill in him a sense of confidence. *As is our confidence, so is our ability,* he had said on more than one occasion. Timothy marveled at the simplicity of the thought. The Asura had always been able to see things with such clarity.

Ivar stood with the others, crossing his arms over his barrel chest, waiting patiently.

And deep down, Timothy knew. It was time.

"Sorry for the delay," Timothy apologized. "Let's see if this thing does what it's supposed to."

Timothy pulled himself up into the seat of the Burrower. A pair of protective goggles dangled from one of the machine's operating mechanisms. He grabbed them up and pulled them on over his eyes. He looked toward his gathering of friends and again felt anticipation crackling in the air. He thought of all the things he would have liked to check one final time, but quickly pushed them from his mind. The time was now, and there would be no turning back.

His hands went to the first of the valves, and he turned it as far as it would go. A hiss like that of a gigantic serpent filled the air. The craft shuddered slightly as the steam that had been building up in a storage tank was released into the main body of the Burrower through a series of pipes. Timothy turned the next knob ever so slightly, and a smile blossomed across his face as the conical-shaped drill at the front of the craft slowly began to turn, with each full rotation growing faster and faster still.

Quickly he pressed his foot on a thick pedal and began to pump it. The rear of the Burrower began to gradually rise as the front of the craft angled toward the ground. As he released the brake, the craft slid forward.

Timothy held his breath as the furiously rotating drill touched the grass, cutting through it with ease and then into the dirt and rock beneath. He pumped the pedal further, and the machine's back end continued to lift. The drill spun faster, emitting a high-pitched whine, digging deeper and deeper into the ground, creating the beginnings of a tunnel. The Burrower was working exactly as Timothy had planned.

Cassandra Nicodemus removed the cover on the old chest and stared down at the rolled pieces of parchment stored within. A musty smell wafted up from within the box, and for a moment she thought that she might sneeze. Suppressing the need, she went about her task. She had an important job to do this morning that required her full concentration, but try as she might, she could not stop thinking about Timothy Cade.

A flush of warmth flowed into her cheeks. She didn't know why, but she found everything about him strangely fascinating, most especially that excited twinkle in his eyes when he talked about the fabulous inventions he intended to build.

Cassandra moved her hand over the top layer of scrolls in the old box, muttering the words of a magical incantation. The rolled parchments on the top slowly rose and began to unroll to reveal what was written on them. And again she found herself thinking of Timothy.

He was unable to perform even the simplest acts of magic. *How different everything must be for him,* Cassandra thought as the contents of the scrolls were exposed to her. She could barely focus on the information they revealed, lost in her thoughts about the boy and how much he had changed the world since his arrival.

"Have you found anything yet?"

Startled from her daydreams, Cassandra turned toward the large, bearded mage who sat behind the desk on the other side of the office. Leander Maddox was surrounded by ancient writings, from the oldest parchment scrolls to more recent texts. He was the one who had found Timothy, hidden away in a pocket world by his father, the great magician, Argus Cade, and had brought him into this world upon the mage's death.

There was an unusual edge of impatience in Leander's voice today.

"Not yet," she told him, attempting to clear her mind so that she could focus on the documents floating in the air before her. But there was so much to think about.

Leander was the current Grandmaster of the Order of

Alhazred, the guild of mages to which the Cade and Nicodemus families had always belonged. Cassandra could not help but wonder how the burly mage felt about the changes that had come since he had brought Timothy into this world where the boy was an oddity.

An outcast.

It had been Timothy who had revealed the insidious plot of the former Grandmaster—her own grandfather—to try to take control of the entire Parliament of Mages, to rule all of the various Orders. Cassandra felt a pang of sadness as she recalled the death of her grandfather during a battle with Timothy, and the resultant chaos that followed in the Parliament of Mages.

So much had occurred in so little time.

She thought about the coming of the Wurm, Verlis. This was seen by many as yet another threat, but in fact, the descendant of the Dragons of Old had come seeking help against a much larger evil, an evil that now threatened to spill into her life—into her world. Long before she and Timothy had been born, the Wurm had existed peacefully on Terra alongside mages. But in time there had been conflict, and the Wurm had been driven from the world and forcibly relocated in a parallel dimension named Draconae.

Now, on Draconae, their leader, Raptus, was planning to breach the barrier that separated the dimensions. According to Verlis, Raptus sought revenge upon the world of mages and planned to take control of Terra and destroy the Parliament entirely. The mages had been manipulated in those dark days by Alhazred, founder of Cassandra's own Order, and thus Parliament had betrayed the Wurm. Raptus and his followers would not rest until they had their vengeance.

With a sigh, she at last focused upon the documents floating in the air. She and Leander had been charged by Parliament with the task of studying the ancient scrolls, searching for anything that might help in their defense against the impending Wurm attack. Cassandra found nothing of use on four of the scrolls, allowing them to roll closed again and drop to the floor. It was something on the fifth that caught her eye.

"Leander," she said, reaching up to pluck the scroll from the air before her. "I think I may have found something of interest."

The Grandmaster looked up from his own work, his eyes red and his face haggard with exhaustion. Cassandra knew the job was a taxing one, but had never really stopped to think about the toll that leading an entire guild might exact upon a grandmaster. Though it was something she would have to seriously consider, if she ever planned to assume the mantle of Grandmaster to the Order of Alhazred. For, as granddaughter of Aloysius Nicodemus, the previous leader of the guild, the post was hers as soon as she felt ready to take it upon herself.

"What is it?" he asked, rising from his chair.

She brought the scroll to him. "It's nothing specific, but in this correspondence between two guild craftsmen, there is some talk about what I presume is the original mining operation near the original Wurm settlement at Tora'nah."

Leander snatched the document from her hand. "Give

that to me," he hissed, and she was taken aback by his abruptness. She had noticed some subtle changes in the Grandmaster of late, and was worried that the pressures of the position may have had an unpleasant effect on the normally unflappable gentleman.

"Yes," he said, scanning the ancient writing. "Yes, this may indeed prove very useful to us on our journey."

Leander, along with Timothy and Verlis and some specially chosen representatives of Parliament, were planning an expedition to the former home of the Wurm race to check on the stability of the magical barrier between Terra and Draconae. In addition, they were to oversee a new mining operation there and begin formulating plans to defend against invasion if the Wurm were indeed able to breach the barrier.

"The writer of the scroll talks about the creation of a map designating the areas of the Wurm territories richest in natural resources," the Grandmaster said, and looked at her intensely. "We must find this map at once. It could save us weeks of surveying the land, allowing us to begin digging for Malleum almost immediately."

"Do you have any suggestions where I should begin my search for the map?" Cassandra asked, returning to the chest where she had found the scroll. "Perhaps it's still in here?" she suggested, kneeling down to begin her search anew.

She heard the rush of air and glanced toward the Grandmaster to see him in the midst of conjuring. The spell struck the wooden chest and Cassandra jumped back, watching in amazement as the remaining contents of the box flew into the air, unrolling in unison.

Leander moved out from behind his desk, his robes of scarlet and black billowing around him as he studied each of the many floating documents. One by one, as they proved not to be the map he sought, they fluttered to the floor, discarded.

"There is no time," he muttered beneath his breath as he walked among the scrolls. "The fate of all we've known hangs in the balance."

Leander stiffened and reached out for one of the floating pieces of parchment. "This is it," he said, turning to her excitedly, and the remaining scrolls fell to the ground. He held the parchment out before him. "Crude, but useful nonetheless."

And then the Grandmaster started to laugh, an eerie sound the likes of which she had never heard from him before, and hoped never to hear again.

"Master Maddox?" she said.

He looked away from his prize to glare at her, and for a frightening moment she did not recognize him. Then his features relaxed, and the older gentleman she had come to admire and respect had returned.

"Yes, child?" he answered in a voice that seemed much too weak for a man of his usual vigor.

"Are you . . . are you unwell?"

Leander slowly rolled the scroll. "I'm quite all right," he told her, forcing a sad smile upon his wan features. "Just a little bit tired. There's no need for concern, my dear."

Yet as she watched him make his way slowly back to his desk, clutching the map to his chest, she wished that she could believe him. For as long as she had known the mage, Cassandra had found him tireless in his exuberance. In fact, she imagined that when the time came for the position of Grandmaster to be passed to her, Leander would be the example upon which she would model her own authority. But something was amiss.

He slid the last of the scrolls into a leather satchel with other documents they had found over the last three days, a spell of closure keeping the contents sealed tightly away. "I think we're just about ready to go."

She watched him carefully, searching for any clue as to what might be troubling him, but all she could detect was weariness. Perhaps the Grandmaster really was just exhausted, his nerves frayed by the demands of his post.

Leander glanced at the large timepiece on the wall and then back at her. "Cassandra, please go tell Timothy that it is time." He gathered up his things. "I shall await him with the other members of the expedition at the main entrance."

She bowed her head and left his study. Cassandra thought she had heard Timothy mention something about testing his new invention in one of the open areas at the back of the estate, so she headed in that direction. She bustled along the seemingly endless corridors, hiking up the hem of her emerald green dress so as not to trip as she descended staircase after staircase. To the uninitiated, SkyHaven would be like a maze, but she had made a study of the place upon her arrival following the tragic death of her parents. She doubted that there was any place left in the floating manor that she had yet to see.

Cassandra descended a set of marble stairs that would take her to the back of the estate through the kitchen. When she entered the room she was a bit surprised that the staff was not hard at work preparing the afternoon meal. Instead, she found them all clustered at the back door, watching with rapt attention some display outside. There was a loud clamor from outside the building, accompanied by a high-pitched whine.

She made her way toward the gathering, nobody taking notice of her approach, and stood on tiptoe to see over the heads of the servants and cooks. Cassandra laughed softly to herself. *Timothy Cade, I should have known,* she thought, watching the boy astride a strange contraption that was digging into the earth, tossing dirt here and there.

Cassandra cleared her throat once, and then a second time, louder. The staff of SkyHaven's kitchen gradually reacted, reluctantly returning to their jobs, fearful that they would be scolded. She didn't blame them for their fascination. After all, how often did people see a boy riding a machine that could burrow down into the earth? Not every day. Never, in fact. Not until Timothy Cade had come into their lives. There was really no one like him in the world.

She stepped through the back door and strolled across the grass toward the gathering of Timothy's friends, who now stood around the hole he had dug, marveling at his latest accomplishment. Cassandra hoped Timothy was smart enough to know when to stop the machine. SkyHaven was a floating island, and if he dug too deeply he could find himself breaking through the bottom and falling into the ocean below. *What a sight that would be,* she thought, and had to stifle a giggle.

"Does he know when to stop?" she asked aloud, cupping

her hands over her mouth and raising her voice to be heard over the sound of the digging machine.

Verlis glanced at Ivar, and the Asura then looked at Sheridan.

Edgar, who was perched upon the mechanical man's shoulder, flew into the air and landed on her waiting arm.

"Are you serious?" the rook asked, speaking loudly. "After everything he's done, you still have to ask that question?" The bird shook his head in disgust.

"I meant no disrespect. I just want to be sure he's careful."

Edgar ruffled his feathers indignantly. "The kid's a genius. Of course he knows not to go too far."

And as if on cue, the engine of the digging machine cut out and the sound of another, far quieter, device kicked in. Cassandra leaned forward and gazed into the hole to see that the machine was now ascending. The new sound was that of its wheels slowly turning, backing the craft up and bringing it to the surface.

"See," Edgar said to her. "Nothing to worry about. He knew just when to stop."

The digging machine backed out of the hole and up onto the grass. Timothy busied himself turning knobs and switching levers to shut down his invention's power source.

"Good thing I remembered to stop," Timothy said, removing the goggles from his eyes and jumping down from the craft to the ground. "I was so excited that it was working, I almost kept going."

Cassandra arched an eyebrow and smirked, glancing at Edgar, who quickly looked away, flying from his perch on her arm to the top of the boy's head.

"Good job, kid," the rook cawed. "The Burrower worked like a charm, just like I knew it would."

"Thanks, Edgar," the boy said, beaming.

Verlis approached the machine, resting a claw upon its metal surface. "Fascinating," he growled. And he then looked toward the boy. "As are you, Timothy Cade, as are you." He then walked to the tunnel dug into the ground and peered down into the darkness.

Ivar and Sheridan went to congratulate Timothy next, but Cassandra hung back, not sure that Timothy had even noticed she was there. The breeze whipped her red hair across her face and she pushed it away from her eyes, trying unsuccessfully to tame it.

"Did you see?" he asked, striding toward her with a grin on his face. "It worked just as I'd hoped."

Cassandra smiled in return. "It's incredible." She wanted to say more but was having difficulty finding the right words with Timothy so close and smiling at her like that.

What's happening to me? she pondered, on the verge of panic.

Their eyes locked for a moment, and then Timothy quickly looked away, scratching the back of his head nervously. He turned his focus back to the Burrower. "Can't wait to tell Leander it worked," he said, reminding her why she had come to find him.

"Oh, right," Cassandra said, her hand quickly going to her mouth. "With all the excitement, I almost forgot. They're ready to leave now. The expedition to Tora'nah . . . they're waiting for you."